Suddenly Desired

ALSO BY KATIE EVERGREEN

APEX BILLIONAIRES' CLUB
Book 1: Suddenly Tempted
Book 2: Suddenly Desired

SUDDENLY
Desired

KATIE EVERGREEN

Choc Lit
A JOFFE BOOKS COMPANY

Revised edition 2025
Choc Lit, London
A Joffe Books company
www.choc-lit.com

First published as *My Antisocial Billionaire* in 2019

This paperback edition was first published
in Great Britain in 2025

Cover art by Alexandra Allden

ISBN: 978-1781898994

For the readers: thank you for being so wonderfully supportive, passionate, and fun. You make this all worthwhile.
With love, Katie.

CHAPTER 1

BLAKE

Blake Fielding gently closed his laptop. The blood had drained from his face, turning his tanned skin ashen. Five people stared at him from the other side of the wide boardroom table, their eyes cold, their mouths thin, hard lines.

"I don't know how this happened," he said, trying to keep his voice calm.

His hands were shaking so much he had to rest them on the shiny walnut veneer. It was the truth — he didn't know how this had happened.

It was impossible.

Every single Heartbook account was secure. And as the founder of the multimillion-pound social media network, Blake's account had been triple-locked. Nobody on the planet should have been able to breach it, yet that very morning somebody had — and in doing so they had set about destroying his life.

"The evidence suggests that you posted these yourself," said Agnes Mason, adjusting her thin glasses and brushing a strand of grey hair from her forehead. There was a sheaf

1

of printouts in front of her and she picked up the top sheet, reading from it. "*'A woman's place is in the kitchen.'* This was posted four weeks ago, and the evidence suggests it was sent from the computer in your office. I'm seventy-two years old, Blake, and this kind of attitude was tiresome enough back when I was young."

"Agnes . . ." Blake tugged at his tie, the expensive suit making him uncomfortable. He didn't feel at home in anything other than jeans and a T-shirt, but David Wyvern, his right-hand man, had told him to dress smart, dress *powerful*. The board were out for blood, and he needed every bit of help he could get. "You know me. You've known me for almost ten years. I would never say something like that."

"What about this one?" boomed board member Mike O'Connell, jabbing a finger at the document in front of him. "You say, *'In my experience, women lack the intelligence necessary to run a business, any business.'* I mean, come on, Blake, half our shareholders are women."

"And apparently you think we should all be at your beck and call," said Michelle Carlson, her glossy red lips curling into a smirk.

Blake glanced at her, trying not to let the dislike show on his face. Michelle sat directly opposite him, looking like a cutout from a fashion magazine. Her blonde hair was perfectly styled, her Chanel dress so new and exclusive it wasn't even in the stores yet. She was the picture-perfect beauty, and it was this that had drawn him to her a year ago when she'd joined the board. Six months into their relationship, though, he'd come to understand that beneath her flawless exterior lay a devious and dangerous mind. Even now, all these weeks after he'd politely and kindly ended things with her, she still bore a grudge. "Were you always such a brute? I can't remember."

"I did not post it." Blake's voice rose as he pushed back his chair. He walked to the window, looking at the bustling plaza ten storeys below. It was his kingdom — he'd built the entire campus from scratch when Heartbook had floated on

2

the stock market six years ago. Over a thousand people worked here, and right now he'd have traded places with any one of them, even if it meant giving up his fortune.

He turned back into the room, blinking the glaring sunshine from his eyes. "I didn't post any of it," he said, looking at each of the board members in turn, holding Michelle's gaze for as long as he could bear it. "You all know me. You know I'd never say anything like that, let alone post it. These posts are an attack on me, and an attack on the company."

"He's right." David ran a hand through his prematurely silvering hair. "This doesn't seem like Blake at all. Let's at least look at other explanations before we start a full-blown witch hunt."

"It's not about if we believe you, Blake. It's about what's happening to the business," said Maurice Becker, checking the time on the fob watch he kept in the pocket of his crimson waistcoat. "What matters is that these posts became public at 6.03 a.m. They went viral at 11.40 a.m. And shares in Heartbook had tumbled nearly twenty-five percent by noon." He shook his head, fixing his old, watery eyes on Blake. "My boy, public condemnation is a powerful thing. It can topple even the mightiest empire. You have to make a choice. Save yourself, or save this company. Take the hit, Blake. Announce your resignation."

"No," he said. He may have been thirty-one years old, his body sculpted from his daily gym routine, but right now he felt weak, small, backed into a corner with no obvious way out. "I won't give up. I won't let this happen."

"At the end of the day, it's not up to you," said Agnes sadly, straightening her papers. "It's a decision for the board. I say we vote on it."

"I agree." Michelle's grin practically split her face in two. "I vote we take out the trash."

"Wait." David held up his hand. "I agree, we should vote, but we shouldn't do anything hasty. Blake founded this company. Without him, none of us would be sitting here. Let's

3

give him the benefit of the doubt. Blake is telling us it wasn't him and I believe him. We need to look into what's happened. We've got time, haven't we?"

Maurice sighed, then nodded. "We've probably got around twenty-four hours before the damage is irreparable," he conceded, standing up. "We meet back here tomorrow."

"But if the shares keep tumbling, then we act immediately." Agnes folded her glasses and slid them into the pocket of her shirt. Her eyes looked tired. "We have to extinguish the fire before it consumes us all. This is our business now, too. Our money that's at stake. So, think hard about how you want to play this, Blake."

One by one the board members left without a backward glance, all except for Michelle. She walked to the glass door, stopped and flicked her hair over her shoulder.

"It's game over, Blake," she said. "If you hadn't walked away from me, I might have been on your side."

She shrugged, and then she was gone too, plunging the room into silence. Only David stayed where he was.

Blake rested his fists on the table, hanging his head. "How did this happen? It doesn't make any sense."

"It makes perfect sense," replied David, rubbing a hand down his face. "Who wouldn't want to take you down? You're worth six billion pounds, you're one of the richest people in the country, Heartbook is one of the most popular platforms on the planet. And you're *you*, Blake. Men want to be you. Women want to be with you. You're like some Greek god who's stepped right off an island into the world of mortals. Personally, I don't get it." David grinned. "To me, you'll always be the guy who tried to teach himself to juggle flaming torches for a charity event, only to set off the hotel's sprinkler system and drench half the board of trustees."

Blake sighed, pinching the bridge of his nose. "It was for a good cause, David. And, for the record, I raised ten grand."

David chuckled. "Yeah, and you nearly raised their blood pressure to lethal levels. But, hey, it proves you're not perfect.

4

That might be your best defence right now. That's if the whole Greek god look doesn't work for you this time."

Blake almost laughed. He'd been blessed with his father's athletic physique and his mother's bright blue eyes, sure, and he'd looked after himself his whole life, the way his mother had taught him to. But he was no Greek god — not in his own eyes, anyway. You had to be strong to be a god. You had to be decisive, you had to be fearless. Right now, he was none of those things.

"You believe me, though, right?" Blake asked, looking at his friend. They'd met at Cambridge, over ten years ago now, and even though Blake had dropped out while David had gone on to complete his degree, they trusted each other like brothers. He didn't know what he would do without David's level head and fierce intelligence. "You know I'd never write those things?"

David walked around the table and opened his arms. They hugged, clapping each other on the back. When they parted, David kept his hands on Blake's wide shoulders, not breaking eye contact. "Blake, I'm probably the only member of the board who knows your mother would tan your hide if you'd even thought stuff like that," he answered. "I know you're not a bad guy. You're one of the most decent people I've ever met."

"Thank you." Blake turned away so David wouldn't see the fear on his face. Once again, he stared out of the window, losing himself in the warm, yellow glow.

"But the trouble is, nobody really knows you," David went on. "You've always been closed off to the outside world — even the press haven't been able to penetrate that great wall of yours. You've always eschewed the public eye. You never do interviews, and even your profile on Heartbook is just the surface stuff. There's no depth there, no *you*."

He was right. Blake had always hated attention, and had done everything to avoid it, even throughout his meteoric rise. He figured people might think him aloof, or arrogant, but

5

that had never really concerned him. Now, thanks to these mystery posts on his page — over a hundred of them, dated from eight months ago to as recently as today, all suddenly public — people had started to hate him. And it was so much harder to defend yourself when nobody knew the real you.

"Look, we've got a day to fix this," said David. "It's not long, but we can do it. Take some time, get away from the office for a while. Let me look into it. I'll round up the tech team and we'll figure this out, I promise."

"Okay," said Blake. "Do what you can. But I'm going to get to the bottom of this myself."

"I know you will," said David. "Go on, I'll hold the board at bay."

Blake wasn't sure if even David could do that. Maurice and Agnes had been lobbying for years for Heartbook to strategically expand into an e-commerce site that would prioritise their profits. Blake had blocked numerous attempts — he didn't want Heartbook becoming a glorified shopping site. He had always wanted Heartbook to be something good, a social network that was a positive force in the world, but as soon as the money had started to roll in, the vultures had arrived.

The honest truth was that Blake didn't even enjoy his job now. All these years he'd thought of Heartbook as his way to escape from the real world, but now he was a prisoner in his own social network. As for Michelle, she simply hated him. This was just the excuse the board needed to send him to the gallows.

He offered his hand to David, who shook it, then he made his way to the door.

"Oh, and Blake," said David. "You might want to keep a low profile. There are a lot of haters out there."

6

CHAPTER 2

ELLIE

Something weird was happening.

Ellie Mae Woodward looked up from her notepad and adjusted her glasses to see a line of people walking swiftly past. They all looked panicked, and for a moment she wondered if the fire alarm had gone off. But it would have to be the world's worst fire alarm, because there was no noise other than the hushed, frantic whispers of the crowd — that and the constantly ringing phones from the wide, curved reception desk on the other side of the lobby. A man and a woman were sitting there, red-faced and flustered as they fielded call after call.

Maybe it wasn't weird, she thought. Maybe this was just how it was here every day. This was the world headquarters for Heartbook, after all. It would be unusual if it wasn't a hive of activity. Wasn't that one of the reasons she'd always wanted to work here?

But she was Ellie Mae Woodward. Things had a habit of turning weird as soon as she got involved.

"Ah, nuts!" said the man who was sitting two seats away from her in the large, sun-drenched lobby. He was staring at his phone with an expression of angry disappointment, and with another grumbled curse he stood up and walked out. There were seven other people there all looking at their phones too. Three of them packed up their things and left silently, joining the throng of people exiting the building.

Ellie dropped her pink notebook into her handbag. It was full of neatly written notes for her job interview today, as well as just about every other thought that had entered her head recently. It took her a while to find her phone in the clutter, and when she did, the ancient Samsung didn't have a signal — even though they were smack bang in the heart of the city. Ellie called out to another young woman, with a face like an A-list actress and clothes to match, who was trotting out of the lobby. "Excuse me, do you know what's going on?"

Either her quiet voice didn't register, or the woman was too rude to answer. She pushed through the doors and disappeared into the crowd that was forming on the plaza outside.

This is really *weird*, Ellie thought, wondering if the Ellie Mae Curse really had struck again. She swallowed her nerves and picked up her bag, clutching it to her chest as she walked to the reception desk. Both receptionists were speaking into their headsets and she listened to them while pretending to study a Heartbook welcome pack in the rack by the desk.

". . . I'm very sorry, all tours are cancelled today. Uh-huh, uh-huh, if you send us an email we'll be able to refund the cost. I'm very sorry . . ."

". . . not in today, all meetings have been rescheduled. No, you'll have to talk to Mr Fielding, and I'm afraid he's not in right now, and if you print that without comment then you'll have to answer to our legal team."

The man pressed the button on his headset and looked wearily at Ellie.

"Can I help you?" he asked, the phone already ringing again.

"Um, yes." Ellie tucked a strand of honey-blonde hair behind her ear. She gave him her best smile, the only thing she

8

ever seemed to be complimented on. "I'm here for the interview, for the design team post. We were told to wait in reception."

The man laughed, but there was no humour there. "Sweetheart," he said, the word instantly causing her hackles to rise. "Look around you. And maybe check your phone. Do you honestly think we're recruiting right now?" He pressed the button on his headset and waved her away like she was a fly. "Heartbook HQ, how may I direct your call?"

Ellie hesitated, stunned by his rudeness. After taking a steadying breath she turned and walked across the lobby, wanting nothing more than to get away. She squeezed through the cluster of people by the doors, all of them speaking furiously into their phones, then stepped out of the crisp, air-conditioned building into a blast of hot summer sunshine.

This was typical. She'd worked so hard to get the interview with her dream company. She'd spent weeks preparing her application, writing at least seven drafts of the cover letter that she had attached to her CV. Hundreds of people would be going for the job, and with her complete lack of experience and failed academic career she really only had one thing going for her — her enthusiasm. Well, that and the fact that she had spent the last few years designing her own social network, LifeWrite, which was based around her love of books.

This interview was her one opportunity to show Heartbook just how perfect she was for the job, and how valuable she would be to the company, and it might even give her the chance to pitch LifeWrite to the boss. And now it didn't even look like she was going to get past reception.

"You really are cursed," she told herself as she pushed and mumbled her way through the crowd. Several times she tried to catch people's eyes as she went, hoping that somebody would explain the situation to her. But everyone was too busy, and she was far too shy to make herself heard. By the time she reached the path that led back to the car park, she was convinced that there was no way she could have done the job anyway, because surely you needed a backbone to work for a company like this.

9

Never mind. Her current job wasn't exactly awful, was it? There wasn't a great deal of stress in waiting tables in a café, and she'd just been promoted to assistant manager with twice the responsibility and an extra pound for every hour. And her intensely irritating ex-boyfriend Josh only turned up once a day — sometimes twice — to beg her to come back to him. It could be so much worse. Couldn't it?

She sighed, kicking a pebble across the path. Who was she kidding? This had been her one chance to escape, and somehow she'd blown it without even really getting inside.

The Heartbook campus was right next to the river, and Ellie took a detour on her way back to the car park so that she could walk beside the water. She wasn't quite ready to head home yet, where her empty flat and empty bed and empty fridge were waiting for her. She was here now, so she might as well enjoy the sights, because she knew she wouldn't be back. Besides, there was nobody down here other than the ducks.

The river gurgled, the trees swaying in the gentle breeze. Her button-down dress, printed with hearts wearing glasses and bought especially for today, swished about her knees, and for a moment she almost managed to convince herself she was on holiday, strolling down the promenade with a gorgeous man by her side.

As if, Ellie, she told herself. She was as cursed with men as she was with her career.

The daydream was demolished by the sound of her phone bleeping from her tote bag, and she pulled it out, seeing that she finally had a signal. A message from her mum was waiting for her:

Good luck, I know you can do this!

"Sorry, Mum, evidently I can't." She opened the internet browser and searched 'Heartbook'. It seemed to take an hour for the results page to load, and her eyes widened as she took in the headlines.

10

HEARTBOOK CEO UNDER FIRE
FOR DISGUSTING POSTS
Blake Fielding denies calling women "bitter, stupid, and greedy" on his Heartbook profile as shares plummet.

She tried clicking on a link, but her phone was too old to be able to load it. Grunting in frustration, she slid it back into her bag, so focused on what she was doing that she collided with a man walking in the opposite direction. Her bag fell to the floor, its contents spilling over the grass.

"Oh! I'm so sorry." She ducked down to pick up her belongings, and he did the same. She was so embarrassed she couldn't even look at him. Could this day get any worse?

"I was just on my phone," she said, grasping for her purse. "I wasn't even looking. Please, I can manage, you don't have to."

She dropped the purse into her bag. He held out her keys, the plush Hello Kitty keyring she'd found in a cracker last Christmas dangling from his hand. They landed with a jingle next to the purse.

"I was just, you know, not with it at all, with everything that's going on," she said, blurting out the words almost at random, in true Ellie Mae fashion. "I was supposed to be interviewing for this job, then it got cancelled, so I was just thinking about what to do next. Oh, thank you."

She took her hairbrush from the man, both of them reaching for her makeup bag at the same time. For a moment their hands touched, and he pulled away. Ellie's glasses were in danger of falling off her nose and she pushed them back into place.

"It's just my luck," she went on, laughing. "Get a chance at the job of a lifetime then the CEO turns out to be a sexist, woman-hating monster."

She tucked the makeup bag back into her handbag, finally letting herself look up at the man who had helped her.

"Oh," she said again.

11

The first thing she noticed was how impossibly handsome he was. The second thing, really, after his height, and maybe the way his shoulders were moulded into his well-cut grey suit. A little older than her, his dark hair had been tousled by the breeze, making him look like he'd been racing to get to where he now stood. His skin was perfectly tanned, his blue eyes so bright in the sun that she decided they must be coloured contact lenses because nobody's eyes were that gorgeous in real life.

When he smiled, little dimples cut through his cheeks and she felt suddenly warmer, as if the summer sun had flooded her internal organs.

His suit may have fit like it was hand-stitched around his biceps, but he seemed uncomfortable in it, tugging at his tie like it was a noose. He passed her a handful of loose change that had scattered on the grass, and it was then that she noticed the third thing.

"Oh," she said for a third time, drawing out the vowel, her brain finally making the connection. "Blake Fielding?"

"The very same," he said, the smile wavering. "The sexist, woman-hating monster, at your service."

12

CHAPTER 3

BLAKE

There are a lot of haters out there, David had warned him.

And he'd walked into the first one within two minutes of leaving the boardroom.

Just hours ago people would have been clamouring to shake his hand, snapping selfies for Heartbook clout. Blake Fielding, the golden boy of the city, the guy with the Midas touch. He'd always had a knack for connecting with people, a gift passed down from his mum — the warm, friendly eyes, the quick, disarming smile, the easy charisma had always felt effortless. It was one of the reasons he'd got so far in business, because people seemed to instantly trust him.

Now? His name was dirt. His reputation scorched earth. The thought of it made his blood boil.

He swallowed hard and forced himself to step back. No point making things worse. "Sorry for bumping into you," he said, giving the woman a quick nod.

She was fumbling with her bag, her hands shaking as she wrestled with a catch that clearly wasn't cooperating. She must have sensed him looking because she glanced up again, a nervous smile on her face. He'd guess that she was a little younger than him, but she looked younger still because of the flush of colour on her cheeks, her thick-rimmed black glasses, and the way her sunshine-yellow hair was haphazardly tied back. He squinted at it, realising that there was a pencil slotted through her blonde bun. She tapped her head, his awkward stare probably reminding her it was there, her face burning even brighter and matching the scatter of pink hearts printed across her dress. Hearts wearing glasses, no less.

She was really, bloody stunning. The kind of stunning that made a man forget his own name.

"No, I'm sorry," she said. "I didn't mean to . . . It's just I was sitting in the— I mean, I only just heard the news. Sorry."

Could this conversation get any more awkward? Blake thought, as he fiddled with the knot of his tie.

Blake Fielding had never struggled to talk to women. In business, in social circles, even in relationships, he'd always been confident — charming, even. But this woman was different, his usual easy confidence evaporated, replaced by something he didn't recognise. The normally smooth, articulate CEO found himself blundering. It was completely and utterly embarrassing — and worse, he had no idea how to stop it.

"Don't apologise," he blurted out, eventually. "Please, I should have been watching where I was going too. It's been a . . . a tough morning."

The woman had sorted her bag and was clutching it to her chest like it was stuffed with her life savings. She used her free hand to brush a strand of hair behind her ear, still grinning nervously.

"I should go." She nodded towards the car park and started to edge around him. "Sorry again."

She'd just started to walk away when he called out after her, the words exploding from his mouth before he knew they were coming. "I didn't say those things."

She froze mid-step and turned, blinking at him like he was speaking a different language. "I'm sorry, what?"

14

"The things on my Heartbook page," he said, quickly. "I didn't say them. I'd never . . ." He paused, rubbing the back of his neck as his voice cracked. "I would never say that stuff. Not about women. Not about *anyone*." He didn't know why he was trying so hard to defend himself to this woman he had just met. Except in his head she somehow represented everyone in the company, everyone in the country, everyone in the world who had heard the news and made up their mind about him. "I was hacked. I can't prove it yet, but I will."

"Sure, of course," the woman said, but she didn't look convinced.

She adjusted the bag on her shoulder, hesitating, as if she wasn't sure whether to stay or walk away. Her gaze stayed on him for a beat longer than expected and Blake felt a bead of sweat gather at his temple.

"Well then," she said after a moment, her tone carefully neutral, "I guess this is goodbye. Good luck with . . . everything."

She offered him a tight smile. The kind that could say anything from *"I don't really believe you"* to *"You're definitely a woman-hating monster".* Then she started to walk away again.

"No, wait," he called. "I just . . . Look, I know you don't really know me, but I'm not that guy. I swear."

The woman raised an eyebrow, a strand of blonde hair tickling it where it had fallen from the pencil-clad topknot, but her expression had softened.

"Okay," she said, elongating the second syllable. "You don't have to explain yourself to me. I'm just some random woman who almost walked into you . . ."

"Technically, you did make contact," Blake smiled. "And you're . . . you know?" *Cute, approachable, seem to have a good moral compass.* "You're, um, someone."

"Well, that clears that up." She tilted her head at him, the corners of her mouth twitching like she was trying not to laugh.

Blake didn't blame her. He had no idea what was happening to him. He blamed the shock of what had happened in the boardroom. That was it, he was in shock. it was the

15

sole reason he wasn't able to form a decent sentence. A decent sentence that this captivating woman seemed to still be waiting for. She hadn't run away. That was a good sign. Blake gathered together some semblance of calm and spoke slowly.

"I'm not going to offload my problems on you, don't worry. But it's hard when people think you're something that you're not." Blake cringed at how desperate he sounded. "Especially when that something is a misogynistic idiot. Why can't they have mistaken me for a conscientious gigolo or something? Will never have a work-life balance, but at least I can twerk it for money when it counts."

Shut up, Blake, right now.

The woman nodded slowly, the grip on her bag tightening.

"I guess," she said, her forehead pinched.

Blake felt his whole body sag with the weight of the world on his shoulders. But then the woman's expression softened, and she reached out and placed her hand on his. Her fingers were soft and warm, and he felt his skin tingle under them.

"It doesn't matter what people think, does it?" she said, with a quiet determination. "As long as *you* know the real truth."

Blake frowned, caught off guard by the simplicity of what she'd said. "Maybe," he said, then he shook his head. "No, actually, I think it does matter. It matters to me. If people think that I could do something like that then I've failed as a person. Not to mention what will happen to everyone Heartbook employs. I will have failed them too."

Her expression softened further and she shifted her weight from one foot to the other. "I don't know," she said, almost to herself. "Maybe it's not about the failing, maybe it's about what you do next."

Her cheeks flushed prettily again as she looked at her hand still on his, dropping it quickly to her side.

"I find out who's hacked me?" Blake blinked, surprised by how much her words resonated and how much he was missing her touch.

16

"Yep." She nodded. "You can't control what people think. All you can do is keep on being you and hope that the truth comes out in the end."

Blake stared at the young woman, momentarily stunned into silence by the way her words had cut through all the noise in his head and made the solution sound so simple.

"Yes," he said, brighter now. "You're so right."

She gave him a small, encouraging smile and glanced at her watch. "Anyway, I should get going."

Blake felt a pang of disappointment, but he nodded. "Of course. Thanks for listening, and for not running away screaming."

She laughed softly. The sound made his chest heat up. "You didn't seem that scary, not really. Just a little intense, maybe."

Blake laughed in return. "Just what I was aiming for."

Their eyes hooked for a beat that made Blake's lungs constrict. Then the young woman readjusted her bag and made to leave, her smile lingering. "Good luck with everything," she called again, looking back over her shoulder.

Blake opened his mouth to say something, anything, preferably *"Can I take you for coffee?"*, but all that came out was a squeak as his brain short-circuited. So instead, he nodded silently and watched as she walked away, the pencil in her hair wobbling as she went.

As she disappeared towards the packed car park, Blake let out a long breath, his shoulders slumping. He replayed the conversation in his head, a strange mix of awkwardness and relief settling in him. Until it hit him. He hadn't asked her name. A laugh bubbled up, surprising even Blake. Of course, the one person who'd stopped long enough to listen, who'd offered him the smallest sliver of kindness among the whispers and glares, and he hadn't even thought to ask.

"Well," he muttered to himself, kicking the earth with the toe of his shoe. "I guess that was on-brand of me."

CHAPTER 4

ELLIE

Ellie squirmed as she walked away, trying to wiggle her hips and look like a strong-minded woman in full control of herself. On the inside, she literally had no idea what had just happened. Her mind was buzzing like there was a nest of wasps inside it. It was weird enough that it had been Blake Fielding she had talked to — who had talked to *her* — let alone that he was now watching her leave as though his eyes were glued to her backside. She stumbled a little and righted herself on the bonnet of a 4x4, inwardly kicking herself for the faux pas.

What was she doing? Did she think Blake Fielding was going to notice her hips, chase her down and declare his undying love? Or even offer her a job at Heartbook, which was the more unrealistic of the two right now. She almost laughed out loud at the idea.

Blake Fielding in the flesh.

She knew all about him, of course, because she'd wanted to work for Heartbook for so long. She knew about his childhood, his breakthrough invention at a school science fair, his enrolment then abrupt exit from Cambridge. She'd followed

18

his career from startups to the moment Heartbook became a household name. Ellie even remembered his quirky, obscure interviews from the early days, the ones where he had talked about his family and the way their lovingly competitive sides came out over a game of charades. He had stopped talking about his family when *he* became a household name, and Ellie didn't blame him. The press were intrusive enough with Blake. What Ellie hadn't imagined, though, was that he'd be *so* handsome.

She'd seen a few photos of Blake, mainly from his Heartbook page, but none came anywhere close to doing him justice. He was an exquisite, imposing presence — sky-tall, biceps not even pretending to be contained by his suit jacket, eyes like a galaxy of bright blue planets that had sucked her into their orbit and—

Ellie, enough. Jeez. Focus.

She had to focus on where she was going because her legs felt like she'd just run a marathon, and her brain wasn't much better. She was so caught up in her thoughts that she bumped into a Ford SUV and apologised to it.

What was it about Blake that was causing Ellie's brain fog? Sure, he was gorgeous, but he had something else going for him that made it seem as though he was the nucleus of his own galaxy. Of course he did, though. People didn't become billionaires by being ordinary, did they?

But he was being really, really weird — even by Ellie's standards. She thought she was bad for wittering on, but he had taken it to a whole new level. That rambling explanation about not saying those things.

It should have come off as suspicious, but it hadn't. There had been something so earnest in his expression, something so desperate. He was a nervous speaker, but there was a confidence there too, and she wondered if that confidence came from the fact he was telling the truth.

And wasn't that the million-pound question? *Was* he telling the truth?

19

Ellie spotted the car, an ancient Toyota that she'd borrowed from her boss Lissa, and wound her way around a few bonnets to get to it.

Oh. My. Gosh, she thought as she climbed in. *What* was *that?*

She sat there for a moment, hands gripping the steering wheel, playing the scene over and over in her head. Her heart raced. That was Blake Fielding, one of the richest men on the planet, one of the cleverest tech entrepreneurs in the business. And there she was wittering on about things being easy. She slapped a hand to her forehead, imagining him laughing at her stupidity. If the headlines were anything to go by, he'd be doing just that — mocking her for being an incompetent female — but she couldn't match those rumours with the honest and open man she'd just met.

He'd seemed sincere, hadn't he? Like he genuinely cared about what she thought. But men like Blake Fielding didn't care about people like her. They didn't stop in the middle of a crisis to explain themselves to nobodies.

"It doesn't matter," she told herself, firmly. It wasn't like she'd ever meet him again, or get her dream job at Heartbook. She'd chalk this whole day up as a disaster, as another example of the Ellie Mae Curse, and then go back to work with a smile on her face and a hole in her soul. She hadn't even told him her name.

Ellie started the engine, feeling like she was about to cry. The rumble of the vehicle cut through the car park as she wound down the window to get some fresh air. She was about to put the car in gear when her phone buzzed. She groaned, fumbling through her bag.

The screen lit up with her mum's name. Ellie hesitated, her thumb hovering over the green answer button, but she didn't have the energy to explain what had happened. Not now.

"Sorry, Mum," she muttered, letting the call go to voicemail.

She threw her phone back in her bag and something caught her eye. Or, rather, the absence of something. Her

20

notebook — the one she carried everywhere, full of the most intimate details of her life — was missing.

Her breath hitched.

"Oh no, no, no, no," she whispered, frantically rifling through the bag again as if her notebook would appear by magic.

But it wasn't there.

And Ellie knew exactly where it was.

CHAPTER 5

BLAKE

Blake stood by the river, hands shoved into his trouser pockets, feeling like his pulse was humming. He'd been dead set on leaving the campus immediately, planning to head back to his penthouse apartment and start going over the code behind his hacked account. But he couldn't quite bring himself to start walking again. His mind was sparking. *Who was she?*

A complete stranger was one answer. He met dozens of people every day, mostly with surface-level charm and hidden agendas. He usually felt drained by the effort of meeting new people, their smiles loaded with expectations: money, influence, validation . . . anything. But for some reason this woman had been something else entirely. She was open, uncomplicated, like she had no idea how much light she was throwing around. And she had lit something in Blake all right.

He shifted his weight from one foot to the other, trying to figure it out.

He'd forgotten what it was like to talk to someone without all the noise getting in the way. And for a few, sweet moments the scandal and hacked account had just fallen away.

It had just been Blake and the cute woman with pencil-stabbed hair and a body that made his own stir in ways he hadn't felt for a long while, completely flummoxing him in the process. He'd left the conversation totally and utterly tongue-tied, yet somehow more alive than he had felt in months.

It made no sense, but weirdly that made it matter more.

Two men were walking in his direction, and he ducked his head and turned to the water to avoid their stares. Blake could overhear them laughing about the comments being on the money, how people were just too afraid of the 'woke' to say it anymore, and his stomach churned with the idea that if he reacted, he'd be adding fuel to a fire he would rather douse. He wanted to shout at them for being neanderthals but knew it would cause trouble.

Instead, he focused on what the woman had said to him as he watched the water trickle over itself, the hot sun reflecting on the surface. *Whatever this is, it will be okay.* There was no way she could possibly know that, of course, but she'd believed it — she'd believed him. How much kindness did it take for her to say that to him? Fifteen minutes ago he'd convinced himself that he'd lost everything, that the world would turn against him and force him into hiding, but this one show of trust from a young woman who'd accidentally barged into him by the river had given him hope.

It helped, too, that she was so attractive.

Are you insane? Blake laughed to himself. That was the last thing he should be thinking about. He was in enough hot water as it was. If the press even caught wind of him talking about women in that way then they'd hang him out to dry, quite rightly. He'd have to put the way that strands of her hair had tickled her face in places he wanted to out of his mind. And he definitely couldn't start thinking about the way the hearts on her dress looked as she'd walked away from him. And if he even dared to remember the way she'd bitten her bottom lip as she'd gazed up at him with eyes he could lose himself in, then he had no hope of retaining control over his own body.

23

Blake cleared his throat and shook his head, turning to see if he was alone again. The men had walked on, seemingly oblivious to who they'd passed. Luckily, because Blake could feel the heat in his cheeks and needed to cool off before he bumped into anyone else.

Ungentlemanly thoughts aside, he was kicking himself that he hadn't even asked for her name.

He shook his head, heading for the secure car park beneath the security gate. He'd only taken a few steps before he caught a glimpse of something pink lying in a clump of long grass. Curious, he bent down and picked up a small, hardback notepad. Brushing the dirt from the cover, he opened it up and flicked through the pages. There were shopping lists, appointment times, at least three notes saying, *Call Mum!* There were lists of resolutions, lists about how to improve posture and gain stamina and increase confidence, lists about how to attract the perfect man. It was like an issue of *Cosmo* condensed into a notebook, complete with cute little illustrations and doodles. There were what looked like diary entries too, but he didn't read them because it felt like an intrusion. He skipped to the last page and couldn't help but smile as he read through what was written there.

Notes on Interview!!!!
1. *DON'T MESS IT UP.*
2. *Talk about Heartbook. Duh, I mean, it's an interview at Heartbook, so you're obviously going to do that.*
3. *Talk about LifeWrite, because you invented it and it deserves to be discovered. EMPHASISE IT'S YOUR IDEA BECAUSE IT IS YOUR IDEA.*
4. *Remember Blake Fielding started with nothing, and so did you. You can be as awesome as he is. Just believe in yourself, and don't forget the most important rule:*
5. *DON'T MESS IT UP!!!!*

There was a cartoonish doodle underneath of a young woman in glasses fighting a monstrous, bug-eyed creature

24

with the word *CURSE* written on it. She was armed with a pencil, another one tucked in her hair, which all but confirmed that the owner of the notebook was the young woman he'd just been speaking to. He almost laughed at the words, and at the picture, but the mention of his name there was like a punch to the gut. *You can be as awesome as he is.* People had once admired and respected him. But after today, would anybody want to be like him?

He opened the first page of the notebook, seeing a *Please Return Me* form. The field for the name had been left blank, as had the address, but where it said *Reward* there was a scribbled note.

> *No money to give you, but come down to The Bookworm Café and I'll make you a coffee!!!*

It wasn't much, but it was something. Blake held on to the notebook, making his way up the river. A bank of acacias meant that he couldn't see the plaza from here, but he could hear the buzz of the crowd that had formed. He wished he could walk among them unseen, if only to find out what more of them were saying. He hoped that some of his employees were supporting him, but even within the company he'd never really let himself get close to anyone. While he knew that most people liked him, there was nobody — outside of the boardroom, anyway — who could vouch with complete confidence that he wasn't a sexist, woman-hating monster.

He followed the bend in the river and saw the security booth up ahead. His Mercedes was there, and he wondered whether he should take it straight to the café mentioned in the notebook. The woman might be heading there now, and surely she couldn't hate him for bringing her book back. That was the right thing to do, wasn't it? It's not like he was being spurred on solely by the idea of seeing her again. He'd hand it back, wish her a bright and happy future, and tell her she was welcome back for an interview any time.

He was so caught up in the plan that he didn't notice the cluster of people hovering around the security booth until it was too late. He heard somebody call his name, and suddenly a dozen men and women were running down the path towards him, microphones and cameras held out like the weapons of a charging army. His first instinct was to bolt, but he stood his ground, gritting his teeth and trying to smile at the reporters. It was more of a grimace, he knew, made worse by the fact that his fist was balled by his side. He forced himself to relax and to make his smile as genuine as possible.

"Mr Fielding!" said the fastest of the group, a middle-aged guy who was dressed for the sports desk. By his side was another man, a video camera mounted on his shoulder. "You're accused of being a misogynist. Would you care to tell us why you posted those comments about women?"

He'd only just opened his mouth to deny the accusation when a woman butted in front of the guy, shaking her perm from her eyes and thrusting her phone in his face. "'Corrupt', 'indecent', 'selfish', 'cruel', 'pathetic', 'asinine'. Just some of the words you used to describe the women in your life. Just how did somebody end up with such a strong and hateful attitude towards the opposite sex. What happened to you, Blake?"

"Look," Blake said, but the questions came too fast and too hard for him to answer. He tried to shout over them, waving them away with the little pink notebook. "I'm innocent. I categorically deny that it was me who posted those comments."

"It was you?" asked another reporter, jamming a padded microphone at him. "Are you admitting it?"

"No, I said it *wasn't* me!" he fired back, trying to control his temper. "I'll make an official statement later today. Please, excuse me."

He pushed past the woman with the perm, a little more forcefully than he'd intended. She dropped her phone, gasping, but he didn't dare stop to help her. He put his head down, striding to the gate that led to the car park. The reporters followed like hyenas, still yelling questions at him.

26

Old Mike, the security guard who was supposed to be manning the gate, was puffing and panting down the path from the booth, his hat in his hands. "I'm sorry, Mr Fielding," he said, his red face drenched in sweat. "I asked them not to come in, but they didn't listen."

"Just make sure they leave," Blake said, using his keycard to open the gate and running into the shade and safety of the building. He heard Mike barking orders at the crowd, ushering them out of the campus with threats of police action. Blake waited until the world had fallen silent, massaging his head to try to ease the ache in his skull.

"That probably wasn't as bad as it seemed," he told himself, replaying the last five minutes. But something told him it was *way* worse.

He walked down the ramp to his Mercedes, opening the door and climbing inside. He stared at the notepad for a moment, then tossed it on to the passenger seat. There was no way he could return it now. The press would be everywhere, and they'd be watching his every move like a hawk. The mystery woman would have to wait.

Sighing, and doing his best to shake the image of her smile from his head, he started the engine, and set off for home.

CHAPTER 6

ELLIE

Ellie pushed through the door into the cool, air-conditioned café, happy to leave the sweltering heat outside. She wasn't due to start her shift for another two hours, but Lissa always needed the help, and it wasn't like there was anything waiting for her at home.

There was *something* waiting for her there, though, something distinctly unpleasant. Josh. Urgh. There he was at his usual corner table, swirling a sad, lukewarm coffee, his pale grey eyes darting around the room. She froze, debating whether or not she could slip out unnoticed, but it was too late. His round face lit up, and he stood so quickly that his chair almost toppled over.

"Ellie!" he called out, running a hand through his thinning blond hair as he approached. "How did it go? I was waiting for you. I wanted to be the first to find out whether you sank or swam." His smile was sharp, almost amused. "I'm guessing by the look on your face you didn't sink so much as drown."

Ellie dragged her gaze over to Lissa, who was busy frothing milk at the machine. Lissa shrugged helplessly, and Ellie walked to the counter. Josh practically sprinted between the tables to meet her there, opening his arms for a hug.

28

Every time. Even though she'd asked him not to. They'd been broken up for nearly two months now, but after two years together, he still didn't seem to understand boundaries.

"Josh, don't . . ." But it was too late. He had her in a bear hug that reeked of the Deep Heat he rubbed perpetually on his sore back.

She gave him the world's most unenthusiastic pat, counting the seconds until he let go and she could breathe again.

"So?" he pressed, his watery eyes blinking at her. "Did you get in?"

"No," she said. She turned to Lissa, watching her boss work the coffee machine. Lissa was in her fifties and was as much a kindly aunt as a boss. Ellie felt like she could tell her anything, even with Josh simpering next to her. "Something happened."

"The curse?" Lissa said. "I'm sorry, Ellie."

"It wasn't me," she started. "There was something—"

"I always said you have to be more confident," Josh interrupted, brushing something off her shoulder, his fingers lingering.

Ellie took a step away from him, but he closed in, oblivious to her efforts to escape. "You should have listened to me. When you come to your senses and we get back together I'll show you the best way to succeed in a job interview. Consider it a perk."

This was coming from the thirty-three-year-old man who still worked in his dad's music shop and hadn't been to a single job interview in his life.

"Interviews are all about personality," he went on, still oblivious. "You've got one — you just have to let it show instead of keeping it hidden all the time. They probably just thought you were shy or something."

Her patience stretched thin, she pushed past him, heading for the stock-room-slash-staff room. She reached out to close the door behind her, but Josh was right there, still going on about her faults. It had been one of his favourite things to do when they were together, and it seemed that being apart was no barrier to his arrogance. She held out a hand to stop him. "I need to get changed, Josh."

29

His eyes ran over her, his wet lips peeling open into a smile.

"Nothing I haven't seen before, babe."

Gross! She slammed the door in his face. *How did I ever think he was attractive, or kind, or . . . urgh.*

Oh right, the music. The stupid, perfect music.

She could still picture the first time she'd walked into his family's shop, years ago. He'd been sitting at a grand piano in the corner, playing Beethoven's Moonlight Sonata like it was the only thing that mattered. It had been mesmerising, and for a moment, she'd thought maybe he was too.

She'd asked him about lessons and he'd offered his services on the spot, all charm and confidence. What had started off as a half-hour class every week in the back room of the shop had fast grown into a full-blown relationship. At first, he'd seemed so perfect for her. Sure, he hadn't been her usual type, but he liked the same music, the same movies, the same books. And the way he played the piano? It felt like a sign. Anyone who could play as well as he did, had to be a good person, right?

For a while she believed it. But after a year, the cracks had started to show. It was her mum who'd started plucking at the strings, unravelling what turned out to be an elaborate sham. One evening, during dinner at the family farmhouse, her mum had pulled the dust sheet from the old piano, opened up some yellowing music books and asked Josh to give them a good, old-fashioned singsong. He'd gone bright red and made every excuse under the sun, eventually storming off in a huff, claiming that they were putting him under too much pressure.

After that, it hadn't taken Ellie long to work out that Josh couldn't play the piano at all, other than a few pieces he'd learned off by heart. He certainly couldn't read a single note of music. He'd been studying online piano courses every week then regurgitating the information to her during their classes, while posing as a master tutor. And all the things he'd claimed to be interested in he'd just lifted from her Heartbook

30

account. He was a fraud, and a conman, and she'd fallen hook, line and sinker for it.

The worst part, though? It had taken her another year to work up the courage to end the relationship. Every time she'd tried, he'd found an excuse to keep it going: *It's just your hormones, you're overreacting. You can't leave me, we're renting this place together and we'll lose so much money. I read an article saying that keeping things from your significant other was a guaranteed way of adding spice. I won't cope without you, I don't think I could even go on living.*

And she'd believed him. Every. Single. Time.

The breaking point came one morning when she caught him logged into her Heartbook account, typing out messages as *her*. He wasn't even subtle about it — replying to her friends, declining party invites, deleting conversations. Worse, he'd been intercepting emails from companies she'd applied to, quietly sabotaging her chances at job interviews.

"I'm doing it for your own good," he'd told her, furious at *her* for being furious at him. "I know what's best for you, I always have. If you don't want my help, then you don't deserve me."

That was it. That had been the final straw.

Ellie slung her bag on the hook and closed her eyes for a moment, trying to push the frustration away. The worst part was that she still hadn't managed to kick Josh out of her life. He was utterly convinced that they were destined to get back together and with her luck — and thanks to the Ellie Mae Curse — he was probably right.

"No," she muttered under her breath, unbuttoning her dress and shrugging out of it. She hung it neatly next to her bag and glanced at her reflection in the full-length mirror wedged awkwardly between the shelves of coffee supplies.

Her mum always said she was beautiful, but Ellie never saw it. She had always been too short for supermodel status, and though her legs were toned from long shifts on her feet, Ellie always focused on what she saw as her flaws. Her eyes were too big, framed behind thick glasses she'd worn since she

31

was six, her lips too full, her nose too freckled, and her hair — a mass of thick waves — seemed to have a life of its own. If she squinted — or took her glasses off — she could almost convince herself she was cute. But most of the time she just felt . . . average.

She exhaled and reached for her uniform, and as she did her thoughts snagged on something unexpected. That moment, earlier, when she'd collided with Blake Fielding. Now where had *that* come from? Even now she cringed at the memory — dropping her phone, tipping the contents of her bag at his feet — but the thought of him didn't make her feel bad. Not at all.

In fact, she was struggling to get him out of her head. He'd been something else. It wasn't just the jawline, or his sun-kissed skin, or even the sparkling blue oceans of his eyes. It wasn't his tousled hair, or the impressive physique barely contained beneath the cut of his suit. No, it had been something else, something about the warmth in his voice and the softness in his expression that she couldn't forget.

Thanks for listening, he'd said.

A scorch of electricity travelled up her body as she remembered the way he'd smiled at her. It was the kind of smile that set her skin tingling with anticipation. Even now, standing in the cool stock room in nothing but her underwear, her face was burning up at the thought of it. She'd been face to face with Blake Fielding, she'd touched Blake Fielding, she'd been close enough to reach out and kiss—

Behind her, the door opened. Ellie yelped, wrapping her hands around herself.

She spun around. "Josh, I swear—"

But it was just Lissa, hefting a box of long-life milk from the floor like it weighed nothing.

"Sorry," she said, blinking at her. "You okay? You look a bit flushed."

Ellie grabbed her uniform, shaking her head. "Uh, I'm fine. It's just hot in here." It wasn't a total lie.

32

"You deserve better," Lissa said, interpreting Ellie's expression as one of disappointment. "As much as I'd hate to lose you, that Heartbook job should be yours."

"I never even got the chance to interview," Ellie muttered. "It was cancelled. The whole 'Blake Fielding hates women' thing."

"I know," Lissa said. "It's on the TV right now."

Ellie scrabbled into her work trousers and shoes, buttoning her shirt as she left the stock room. She cleaned her glasses on her shirt and squinted at the little TV. Sure enough it was tuned to the news, a picture of Blake splashed behind the anchor. They'd obviously trawled the internet to find the least flattering photograph they could — a grainy corporate shot with a suited, miserable-looking Blake glaring at the camera, his arms folded arrogantly over his chest.

"Turn it up," said Ellie, pulling an apron from the side of the counter and tying it behind her back.

Lissa fiddled with the volume until it could be heard over the hiss of the coffee machine and the chatter of customers.

"... continue to fall as Heartbook CEO Blake Fielding battles allegations of sexism. The company has yet to offer a formal statement, but earlier today Fielding addressed reporters at the Heartbook campus."

"What a creep," said Josh, who had sneaked up behind Ellie, his breath hot on her neck. "That guy is gonna get canned."

Lissa hushed him as Ellie squirmed away. On-screen, Blake was standing in front of a camera doing his best to smile. Ellie's heart did a somersault as she watched him. The screen had diminished his looks a little, but when he looked at the camera Ellie shivered — feeling once again like he was staring directly at her.

And then she saw it in his hand.

Her heart plummeted as her eyes locked on to the notebook he was holding. Her notebook. The same one she'd dropped by the river. She gripped the counter to steady herself, biting back a gasp.

33

That notebook hadn't just been where she'd written the notes for her interview — it contained a million and one other things, ninety-five percent of which were unbearably embarrassing. *Please don't read it, please don't read it.*

Blake was waving the notebook like it was a sword. The noise of the reporters all but drowned out his voice, but it almost sounded like he was saying, "It was me who posted those comments."

"What?" said Lissa. "He's admitting it?"

"No," said Ellie, shaking her head a little too much. "I think he was denying that it was him who posted the comments. He didn't do it."

"You seem pretty sure about that," said Lissa. "How can you be so certain?"

Ellie hesitated, the story on the tip of her tongue. But it felt wrong to share the experience. It had been a moment between the two of them. His words had been for her.

"Oh, God, do you fancy him?" Josh sneered, his face clouded with jealousy. "Stupid girl."

Ellie ignored him. "I just have a hunch," she said, simply. "He's innocent."

The shot ended with Blake pushing past a reporter and knocking the phone from her hands. He stormed off, and Ellie frowned. That wasn't exactly a gentlemanly thing to do, and he hadn't even apologised. Maybe the stories *were* true.

But no — she refused to believe it. There had been something real in his words, and the way he'd not hesitated to help her pick up her things. There was something genuine about Blake Fielding.

". . . *Time will tell whether the actions of the founder will have long-lasting implications for one of the world's best known social media companies.*"

The story flicked to something else and Lissa turned the volume down. Josh made his excuses, heading for the customer toilets. Lissa offered Ellie a sympathetic smile. "Like I said, you deserve better," she said, softly. "Better job, better man, better life."

34

Ellie nodded but didn't reply. The knot in her stomach tightened as she stared at the counter. Instead of feeling hopeful, Ellie felt something close to hollow. 'Better' might exist out there somewhere, but right now, all she felt was the weight of being stuck.

Alone.

CHAPTER 7

BLAKE

The drive back to his apartment felt like it took for ever, even though it was just three miles from the Heartbook campus. Every car seemed to crawl in front of him, every traffic light turned red at the worst moment, and it felt as though every pedestrian on the pavement was throwing silent accusations his way. Even the doorman at the exclusive luxury apartment block he called home seemed annoyed, offering Blake the briefest of nods as he walked past the desk.

Only when the lift doors slid shut did he allow himself a long, deep breath. The soft hum of the lift and the solitude calmed him, but only slightly. He leaned back against the mirrored wall and closed his eyes. For a moment he debated keeping them closed. At least with his eyes shut he wouldn't notice how empty it was there, how quiet.

The penthouse had been his idea — a way to shield himself from the chaos that came with being *Blake Fielding*. He had never cared for the celebrity status that his wealth had brought him, but avoiding it had been near impossible. The press, the speculation, the endless scrutiny — it followed him

36

everywhere. Here, though, in this sleek, high-rise sanctuary, he had been untouchable. The building's security was airtight, the lifts private and locked with codes. No cameras, no unwanted visitors. Just silence.

At least, that's how it used to be.

Now, even within these walls, he couldn't escape what was happening. The headlines had seeped through. The accusations clung to him like smoke.

Blake stepped out of the lift and into his lair, the floor-to-ceiling windows framing the glittering city below. The penthouse had once felt like a retreat. Now it felt like a cage.

He composed himself and headed straight for the walk-in wardrobe inside his master-bedroom suite, pulling the tie from his neck with a frustrated tug. He shrugged off the jacket and slid off the trousers, tossing them on to the bed. The shirt was next, and he balled it up and lobbed it into the laundry basket on the other side of the room.

He put on a pair of jeans, complementing them with a plain grey T-shirt that clung to his athletic frame. For the first time all day he felt like he could breathe. Recovering the bright pink notebook from his jacket, he walked through to the living area and sat on the sofa.

The penthouse stretched out before him, vast and hollow. It hadn't always been this empty, though. Michelle had moved in quickly, and with her came the slow, insidious takeover. The sleek, designer furniture. The strategically placed abstract art. The state-of-the-art tech built into every surface. At first, he'd told himself it didn't matter — he didn't care much about aesthetics, and Michelle had an eye for these things — but it had never felt like *his* home. Everything had been sharp edges and curated perfection, a reflection of her.

David had always disapproved of Michelle. Even before they got together, he'd made offhand comments — warnings Blake had ignored. "She's all ambition, Blake. And you? You're the prize." Back then, he'd written it off as jealousy or cynicism. Now, he wished he'd listened.

37

His gaze flicked to the bright pink notebook, an absurd splash of colour in the monochrome surroundings. He smiled to himself. She was all mismatched hues and creative chaos. She was notebooks spilling out of bags, doodles in margins, ideas scrawled in ink-smudged pages. Nothing about her was carefully curated, and that was precisely why she had got under his skin so quickly.

He ran a finger over the cover, frowning at the idea that he'd kept it. It wasn't his, and returning it was going to relive the awkward moment when he'd met the woman it belonged to. Blake had staff to deal with lost property, so why was this notebook resting on his palm, willing him to open it?

Her handwriting was small but full of loops, straying from the line. His mum had a knack of reading people from their handwriting. She'd have taken a look at it and given Blake an instant report on the owner's personality. The small letters indicated that she was shy, introverted maybe. But the loops showed that she was creative and expressive, not afraid to do her own thing. The fact that she'd missed out the first two fields for name and address, then added a cute message into the space for the reward, gave the impression that she didn't always follow the rules. And the three exclamation marks matched her smile perfectly, her contagious energy.

Blake leaned his head against the back of the sofa, letting the notebook lie in his lap as his thoughts wandered back to the woman with the wide-eyed expression. A slow heat uncurled in his chest. It had been a long time since he'd felt this kind of unfiltered, raw pull, and it wasn't an awful feeling. Her messy hair, her freckled nose, the soft curve of her lips — the memory of her made him stir.

Blake adjusted his jeans where they were growing tighter and snapped the book closed.

"Focus!" he ordered himself. There were more important things he needed to do.

He got up from the sofa, leaving the notebook behind. He walked across the living area into the small extra bedroom

38

he used as a home office and opened up one of the three laptops he kept there, logging into the Heartbook mainframe. On another he opened Google, searching for his name. He instantly regretted it, the landing page lighting up with articles about the things that had been posted on his account.

He scrolled through the first few entries, his anger and frustration growing with each one. The posts weren't just controversial, they were hateful. Whoever had posted them had a serious problem with women. Nobody sane would say the things that they were saying, even if they were just doing it to frame him. It made him feel physically sick.

The comments were worse. It seemed as if the world had already judged him to be guilty. On all the social media networks, including his own, people were calling on him to resign, to leave the country, to leave the *planet*, and a whole lot worse as well. He wanted to respond to them all, to protest his innocence, but he knew that would be a mistake. He needed evidence first, then he could clear his name.

He snapped the second laptop shut and focused on the first, using his Heartbook passwords to access the site databases. Pressing 'enter', he was greeted by a pop-up message denying him access.

Weird, he thought. He tried again, but it wasn't letting him in.

He pulled his phone from his pocket, calling David.

"Hey, Blake," his friend said, answering after a single ring. "Hope you're staying away from the news, buddy. They're not taking any prisoners."

Blake got straight to the point. "I'm trying to log in. What's going on?"

He heard David sigh, and instantly knew the answer.

"They've locked me out," Blake said. "Who gave the order?"

"Blake," said David. "It's protocol. The whole network is in lockdown. We've lost a quarter of a million users already. It's for—"

39

"Who, David?" he interrupted, getting out of his seat so that the full authority of his voice made it across the airwaves. "Tell me, now."

"Michelle," David said, telling Blake what he already knew. "She ordered it the moment the meeting ended. I only just found out myself."

"She doesn't have the power to do that." Blake's whole body was shaking with rage. "It's my company."

"Not since it floated," David said. "She had Maurice's backing. Agnes's too."

Blake bit his tongue. David was right. Even though he and David had built Heartbook together, they didn't control it anymore. If the board had a majority, then any decision they passed was law.

"I'm doing what I can," said David, his voice crackling over the line. "But the posts are still appearing, going back further. They're getting worse, too. There's nothing you can do from there. Let me handle it."

Blake nodded. "Handle it," he said. "Please."

He ended the call and dropped his phone on to his desk, gripping the edges to steady himself. His pulse pounded in his ears, rage simmering just beneath the surface. He wanted to fight back, to wrest control of his company from Michelle, from Maurice, from Agnes — from whoever thought they could manipulate the empire he'd built from scratch. But right now, all he had was anger and no direction to channel it.

He stared at his phone, hesitating for a moment before picking it back up and scrolling through his contacts. If anyone could give him clarity in this context, it was his old friend and fellow APEX Billionaire Club member Devlin Storm. Devlin had once been the target of a lot of negative press — he'd know what to do.

The line barely rang before Devlin's voice came through, steady and grounded. "Blake, I didn't expect to hear from you. What's happened?"

"Have you not seen the news?"

40

"I've been out on the mountains," Devlin replied, and in the background Blake could hear the thrum of the blades on Devlin's rescue chopper. "Give me the bullet points."

"I need advice," Blake said, his voice tight. "I'm in a mess. Someone has hacked my Heartbook account and made misogynistic comments in my name. My company is in lockdown, my access blocked, the board's made a move against me, and the whole of the internet is convinced I'm a prejudiced arsehole. It's bad, Devlin."

There was a pause, the sound of muffled voices and the faint whir of helicopter blades.

"Damn," Devlin said, eventually. "I'm online and I can see why you're calling."

Blake let out a sharp exhale, running a hand through his hair, afraid of what Devlin was reading.

"I didn't say those things."

"Of course you didn't. Did you think I'd even think it, let alone believe this crap?"

"So, what should I do? What would you do?"

"Have you talked to Nate? If anyone can help, it's him," Devlin said, his tone calm. "But I'd start by deciding what matters most. Is it the company? Your reputation? Or something else entirely? You can't fight everything at once, Blake. Pick your priority and hit it hard."

Blake swallowed, his throat tightening. "The company. Heartbook. It's everything I've built."

"Then focus on that," Devlin hit back. "You don't need to defend yourself to the mob. Let the noise die down while you dig for the truth. Find out who's really behind this, and don't stop until you have answers. But Blake . . ."

"What?" Blake's grip was tightening on his phone.

"Don't lose yourself in the process. Your company might be hugely successful, but you're more than that."

Blake nodded, even though Devlin couldn't see him. "Thanks, Dev. I appreciate it."

41

"No problem," Devlin said as the whir of the blades increased. "Look, I've got to go. I'm about to lift off. But remember, stay clear-headed, focus on your priority, and don't let them pull you under."

"Love you, man," Blake said.

"You too." The line went dead.

Blake laid the phone gently on the desk and leaned back in his chair, staring at the ceiling as Devlin's sage words echoed in his mind. *Pick your priority. Hit it hard.*

He knew what he had to do. It was time to stop reacting and start taking control.

But first . . .

He made his way back to his bedroom, grabbed a grey sports hoodie from his wardrobe and zipped it up. He put up his hood and donned a pair of aviator sunglasses from the table by the door. Glancing in the mirror, he decided he could be anyone, just an average guy out for a walk. He picked up the pink book again, reading the note:

> *No money to give you, but come down to The Bookworm Café
> and I'll make you a coffee!!!*

It might all end in nothing. She might not even be there. But it felt like the right thing to do.

Heaven knew he needed a coffee. And maybe, just maybe, he needed to see her too.

Smiling, he stepped into the lift.

42

CHAPTER 8

ELLIE

"Honestly, Ellie, take the hint and go home."

Lissa was unloading cups from the dishwasher, drying them with quick, efficient movements before stacking them neatly on the shelf. The café was empty now, just the hum of the fridge and the occasional clatter of dishes breaking the silence. Even Josh had slunk off an hour ago, probably to mope somewhere else. Ellie had scrubbed the tables, mopped the floor — twice — and even deep-cleaned the small bathroom. She was out of tasks, but she still wasn't ready to leave.

"Go," Lissa said again, exasperated. "You're twenty-seven, Ellie. Don't waste your life hanging around here."

Before Ellie could argue, the bell above the door jingled, and a couple strode in. The man was broad-shouldered, dressed in an expensive suit, his hair slicked back. The woman wore a silk blouse, her lipstick applied with surgical precision. They looked like they belonged in a high-end bar sipping martinis, not in a tiny indie café that smelled of old books and freshly baked scones.

Ellie straightened. "Good evening, what can I get you?"

43

The woman didn't acknowledge her, instead wrinkling her nose as she surveyed the café. "Black coffee. No sugar. But make sure it's hot. Not lukewarm, not scalding, just . . . hot. Can you remember that?"

Ellie's hackles rose. She opened her mouth to respond, but the man kissed his wife and then leaned in to Ellie with an easy, almost condescending smirk. "Make that two."

Ellie forced a polite smile. "Coming right up."

She turned towards the counter, her fingers clenched around the dish towel with a death grip, her knuckles white.

Lissa noticed instantly. With a sharp tug, she prised the towel from Ellie's fingers.

"Go," she whispered, her tone gentle but firm. "You're done. You're just getting wound up, and I don't need you snapping and throwing coffee at the customers."

Ellie blinked at her. "I wasn't—"

Lissa arched an eyebrow. "Weren't you?"

Ellie opened her mouth to argue but closed it again. "Fine. I'm going."

Lissa smirked. "Damn right you are. And I'd better not see you here before your shift tomorrow. Go do something reckless. Or, I don't know, *fun*."

Ellie rolled her eyes but couldn't fight a small smile. "Define 'fun'."

"Literally anything but this."

Shaking her head, Ellie grabbed her bag and coat, casting one last side-eye at the couple. It was early evening, and even though the temperature was mild it didn't seem like dress weather anymore so she kept her uniform on. Slinging her bag on her shoulder, she marched out of the café, calling a goodbye to Lissa. She dug her phone out, trying not to notice the depressing lack of text messages — apart from another two from her mum demanding to know how the interview had gone.

Sorry, Mum, she thought, heading off in the direction of her flat. She was just hitting dial when she thumped into something — or someone — solid, the shock of it making her drop her phone.

"Ah, crap, sorry!" she said, flustered, as a low, pained "*Oof!*" came from the person she'd run into. She crouched down quickly, snatching up her phone. "I wasn't looking where I was—" She glanced up and froze mid-sentence.

Her heart slammed against her ribs.

Blake.

He looked different, dressed down in jeans and a hoodie, the shadows of his hood and his aviators obscuring part of his face, but there was no denying it was him. Her body recognised him before her brain did, a rush of heat creeping up her neck. He rubbed his stomach, wincing slightly, but his lips quirked into a lazy half-smile that sent her pulse into overdrive.

"We really should stop meeting like this," he said, his voice soft and laced with humour.

Ellie blinked hard, her brain short-circuiting. "What are you . . . ?" she stammered. "I mean, why . . . *How* . . . ?"

Was she hallucinating? She'd been thinking about Blake all afternoon, and now here he was, like some impossible hoodie-clad mirage. Her words refused to cooperate, leaving her scrambling for something to say. Meanwhile, her traitorous eyes drank him in, noting how well the hoodie fit over the curve of his chest muscles and strained somewhat over his biceps, the way his jeans fit him just a little too well. Casual Blake was somehow more dangerous than Suit Blake.

He tilted his head slightly. "Hi," he said.

"Uh . . ." she managed, her voice barely a whisper. "Hi."

"Hi," he said again, giving her a smile.

"What are you doing here?" she blurted out, wondering if he'd somehow used his Heartbook billions to track her down. "How did you know where I . . . ?"

Blake pulled something from the back pocket of his jeans, holding it out to her. Her pink notebook.

Her eyes widened and she almost slapped a hand to her head again, only just managing to stop herself — she'd already

45

made a complete fool of herself in front of him, twice, and her embarrassment was burning hotter with each second.

"I believe this belongs to you," he said, his tone easy, but there was something in his smile, warm and deliberate, that made her stomach flip.

"Thank you so much." She clutched the notebook like it was a buoy. "You have no idea what it means to me to have this back."

"It's really not a problem," he said, low and steady. "It's the least I could do. I'm just glad I found you."

The way he said it sent a shiver down Ellie's spine, and for a moment, the rest of the world seemed to blur.

"You didn't, um, read it, did you?"

"No," he said, and Ellie barely had time to be relieved before he added, "I mean, I tried not to, I didn't *read* it, not like a book or anything, but I wasn't sure who it belonged to, so I *glanced* at it. Not all of it, just enough. Just a couple of pages."

He was blushing too, she saw, and it made her heart skip a beat. It softened his handsomeness to something a little more approachable, adorable even. The idea that Blake Fielding, billionaire and global icon was as nervous as she was felt almost impossible, especially given her self-proclaimed moniker of Ellie Mae Woodward, Queen of Nobodies. But here he was, fidgeting slightly, hands in pockets, looking like he wanted to apologise all over again.

"I'm so sorry," he blurted out. "Please forgive me."

"I forgive you," she said, her tone light but her pulse doing backflips. "You made up for it by bringing it back."

They fell into silence, eyes snagged on each other. Something raw tugged in her stomach as the silence grew with a buzz of energy that promised so much. She was aware of the small gap between them, fully charged and vibrating so that it made her ears ring. The ringing sounded like a voice in her ear. Which was weird, when Ellie started to think about it. The voice sounded familiar, and was incessantly calling her name. She suddenly realised that it wasn't the anticipation of

46

something between her and Blake — it was an actual voice. Her mum. Lifting her phone to her ear, Ellie heard her mum hollering down it.

"Ellie? Ellie, are you there?"

"Oh, Mum, hey, I'm sorry," she said, fumbling her words. "Give me a minute, I'll call you back."

"Don't you dare—" her mum said, but Ellie ended the call and stuffed the phone back into her bag.

She half wished she'd kept the call going because now she had no idea what to say. And from the look on his face, neither did Blake. The realisation was both intimidating and nauseating. Ellie knew the odds of her blurting out something daft were pretty high. She'd probably crack an inappropriate joke, or tell Blake that his face made her feel funny, so when she landed on something totally sensible to say she got it out as quickly as she could.

"I owe you a reward." Her words blended into one long, breathless syllable. "It's not much, I'm afraid," she added. "But let me get you a coffee."

"I was really hoping you were going to say that," Blake replied, his voice velvety. "I mean, about having coffee, not you buying me one — though I wouldn't mind that. I just don't want you thinking I expect you to pay. Or don't expect you to pay because I can afford it . . . Do you know what? I think I'm going to stop talking now. Today has messed with my head. Sorry."

Ellie couldn't help it. She laughed and Blake faltered, his mouth in a grimace. He rubbed the back of his neck. "Sorry, I'm not normally this bad with words."

"It's fine," Ellie replied, glad to have met someone who wittered on as much as she did. "You're better at it than me. Marginally."

He tilted his head, studying her with a teasing glint in his eye. "I don't know about that."

Before she could reply, he slipped off his sunglasses, tucked them into the neck of his hoodie and fastened his eyes

47

on Ellie. The ground tilted slightly as she noticed his pupils grew to large black holes in the pools of his irises. For someone who was struggling with getting his words out, he was still top notch at the whole flirting game.

"I *really* wouldn't mind you taking me for one," he said again, his voice soft. He didn't look away, not even for a second, and Ellie felt like she might melt into a puddle right there on the pavement.

Trying to keep herself collected, she slid the notebook into her bag and busied herself by fussing with things that really didn't need fussing with. Anything to stop herself from drowning in his eyes — as corny as that may sound, they were so blue she felt her cells flooding as she thought it. Turning back towards the café, she spotted Lissa leaning out the doorway, the dish cloth frozen in her hands. Ellie could see her mouthing, *Wow!*

Ellie's cheeks burned, and she glanced back at Blake.

"Uh, I know the reward said Bookworm's," she said, "but can we go somewhere else?"

"Anywhere," he said without hesitation. "You name it." He popped his lips, looking down the street. "Just maybe not anywhere too public, if that's okay?"

She nodded, remembering why he was dressed down and out here in disguise. The pleasant glow she'd felt just moments earlier dimmed slightly as reality set in. Right now, everyone in the city thought that Blake Fielding was an utter twat, his name plastered across the headlines for all the wrong reasons. And, for all she knew, they might be right. But she couldn't quite reconcile *that* man, with his outdated, derogatory views, with the guy standing in front of her, no matter what image the press had painted. She was amazed he'd dared to even leave his office with the pitchforks out baying for blood.

He'd told her he was innocent, and she'd already decided to give him the benefit of the doubt. Besides, this might be the perfect opportunity to find out for certain.

48

"I know the perfect place," she said, resisting the sudden urge to slide her arm through his. "Just give me a second to call my mum back first."

Blake smiled, sliding his sunglasses back on his face, the corners of his mouth quirking up in a way that made her stomach flip. "Take your time. I'm not going anywhere."

CHAPTER 9

BLAKE

It really was the perfect spot. A cosy but dingy, dimly lit basement venue with soft wall lights and flickering candles. The only other customers were an old guy propping up the bar and a couple talking quietly at a corner table, their hands intertwined, their eyes full of love. Blake glanced at them briefly, then let his eyes settle on the mystery woman as she rummaged in her bag. The soft glow of the candles reflected in her glasses, and the little hearts on her purse matched the pattern on the dress she had been wearing earlier. Everything about her felt warm and easy, *real*.

"So," she said, snapping his attention back, "what's your poison?" She tipped a pile of coins from her purse on to the bar, and Blake's eyebrows lifted in surprise.

"I can't let you buy me a drink," he replied, taking off his sunglasses and pulling down his hood. It would make him instantly recognisable, he knew, but there were so few people in here he hoped it wouldn't matter. "Please, let me."

"No way," she said, pushing her glasses into place again. Every time she did it her nose wrinkled, something he found indescribably cute. "A deal's a deal. You returned my notebook, I buy you a coffee."

Blake chuckled, shaking his head in surrender. "In that case I'll take a double-shot espresso, no milk, no sugar, please."

She whistled, clearly impressed. "That's a serious coffee," she said. "One serious coffee coming up."

She turned to the bar, her energy so casual and confident that Blake was momentarily at a loss. He wasn't used to this. He was always the guy who made the orders and who paid. He could buy this whole bar with a cheque right now. He could buy the whole *street* without making a dent in his bank accounts. Yet here was his mystery woman, counting out battered coins on to the bar to buy him a coffee.

"Keep the change," she said, sliding the coins across.

"Cheers," said the barmaid. "I'll bring the drinks over to you if you want to take a seat."

The mystery woman turned to Blake with a bright smile. "How about right over here?"

Without waiting for his reply, she led him to a small booth along the back wall. She slid into one side and he slid into the seat opposite. The candlelight flickered between them, soft and warm and casting golden highlights across her face. Blake stared for a moment too long, completely disarmed by how beautiful she looked. His mind went blank, devoid of all rational thought. Luckily, she was a little more composed than he was.

"Is your day getting any better?" she asked.

He laughed, the sound surprising him. Somehow, in the span of a few minutes, she'd made him forget everything. Heartbook. The scandal. The headlines. But it all came flooding back with her question.

"Not really." He sighed, thinking of the last news story he'd read on the way over to drop back the notebook.

"Well, I'll try not to take that personally." The little laugh she gave made his skin tingle.

"Oh, God, sorry. I didn't mean you." He laughed in return. "You're not worse. You're the opposite of worse." He

51

caught himself before he said too much. "I just mean, it's nice to be with someone who doesn't hate me. Or someone who hides it very well, at least. You might hate me. I don't know. I don't even know your name."

She laughed, covering her mouth with a slender hand. "Oh, yeah," she said. "It's Ellie. Ellie Mae Woodward."

She stretched the same hand over the table and he took it, holding it for a fraction longer than he should have. Her skin was soft, but her handshake had purpose, a quiet dominance that sent a jolt straight to his groin. He didn't want to let go, not of her hand, nor the ache she'd stirred in him with a single touch. But if he didn't, he'd blow whatever it was growing between them.

"I'm Blake," he said quietly, feeling like an idiot as soon as the words had left his mouth. "But of course you knew that already."

"Yeah," she said. "Pretty sure the whole world and their cats know who you are by now."

"You're not wrong." His heart sank a little. "I'm honestly surprised I managed to get here without being mobbed."

Ellie tilted her head, curiously. "Why did you, then? Come here, I mean? You could have just posted my notebook."

"Would you rather I'd posted it?" His voice was so deep it reverberated across the table.

Ellie's eyes looked heavy as she replied with a quick shake of her head.

"Good," he went on, his chest a tight band. "I'm know I'm pretty antisocial when it comes down to it, but I felt I had a civic duty to return it in person."

"I'm glad," she whispered.

The way she was looking at him made Blake want to leap over the table and devour her. He shifted in his seat, trying to release some of his pent-up tension. He could actually hear his pulse in his ears, racing into overdrive. What was wrong with him?

52

"Here you go," said the barmaid, appearing with a tray and breaking some of the tension.

She set down a tiny espresso in front of Blake and a towering mocha latte, complete with whipped cream and chocolate sprinkles, in front of Ellie.

"Can I get you guys anything else?" she asked, her gaze lingering on Blake like she was trying to place him.

"Not for me, thanks," he replied, offering a polite smile and secretly hoping she wouldn't connect the dots.

"I've got everything I need," said Ellie. "Thank you."

"No worries." The barmaid gave Blake another curious glance before retreating to the bar.

Ellie scooped a dollop of whipped cream on to her finger and licked it off without a second thought, leaving Blake wheezing into his espresso. There was a tiny dot of cream left lingering on the corner of her mouth and Blake's eyes strayed to her lips. He forced himself to look away before his thoughts strayed again too.

"Is this your regular spot, then?" he said, trying and failing to keep the croak from his voice. "It's got a good vibe."

Ellie shook her head, dipping her finger in for another swipe of cream. Blake wanted to reach across and grab her hand, to draw it to his own lips and suck the cream himself. He could barely breathe, yet, looking at how sweet she was being, he knew Ellie had no idea the effect she was having on him.

"Not really," she replied to the question he'd totally forgotten he'd asked. "Sometimes my boss, Lissa, and I come here after work. It's close, it's quiet and no one really bothers us. I'm not big on crowds."

"Same," he agreed. "Why surround yourself with a hundred people when you only really need one good one?"

Ellie paused, her lips twitching upwards. "True." She dipped her spoon in her drink and scooped up more cream. Looking sheepish, she added, "Sorry, it's been a long day. I need the sugar hit."

"Hey—" he held up his hands — "you never have to apologise to me for eating what you like. You're talking to a helpless brownie addict here."

"Yeah, sure." She glanced at his chest and arms, her eyebrow raising. "I can tell."

"I have to work it off," he said, laughing. "But it's worth it."

"My boyfriend," she said, and his stomach almost twisted into a knot. For a second the room went darker, and the feeling of dread that gripped him took him by surprise. Ellie shook her head, staring at her drink. "Not my boyfriend. My *ex*. He always told me I drank too much coffee and ate too much sugar. He said I needed to watch my figure more. Apologising for it is an old habit."

Blake's jaw tightened, a flicker of anger igniting in his chest. *What a jerk*.

"Well, in my opinion, chocolate sprinkles are too good to refuse," he said lightly, trying to lift the mood.

"Exactly!" Ellie's eyes lit up again. She ran the tip of her tongue over her lips, catching the errant cream, sending a ripple of heat through Blake. "You want some?"

When she looked at him her eyes were all pupil.

"Sure," he croaked, and she pushed the cup across the table.

He dipped his teaspoon into what was left of the whipped cream and sprinkles and slid it into his mouth, savouring the sweet, velvety taste. Chocolate really was one of his weaknesses. Along with Ellie, it would seem.

"Good, right?" she said, grinning.

"Really good," he replied. "My espresso seems massively disappointing after that."

"Way too serious," she said. "Do you want one of these?"

"Sorely tempted," he said. "But after this double-shot, a hit of sugar might have me on top of the table belting out Celine Dione, and I'm supposed to be lying low."

Ellie laughed again, the sound soft and infectious. He decided in that moment that he loved making her laugh

Slow down! Blake ordered himself. *Better yet, stop.*

54

Her laugh, her smile, the easy rhythm of their conversation. Blake had spent years drowning in stiff, transactional interactions. Dinners with Michelle had been all business, usually while dining on an eye-wateringly expensive meal in an upmarket restaurant. Michelle had always demanded one hundred percent perfection everywhere she went — anything less was a failure in her eyes. If Blake had so much as used the wrong fork, or worn the wrong socks to complement his tie, she would berate him about it all night. It had been miserable.

The contrast now was intoxicating. He couldn't remember the last time he'd just sat and talked like this, with no agenda, no pressure to impress or perform. It was as if he'd known Ellie for months, *years*, not half a day. There was something so natural about the way they spoke with each other, something so effortless. Ellie knew who he was, knew what he was worth, but there was none of that fake flirting he was so used to, the blatant body language, the sickening insincerity.

But he wasn't entirely free of his thoughts. His company was sinking, and the board were getting ready to throw him overboard. Every single move he made was being scrutinised and sitting here with Ellie like this felt like walking a tightrope. It wasn't a date, not technically, though Blake kind of wished it was now he was here. But being like this — happy, smiling, relaxed in the company of a gorgeous woman — might be enough to drag the whole thing down to the bottom of the ocean.

Still, he couldn't bring himself to leave. Not yet.

"Are you okay?" Ellie asked, her head tilting slightly, a genuine curiosity in her eyes.

Blake smiled, but he could feel that it wasn't quite reaching his eyes. "Not exactly," he said, honestly. "I mean, this day has been . . . interesting, to say the least. One minute I'm just a guy running his own company. Next thing I know, I'm public enemy number one." He finally took a sip of his espresso, savouring the bitter edge. "It's a bit surreal, to be honest. I feel like I'm living in a TV series, and not a very good one at that."

Ellie leaned forward, her expression still soft, but with a trace of humour laced through it. "So, you're telling me the big, bad billionaire in the show has bad days too? I thought he was just there as comic relief."

"Plenty of bad days." Blake leaned forward too, his elbows on the table. The gap between them narrowed and he could see the scattering of freckles on her nose under the frames of her glasses. This close she smelled of strawberries and cream and Blake didn't want to admit that was probably the sprinkles. "Though, to be fair, this one is shaping up a little better than planned."

Ellie arched an eyebrow. "Really?" she teased. "And why is that?"

Well," Blake whispered, pulse spiking as her eyes flickered to his lips. "I don't often get rescued by mystery women who also happen to have impeccable taste in drinks."

Ellie laughed and sat back in her chair, throwing her head back in glee. "You're just lucky I didn't bring the full works — marshmallows, syrup, the whole sugar coma in a cup."

"I wouldn't have complained." He sat back too, missing the scent of her already. "Honestly, I'm just glad I have someone who I can talk to who doesn't want to throw coffee in my face or write the next headline about me."

"Oh, don't worry," Ellie said with a grin. "I'm saving my coffee throwing for our next meeting and it'll be a flat white because there's no way I'm wasting good toppings on teaching someone a lesson."

Blake chuckled. "Noted. I'll bring a spare shirt."

Ellie rolled her eyes, but she sounded serious as she placed her hands on the table in front of her and looked him right in the eyes. "You'll figure it out. People love a scandal, but they love a good comeback even more. You'll just have to ride out the storm for now."

He glanced at her hand, so close to his on the table. Without thinking, he reached out, his fingers brushing hers lightly. "Thanks for saying that. It helps."

56

Ellie's smile softened as she turned her hand, letting her palm meet his. He felt the heat travel all the way up his arm and shoot like a bolt to his groin.

"You're welcome," she said. "And, for what it's worth, you don't seem like the type to stay down for long."

Their eyes met, and for a beat the world between them buzzed.

"Maybe I just needed a little reminder of who I am," he said, his thumb grazing her palm almost absentmindedly. "And maybe someone to tell me I'm not completely doomed."

"Doomed?" She shook her head, her smile wide. "You? You've got more resources than most people combined. You'll bounce back. Probably quicker than you think."

"I guess I'm going to have to keep you around for motivational speeches," Blake said, his smile teasing.

Ellie's eyes narrowed and she pursed her lips. They looked delicious, like ripe strawberries. "Careful," she whispered. "You might not be able to afford me."

Blake's gaze locked back on her eyes. His pulse quickened. Afford her? He wasn't sure he'd survive her.

CHAPTER 10

ELLIE

What are you doing?

"Trust me," Ellie said, her voice softer than she intended, her heart thudding wildly in her chest. She could almost hear her brain screaming at her. *You've known this guy for five minutes, and now you're telling him he can't afford you and holding his hand like it's a scene from some romantic drama.* "It will get better."

Her fingers still tingled from the contact, the warmth of his hand lingering even as she pulled hers back. The sensation spread like a slow electric current, settling low in her belly and leaving her slightly breathless.

Her cheeks flushed, and she glanced down at the table, unable to meet Blake's gaze. The flickering candlelight felt too intimate, the air between them too charged. She darted a glance at the bar, then at the couple laughing quietly in the corner, before finally settling on the ceiling fan, as if it held the answers to all her questions.

For a moment, neither of them spoke. The silence felt heavy, not awkward, but loaded with something unspoken. Ellie's pulse raced as she dared another quick look at Blake.

His face was unreadable, but his jaw was tight, his eyes dark and stormy beneath his hooded brows. He looked like he was fighting some internal battle, one she couldn't quite decipher.

Finally he sighed, rubbing a hand over his face. "You have a way of making things sound so . . . simple."

"It doesn't feel simple to you?" Her voice was barely a whisper.

Blake shook his head, a faint, rueful smile tugging at his lips. "Not even close."

Ellie swallowed hard, her fingers fidgeting with the edge of her napkin. "Maybe you're overthinking it," she said, trying to keep her tone light. "Sometimes you just need to . . . let go."

Blake's eyes snapped to hers, and the intensity in his gaze sent a spark rushing through her. The corner of his mouth curved into something that wasn't quite a smile — more like a challenge.

"Let go, huh?" he murmured, his voice low, almost teasing. "And what would that look like?"

Ellie's breath caught, her mind scrambling for a response. "Well," she said, forcing a small, nervous laugh, "it probably wouldn't involve brooding over an espresso."

Blake chuckled, the sound deep and rich, sending a delicious shiver down her spine. "Point taken," he said, leaning forward slightly, his forearms resting on the table. "But maybe I need some inspiration for what else to do. Any suggestions?"

Her heart skipped, the space between them suddenly feeling much too small. She tried to focus on her drink, but his gaze was magnetic, pulling her back to him.

"I don't know," she said, her voice softer now, almost breathless. "Maybe start with something easy. Like . . . relaxing."

Blake smirked, his eyes flicking briefly to her lips before meeting hers again. "You make it sound so doable."

"It is," she shot back, her confidence building under his scrutiny. "You just need the right company."

His smile deepened, and he leaned in just a fraction closer. "Lucky for me, I seem to have found that."

59

Ellie felt her cheeks burn, the heat spreading down her neck as her pulse thundered in her ears. The tension between them was palpable, a slow, simmering heat that made her feel like the room had grown ten degrees warmer.

She cleared her throat, trying to regain some semblance of composure. "Let's hope I'm as good an influence as you think I am," she said lightly, though her voice trembled just enough to betray her.

Blake's lips curved into a slow, deliberate smile, and the look in his eyes made her stomach do somersaults. "Oh, I'd say you're doing pretty well so far," he said, his voice low and smooth, sending another ripple of heat through her.

"Mr Fielding," she said, leaning back and crossing her arms, her confidence blossoming. "Is that your way of saying you're impressed?"

Blake raised an eyebrow, clearly amused. "Maybe."

"Not too sweet for your bitter, coffee soul?" Ellie replied, her smile growing.

His eyes gleamed, a spark of intrigue lighting them up. "Oh, I can handle it," he said, his voice dropping slightly. "The question is, can you?"

Her heart skipped, but she didn't look away. "Guess we'll find out."

The playful tension between them simmered, and Ellie felt like the world outside the booth had melted away. It wasn't just the flicker of candlelight or the quiet hum of the café — it was him. His presence, his voice, the way he looked at her like she was the most interesting person in the room.

And for the first time in a long time, she liked how that felt.

Ellie traced her finger around the rim of her cup, her gaze flicking up to meet Blake's. She felt relaxed in his company, not scared that he was going to change his whole persona the way Josh used to, depending on who he was trying to impress.

"You ever meet someone who seems like they have it all together, but underneath, they're just . . . pretending?"

60

Blake raised an eyebrow, intrigued. "All the time," he said, leaning forward slightly. "Why?"

She shrugged, a small, rueful smile tugging at her lips. "I used to know someone like that. They wanted everyone to think they were perfect — untouchable, even. But the cracks always showed when they thought no one was looking."

"Your ex?" Blake probed, kindly.

Ellie nodded.

Blake's expression darkened slightly, his hands resting on the table. "Sounds exhausting," he said. "For him and for you."

Ellie let out a short laugh, shaking her head. "You have no idea. Josh was so obsessed with being this picture-perfect version of himself that he couldn't handle real emotions. If I ever got upset, he'd act like I was the problem. Either he'd sneer and fold his arms, or he'd just walk out of the room like I wasn't worth his time."

She glanced up, catching the flicker of anger in Blake's eyes. It surprised her how much it reassured her.

"He just," she continued, her voice softer now, "couldn't let me see him as anything less than perfect."

Blake's jaw tightened, and Ellie could feel the heat radiating off him, his frustration palpable.

"He never wanted a real connection," she said, her voice gaining a sharp edge. "It was all for show. Everything about him was so . . . shallow."

She stopped abruptly, realising she was venting way too much. "Sorry," she said quickly, shaking her head. "I didn't mean to dump all that on you. That was probably way too much. I just wanted you to know that I can see you're not pretending to be someone you're not, but it just came out in a stream of crap about my ex."

She blurted out a laugh and cupped her hands over her face.

Blake pushed his cup aside, his hands now stretched across the table, like he wanted her to take them. "It's not

61

too much," he said, his voice steady. "It's honest. And you're right — there are a lot of people like that. And I'm glad you can see I'm not one of them."

Their eyes met, and the intensity in his look nearly stole her breath. There was no mask, no pretension — just the raw pull of him and the quiet strength that seemed to radiate from every part of him. His voice slid over her skin like a touch she was already craving.

"I'm starting to see that," she said, her voice barely above a whisper, the air between them almost crackling.

Blake glanced down at their outstretched hands, their fingers so close they may as well have been touching. For a second, Ellie thought he was about to close the gap, but then his eyes flicked to his watch. A pang of disappointment shot through her. Was this it? Had she got too personal, pushed too far?

"Shall I get you another?" she blurted out, speaking before her brain had the opportunity to stop her. "I haven't quite hit my caffeine buzz yet."

He chuckled, low and warm, shaking his head. "As tempting as that sounds, I think I'll pass. I'm already going to be wired enough just from being here." His smile softened. "I'm glad I could get your notebook back to you."

They both stared at the little pink notebook that sat on the table. Ellie felt a creeping sense of embarrassment at what he might have seen inside it.

"It's just a silly thing," she mumbled. "I use it to jot down random ideas. Helps me keep track of my thoughts because I'm so scatterbrained."

"I think it's great," he said. "When I was first setting up Heartbook I wrote everything in notebooks. There were hundreds of them, overflowing with messy ideas, terrible pitches and sketches."

She smiled. How did he have a way of making her feel so much better about herself? Josh had always kicked her notebooks under the bed, hating the way they cluttered their apartment.

62

"My mum is the same," he went on. "When I was growing up she used to fill a notebook a week. I got the habit from her. I count those notebooks as one of the reasons I am where I am. They're not silly things at all."

Ellie's cheeks burned as she thought of her notebook's contents. "Well, you obviously didn't read too much of mine," she teased, though her voice wavered slightly. *God, please don't let him have seen the boyfriend lists.*

Blake's lips twitched. "I just glanced through," he said. "I'm so sorry. It was the only way of finding out who it belonged to. I didn't read much, just the odd line here or there."

"That's a relief," Ellie said.

"But I did catch the thing on the last page," he went on. "The interview material."

"Oh crap, you *didn't.*" she said, mortified. "It was just to help me focus. I—"

He was holding up a hand. "Can I show you something?"

"Sure," she said.

He dug a hand into the back pocket of his jeans, pulling out a small, black book. Flicking through it and shaking his head as if he couldn't believe what he was about to do, he placed it on the table, facing her. His handwriting was small, and a little messy, and she couldn't help but smile as she read it.

Board Meeting
Don't let Michelle steer the conversation.
Reassure Mike and Agnes and they will reassure the shareholders.
DON'T DAYDREAM. PAY ATTENTION.

There were other notes too, but Blake shut the book and put it back into his pocket.

"If I let you read any more," he said, "I will literally die of embarrassment."

He was smiling that big, warm smile again.

63

"The only thing it's missing is the doodles," he said, and she laughed. She swatted his hand and he laughed too, feigning injury. "Ow! Easy, tiger. But seriously, there was something in the book that caught my eye. You mentioned LifeWrite. What is that?"

Ellie sat up straight. She'd been so wrapped up in the real-life Blake sitting in front of her that for a moment she'd forgotten who she was speaking to. Wasn't this why she'd pushed so hard for an interview, and for a job at Heartbook? She'd been hoping that one day she'd be able to pitch her idea to the company and hope that it filtered up the chain to the CEO. Well, now here she was, face to face with him. Opportunities didn't come any better than this.

"It's something I've been working on for a while now," she said, fighting to keep her tone calm. "For years and years, really. A social network based around books and reading. It's part friendship, part dating, part business connections, but I want it to focus on stories. It's really about being able to write the story of your life, using the power of books."

He was interested. She could tell that by the way he was watching her intently, nodding with increasing enthusiasm.

"I've always loved to read," she went on. "Books have saved me so many times — from broken hearts to broken dreams. They're so powerful. But hardly anyone uses that power to connect people."

"That's so true," he said when she paused. "Books can save lives. If I'm having a bad day I usually head to the library. Just being around all those books makes me feel better."

The image of him, this powerful, commanding man, sitting quietly in a library, sent her heart fluttering. She smiled, her excitement bubbling over. "Exactly. Books unite us, stories connect us. That's my dream — to bring people together through the power of reading. That's what LifeWrite is. It's a safe place for like-minded people."

She smiled nervously, waiting to be shot down like she always had been with Josh. *That's been done a million times*, he'd said. Or, *You'd never be able to do it, it takes a genius to code.* He'd always looked at her with pity and sometimes even anger, as if she was a young Victorian girl who had ideas above her station. But Blake was genuinely interested. He opened his mouth to reply, but before he could get a word out, the barmaid appeared again.

"Here's the drink you ordered," she said to Blake. She was holding a pitcher of something in one hand, and in the other she held a phone. An alarm bell was going off in Ellie's head.

"I didn't order any drink," said Blake. "Sor—"

Before he could finish, the barmaid tipped the pitcher over Blake's head. A disgusting smell of old coffee grounds and waste water filled the booth, ice cubes smashing on to the table. Blake gasped as the cold water soaked him, and he jumped up so hard his legs cracked into the table.

"You're not welcome here, you chauvinistic prick!" the barmaid yelled. "Take your woman-hating thoughts somewhere else."

Ellie was up on her feet, her head full of anger.

"What the hell?" she said, her voice shaking. "You didn't even give him a chance to defend himself."

"You should be ashamed," the barmaid said, turning her phone to Ellie. "You can do a whole lot better than this trash."

She stormed off, and Ellie walked around the table, shaking out a napkin.

"Are you okay?" she asked. "Let me—"

"I'm fine," he said, his face carved from stone, his eyes suddenly cold. "I'm sorry, I never should have come. Goodbye, Ellie. Thank you for the drink."

And without another word, he walked past her and out of the bar.

65

CHAPTER 11

BLAKE

Blake strode up the steps so fast he almost tripped, flying out into the street. The hot evening air hit him like a slap, but it wasn't enough to clear the frustration buzzing under his skin. His soaking wet hoodie clung to him, stinking of stale coffee and worse.

The light had started to fade, but there was still enough of a glow to catch the attention of passersby, and the last thing Blake wanted right now was another round of unsolicited recognition. He yanked up his soaking wet hood, fumbled his sunglasses on, and kept his eyes firmly fixed on the pavement as he walked swiftly away from the bar.

He was in shock at what had happened, his pulse hammering. The barmaid's voice — sharp, cutting, and laced with fury — echoed in his ears. But worse than the foul-smelling, dripping mess from his clothes, had been the way she'd looked at him when she'd thrown the drink. She'd looked as if she hated him.

And then there was the phone.

Blake clenched his jaw, his hands balling into fists in his damp sleeves. He was certain she'd been filming. The angle of

66

her phone had been too deliberate, too practised, and Blake knew what it felt like to be filmed. He could only guess the headline that would be emblazoned above the footage.

Chauvinistic prick. That's what she'd called him. The words churned in his stomach, mixing with the sharp sting of realisation. This is what his life had become. Every interaction would be scrutinised. Every misstep magnified and dissected for the world's entertainment. Though he missed them with a pain that felt visceral, Blake was glad he'd created a distance between himself and his family. It would kill him to see them scrutinised in the same way.

He swore under his breath, quickening his pace. How could he have been such an idiot? He'd known something like this was going to happen. He should have known better than to leave the apartment. His gut had told him it would be a mistake. And it had been right. He'd let himself get caught up in the moment. In her.

Ellie.

Her name drifted through his mind, uninvited, but impossible to ignore. He didn't know why he felt so drawn to her. She wasn't just another face, another voice clamouring for attention and validation. No. When he'd first met her, by the river, he'd felt something special. And now, after just half an hour in a bar, he knew for sure.

Blake shook his head, trying to banish the thought. He'd only known her for a matter of hours. Whatever spark there was between them couldn't be worth more than his business. Heartbook was his life, his legacy, and right now it was teetering on the edge of ruin.

He crossed the street, seeing a taxi coming the other way and flagging it down. The driver must have taken one look at his ruined clothes and decided he was penniless, because it roared away almost immediately. He had more luck with the second one, climbing inside and pulling out a wad of notes.

"You can keep it if you don't ask any questions." He gave the address.

The taxi driver's eyes flicked to Blake in the rearview mirror, widening as he spoke. He took the money without a word and pulled out into the traffic.

Only when they were accelerating down the street did Blake let himself relax, leaning his head against the back of the seat and listening to the hum of the engine and the noises from the city. But it didn't take long for the tension to creep back in, as his mind replayed every second of the bar incident like a broken record.

He could already picture the fallout. The video would circulate online, then the snarky captions, the anger and hate would follow, along with the steady plummet of share prices. The board wouldn't even wait for him to have a say — they'd pounce on this like wolves, using it as leverage to push him out of his own company.

Blake needed to speak to David.

His phone buzzed in his pocket and he pulled it out, seeing David's name there. Had the news reached the board already? That was not good. He thought about not answering, but this was no time to be an ostrich, and he really did need to hear the voice of a friend right now.

With a resigned sigh, he swiped to answer. "I know," he said, before David could speak. "Don't say it."

"Say what?" snapped a familiar, cutting voice. "That you're single-handedly throwing this company under a bus? What's the game here, Blake? Are you trying to burn it all down?"

Blake froze, the tension in his shoulders ratcheting up a notch. "Michelle," he muttered. Of course she'd muscled her way into this.

"Don't play dumb," she hissed. "This is a disaster. You've got the public screaming down my neck, the media are frothing at the mouth. Are you doing this deliberately or are you really that stupid to *go out and get coffee*?"

"Michelle," he said again, choosing his words carefully. "There was a reason I was there, and it's not the reason you're thinking of."

68

"Sure, Blake. There's always a reason."

He heard David mumbling something, then the sound of the phone being passed over.

"Sorry," David said. "She knew you wouldn't answer if it was her."

Blake pinched the bridge of his nose, exhaling sharply. "Yeah, no kidding. What's the situation?"

"I'm not going to sugarcoat it," David said, his voice serious. "This is bad. Really bad. Let's just say my media alerts are working overtime. Your name has been trending all day, but this video? It's blowing up."

"The bar?"

"Yeah," David confirmed. "Someone sent it to me five minutes ago and now it's everywhere. I've forwarded it to you, but timing couldn't be worse. Agnes is pushing for an emergency board meeting. I think I've managed to hold her off until tomorrow, but she's rallying the troops."

Blake's chest constricted. "Don't let them meet without me."

"I'll stall them as long as I can," David said. "But you need to be ahead of this, Blake. And whatever you do, *stay inside.* Don't give them more fuel. If you're not careful, you're going to lose everything."

David ended the call, and Blake froze for a moment, the weight of the man's words sitting heavy. Slowly, he unlocked his phone, trying to ignore the flurry of notifications that had been setting it alight. He'd intended to go straight to his emails and deal with what David had sent him, but his thumb hovered as a familiar group chat lit up:

APEX Broadcast Channel: Always be closing.

Blake couldn't remember which of his friends had come up with the tongue-in-cheek chat name, but it had stuck.

The message preview caught his eye and, before he could stop himself, he tapped into the thread.

Devlin: *Saw the video. Tough break, man, but you've been through worse. You'll handle this.*

Christian: *Yeah, bro, nothing new. Haters gonna hate, but you're Blake freaking Fielding.*

Nate: *Ignore the noise. But hey, can we talk about the girl? She's a knockout.*

Blake's lips twitched despite the tension in his chest.

Devlin: *Agreed. Who is she, and why haven't we heard about her before?*

Nate: *If I didn't know you better, I'd say she's the reason you're in this mess.*

Christian: *Don't blow it. She's got that "make you forget your own name" vibe.*

Blake sighed, his thumb hovering over the keyboard. He wasn't about to get into a deep conversation about Ellie with these guys, not yet. But the way they talked about her only reinforced what he already knew — Ellie was special. And that scared the hell out of him.

Still, the messages carried an undercurrent of warmth, a reminder that no matter how much pressure he was under, he wasn't completely alone.

Blake: *Appreciate it, guys. Let's focus on not letting the company implode first, yeah?*

Devlin: *Fair. Just don't let the girl slip through your fingers in the meantime.*

He locked his phone again, leaning back against the cab seat and letting out a long breath. The weight of the situation pressed down on him again, but this time, it didn't feel as suffocating.

Still, there was no time to get distracted. He unlocked his phone once more, this time going straight to his inbox. David's email sat at the top, its subject line a blunt punch to the gut: *You need to see this.*

He tapped the link and a YouTube video loaded. The title read, *Blake Fielding gets what's coming to him.*

The wobbly footage started behind the bar, showing the barmaid's perspective as she crossed the room. Blake watched, his throat tightening as the camera zoomed in on him sitting in the booth, Ellie across from him.

And then, something strange happened. The dread that had been clawing at him shifted, replaced by a flicker of something entirely unexpected.

Ellie.

Even through the grainy lens of someone else's phone, she was captivating. The way her lips curved into a small, nervous smile, the way her eyes sparkled with genuine curiosity as she leaned towards him — it stirred something deep in his chest. Something that felt dangerously close to happiness.

He saw the way he was staring into Ellie's eyes, the way his body language leaned into her. He saw his own smile, and he couldn't quite believe it was real. He didn't look like the man he'd seen in the mirror for the last few years, or the man they had photographed for the company brochures. That Blake had always worn a fake smile, even though he'd convinced his friends and family it had been real. He could see why they had never believed him now.

On the video, she mirrored his posture over the table, something he hadn't noticed until now. Her eyes were locked on to him, her chin resting on her hand, her whole body pressed to the table edge as if she was trying to flow right through it to get to him.

Blake blinked, his mind warring with itself. This wasn't how he was supposed to feel. He was supposed to be furious, panicking, strategising his next move. Instead, all he could think about was the way Ellie had looked at him. Like she

71

could unravel him with a glance. Like she already had — and he wanted more.

He rewound the video, watching her again, the faint smile that tugged at her lips, the way she'd gestured as she spoke. Her presence in that booth, across from him, felt like the only solid thing in an otherwise crumbling world.

Blake closed his eyes, gripping the phone tightly. He couldn't afford this. He couldn't afford her. Not now, not with everything at stake.

But, God, how he wished he could.

He went back to the video, not wanting to put himself through the next bit, but knowing he had to. The shaky footage captured the waitress as she walked towards their booth. He saw himself reluctantly turn away from Ellie, the faintest flicker of hesitation in his movement.

He'd been so shocked that he hadn't really noticed what had happened next, but the way Ellie leaped to his aid took the edge off the incident.

The way she shot to her feet, her eyes blazing with anger, her body leaning forward like she was ready to throw herself into the fray for him. She hadn't flinched, hadn't second-guessed him, even when the world was screaming for his downfall. Why? Why was she so willing to believe him when everyone else had already made up their minds?

And, more importantly, would she still believe him now that this video was everywhere?

The taxi jolted to a stop, snapping him out of his thoughts.

"Here we are." The driver nodded towards the sleek, glass building.

Blake thanked the man and climbed out of the car.

David's words echoed relentlessly in his head. *If you're not careful, you're going to lose everything* — his company, his shares, his money, his future. But standing there, staring at the towering building that represented all of it, Blake found he couldn't summon the usual fear or urgency. For once, the

72

weight of Heartbook didn't feel like the most pressing thing in his life.

Instead, he found himself thinking about Ellie.

He should be heading upstairs, cleaning up the mess from his hair, and calling David to strategise. Maybe even shooting another message to the APEX group for their take on how to deal with the situation. That had been the plan.

But right now, the thought of explaining himself to David or enduring Michelle's sharp commentary felt exhausting. What he really wanted was something far simpler.

He wanted to hear Ellie's voice. Her laugh, the way she teased him without trying too hard, the fire in her eyes when she talked about her dream for LifeWrite. She'd made him feel like a person, not a headline or a cautionary tale.

Blake rubbed the back of his neck, letting out a slow breath. He'd never been one to lean on others, but there was something about her that made him want to open up, to keep the conversation going.

He slipped his phone into his pocket and headed inside, his footsteps echoing in the lobby's marble-clad quiet. He still had a business to protect, a reputation to salvage, and a board of directors to face, but in the back of his mind, one thought lingered, clear and insistent.

If he could choose, he'd be talking to Ellie right now.

CHAPTER 12

ELLIE

Ellie was a mess by the time she arrived back at her flat. The evening air clung to her like a second skin, thick and humid, and the hour-long walk home had left her drenched in sweat. She'd used the last of her money on the coffees and hadn't been able to afford a taxi. The evening was hot and clammy, and she still felt like she was in adrenaline mode after the incident at the bar. Her pulse was racing, her body like a furnace. She couldn't believe that had happened. It didn't feel real. How could anybody be that cruel to another person? Even if Blake had been guilty, it didn't give somebody the right to tip a whole pitcher of rancid water over him.

She unlocked the door, picturing Blake's face. He'd looked so horrified, so upset. She had no reason to believe his claim that he was innocent, but in the short time she'd spent with him tonight she felt she already knew him. Either he was telling the truth, or he was the world's best liar.

Of course, it wasn't like she hadn't been taken in by a liar and a cheat before.

Ellie pushed the door open and stepped into her dimly lit hallway, her bag slipping from her shoulder. Her flat was small

74

and cluttered, but cosy, the faint smell of strawberry milkshake from her diffuser hanging in the air. She barely had time to let out a breath when a figure lunged at her from the shadows.

"Jesus," she yelped, leaping backwards into the console with a clatter.

"Oh, sorry," said Josh, not sounding sorry at all. "I just needed to collect some of my things."

Ellie's initial shock gave way to anger, her jaw tightening as she flicked on a light. She pushed past him, hanging her bag in the hall next to the lightweight raincoat he wore whatever the weather.

"You don't have anything left here," she said, trying to keep her voice calm. "You haven't had anything here for weeks."

"I beg to differ," he said, holding up a razor.

She was certain it hadn't been here before today. She'd gone through the place in forensic detail after he'd left and chucked everything that belonged to him — and everything that they owned together — in a bin bag. But Josh had insisted on keeping a key, and she was too poor to have the locks changed, and technically the lease on the flat was in both their names so she couldn't even complain to the landlord.

"Great," Ellie said. "You've got it so now you can go."

Josh ignored her and sauntered into the kitchen. "Coffee?" he called over his shoulder. "I've put a pot on."

Ellie screamed internally, following him into the kitchen to see that as well as the coffee bubbling in the pot, there was something spinning in the microwave. The smell of cheap burgers filled the air. His laptop was open on the counter.

"You don't mind," he said, a statement rather than a question. "I won't be long. Besides, I figured you could use the company."

"I'm tired, Josh," she said. "It's been a long day."

"You and me both, honey." He poured himself a mug of coffee and added a large glug of her favourite creamy milk. He leaned against the counter. "Where have you been?"

"That's none of your business," she snapped, wondering if he'd leave the flat if she picked up a knife and chased him

75

out. But that's the kind of thing Josh wanted her to do. That's how he operated. He drove you insane, made you feel like you were losing your mind, then stepped in and told you he could make it all better. "Just eat and leave."

"Relax." He tapped the keys on his laptop. "I was just curious to see if you'd tell me."

Ellie didn't reply, her arms crossed tightly over her chest as she leaned against the counter. But when Josh turned his laptop towards her, her stomach sank.

"I know where you've been," he said smugly, tapping the trackpad.

A video started playing on-screen, so dark and so fuzzy that it took her a moment to recognise herself and Blake in the bar. She watched with a growing sense of panic as the barmaid threw the drink over Blake's head, as he shot up in shock, as she defended him. Then it cut to black.

"Solid choice for a date," Josh said, revelling in it. "You've got a real knack for public humiliation, haven't you? Silly girl."

Ellie was speechless. She felt terrible. This had all happened because of her. If she hadn't gone for that interview then she never would have bumped into Blake. If she hadn't dropped her notebook then he never would have had to bring it to her. If she hadn't suggested the bar then Blake never would have been filmed. He was in enough trouble as it was. This could ruin him.

"Have you seen the comments?" Josh grinned. "People really do hate him. I'm surprised you don't feel the same way, being a girl. In the latest bunch of posts on his page he claimed that girls shouldn't be allowed to drive because they don't have the coordination for it. Maybe he's right, though. I mean, look at you. You were left to your own devices tonight and you picked the very worst person on the planet to go on a date with."

Rage was boiling inside her skull and she stormed into the bedroom, slamming the door behind her. There was nothing to lock it with, so she sat with her back to the door, planting her head in her hands.

76

Could Josh be right? Could Blake really have said those things? She pulled out her phone and opened up the browser, searching for Blake's name. His Heartbook page had been taken down, but there were a million screenshots of what had been posted there. They really were vile and disgusting statements. She couldn't understand how they could be made by the same person she had met tonight. These remarks were blunt and lazy and cruel. Blake had been talkative — he'd wittered more than her — and imaginative and kind. The posts were offensively demeaning to women, but Blake had spoken to her with care and consideration. Not once had she felt objectified or belittled.

No, it couldn't have been him. Ellie had no idea what was happening, but she was certain that he was being set up. The thought made her feel like a territorial animal. It made her want to run to his side and fight for him. But even though Blake was one of the strongest men she'd ever met — even now she could picture the muscles straining against his hoodie — there was a vulnerability to him. Maybe he'd spent so long being in charge that he'd forgotten what it was like to be looked after.

But how was she supposed to look after him when he'd left without giving her his address, or even his phone number?

"I can hear you in there," said Josh from the other side of the door. He was chewing loudly. "Come on, babe, come out and spend some time with me. It will make you feel better."

She couldn't think of anything that would make her feel worse. She stayed where she was, browsing through the search results until she found an article that wasn't about the comments Blake had supposedly made. She opened up a business site, seeing a photo of a younger Blake with a woman who could only be his mother. She had silver hair, styled in a bob, and she was dressed in a sleek, powerful black suit, a string of pearls around her neck. Her face was kind, her eyes crinkled with laughter lines. She was holding on to Blake's arm, his hand resting on hers. He was looking down at her with such love that it almost broke Ellie's heart.

77

The headline read: *Blake Fielding — Is Silicon Valley's Most Secretive Entrepreneur Actually The Tech Industry's Nicest Guy?*

Was this the real Blake? How had his reputation sunk so quickly? Ellie wanted to copy this article and send it to everyone on the planet, but there was no way to do it. She brushed a finger down Blake's cheek, then put the phone on the floor. Outside the door she heard Josh drop his dishes into the sink.

"Place could do with a clean," he yelled. "You never know when the landlord is going to drop by."

He left, closing the door behind him and whistling his way down the corridor. Ellie shot up, ran to the front door and slid the deadbolt across to stop him making any more unannounced visits. Even though he was the world's biggest idiot, he was right, the apartment did look a little neglected. She'd been so busy at work and planning for her interview that she hadn't hoovered in a while, and there were coffee mugs on practically every surface. It was too late to do anything about it now, but tomorrow she would blitz the place. In fact, she would blitz everything. It was time to get serious about her life. No more working in a café. No more letting Josh just walk through the door whenever he liked.

And no more daydreaming about Blake Fielding.

* * *

Ellie may have sworn off daydreaming about Blake, but apparently, her subconscious hadn't got the memo. Her dreams last night had been so vivid, so electric, that when she woke up, her body pulsed with want. Stretching languidly beneath her covers, she could almost feel his warmth lingering beside her — his breath on her neck, his hands trailing lower.

For a moment, she lay there, blinking in the soft morning light streaming through the curtains, her fingers stroking her naked body. Her pulse was still racing, her skin humming as fragments of the dream flickered through her mind. They'd been in the bar, the same booth where they'd sat drinking

78

coffee. Only this time, no one else was around. The lights were low, shadows dancing across the walls, and Blake had pulled her in to his lap, hands sliding beneath her top, his mouth hot and hungry on hers.

It had felt so real — so unbearably, heartbreakingly real — that waking up alone felt like a cruel joke.

Get it together, Ellie, she scolded herself, running a hand through her messy hair. *You barely know the guy.*

Still, her fingers curled into the duvet as her mind betrayed her again, flashing images of his dark, unruly curls, the way his fathomless blue eyes had locked on to hers like she was the only person in the room. And that body . . . carved from stone, his hoodie doing little to hide the sculpted strength beneath.

She groaned, flopping back against the pillows. "Nope. Not doing this," she muttered aloud, throwing an arm over her eyes. "One day. That's all I'm asking — just one day without thinking about Blake freaking Fielding."

But as she lay there, the ghost of his smile teasing the edges of her memory, she knew she was already doomed.

She clambered out of bed, yawning. It wasn't even seven yet so she put some coffee on and some bread in the toaster. Josh had spilled a load of coffee grounds on the counter and instead of clearing up the mess, he'd drawn a heart in them. She scrubbed it out with a dish cloth, pressing so hard she was in danger of leaving a mark on the Formica surface. She wished she could get rid of Josh as easily, and the thought of having to put up with him at work made her want to climb back into bed and stay there for the rest of the year.

No, she told herself. She wasn't going to do it anymore. Last night she'd shared coffee with a billionaire — although admittedly one hated by pretty much the whole world. She wasn't going to let Josh push her around.

She wasn't sure if she had the courage to say it to his face, though. He could be irritatingly persuasive. Instead, she took out her phone and texted Lissa, asking if she could come

79

in later. Rob would be covering the morning shift as well and there was never enough for them all to do. Besides, even though yesterday had been a complete washout, it had given her renewed enthusiasm for LifeWrite. Blake had seemed genuinely interested, and even though he might not be in any position to work with her now, maybe somebody else was. She certainly wasn't going to find success for her own business while serving coffees in a café. And besides, who was to say she wouldn't have another chance to pitch her idea to Blake?

You're thinking about him again, said her brain, and she slapped herself gently on the side of the head.

Her phone buzzed, Lissa's message appearing.

Sure, hon, after yesterday I don't blame you. Take the day if you like.

She was about to reply when another text came through.

And be careful. Josh sent us all the video. Remember, you deserve better. You deserve the best. Love you.

She fired back a thank you, then poured herself some coffee. Sunlight flooded the room and she basked in it, her mood lifting. Yeah, she'd take the day, clean her little flat and work on some designs for LifeWrite, then maybe the next time she met Blake she'd have something concrete to show him.

Enough about Blake!

It wasn't like she'd ever see him again. The odds were practically non-existent — he hadn't left her his number, hadn't even hinted at wanting to see her again, aside from those fleeting, soul-igniting looks. Sure, he'd mentioned a few places he frequented, but what was she supposed to do? Stalk every café in the city, hoping for a chance encounter?

Even if she did see him again, would he even remember her? Probably not. Guys like Blake Fielding didn't have time to linger on ordinary women like her, no matter how much

80

she wished otherwise. She needed to get a grip, forget about him, and bury the memory of yesterday deep in her mind where it couldn't haunt her.

But then there was that damn smile.

Curled at the corners of his mouth like a secret she needed to know. It hit her low and hard every time she remembered it.

Her cheeks flushed, a soft heat spreading through her that she hated to admit was entirely Blake's doing. She could almost hear his low, velvet voice again, the way he'd said her name, the way his lips had curved as if he'd known exactly what kind of effect he had on her.

"Stop it," she muttered to herself, shaking her head as though she could physically dislodge him from her thoughts.

She grabbed her phone and called her mum. She'd barely scratched the surface in last night's rushed update, and she definitely hadn't wanted to say too much with Blake right there. But now, maybe spilling the whole story would help her shake this . . . whatever it was.

"Honey," said Mum. She could hear the idyllic sounds of cows lowing and birds singing in the background. "I'm so glad you called. It's not like I spent *all* night wondering whether your date had thrown you into the sea."

"One, he wasn't a date," said Ellie, crunching toast as she spoke. "Two, we were nowhere near the sea, and three, he definitely wasn't a date."

"How would I know?" asked Mum. "You never tell me anything. Are you off to work today?"

"Yeah," she lied. Her mum had instilled in Ellie a strict work ethic, and she didn't tolerate any excuses for slacking. Especially not excuses of the boy variety.

"I'm sure the café would fall apart without you," she said dryly. "Just remember, there's plenty of work back here at home, I can set you up in a good company — they're looking for bright young things. And you're always welcome back on the farm. I could use you."

81

"I'm fine, Mum," Ellie said, not feeling particularly young or bright. "I'm working on something big. There's been some . . . interest."

It wasn't a complete lie, was it?

"Well do what you have to do," said her mum. "You know I believe in you. And Ellie?"

"Yeah?"

"You seem pretty insistent that the man you were with last night wasn't a date. But if that was the case, why did you sound like a giddy schoolgirl when you spoke to me?"

Ellie's cheeks blazed. "Gotta go," she said. "Love you, Mum."

She ended the call. How ridiculous was her mother? She hadn't sounded like a giddy schoolgirl at all. She'd just been tired, and Blake had caught her by surprise.

Definitely not a date.

She finished her coffee and toast then showered, dressing in a light, summery dress and flats. It would be nice to sit and work here all day, but she knew that as soon as Josh found out she wasn't in the café, he'd come over to keep her company. There were plenty of other cafés nearby she could use, but she found the hustle and bustle distracting. A bookstore was out of the question, too, because she'd end up returning home with a pile of new books and she was poor enough as it was.

No, she needed somewhere quiet, somewhere where she'd be surrounded by books but wouldn't have to pay for any. Somewhere she wouldn't be interrupted by Josh.

Checking she had enough money for the bus, she grabbed her bag and headed for the library. It was only as she was walking out the door that she remembered to pick up her laptop too, scolding herself for not focusing.

Because the truth was, work wasn't the only reason she was heading into town.

82

CHAPTER 13

BLAKE

Blake stepped out of the heat into the glorious, air-conditioned interior of the public library. The faint hum of the lights, the smell of the books, the quiet tapping of the librarian's keyboard — it was like Xanax to Blake's senses.

No one appeared to be paying him any attention — just a couple of students hunched over laptops, an elderly man thumbing a dog-eared paperback, and a woman stacking shelves. But he kept his head down anyway, his heart racing in case anyone recognised him. He was wearing a white polo shirt and jeans, white Adidas trainers, and a 49ers cap that he'd picked up on the way over. In addition, he'd shaved off his stubble and found a pair of black-rimmed glasses from before he'd had his eyes LASIKed. They made everything wobble like he was underwater, but they completely changed the shape of his face. Even with the disguise he felt like a spy, creeping into a government building to steal secrets and knowing that one wrong move would lead to instant death.

Of course, it wasn't a life-or-death thing really, not for him anyway. For his company, though, it could well be. David had told him to stay hidden, and after the incident in the bar that seemed like a good idea. But the thought of being imprisoned in a cell — even if that cell was a 4,000-square-foot luxury penthouse — was enough to bring on a panic attack. It was risky being here, but he'd used a driver today, and the car would be waiting right outside in the event he needed to make a quick getaway.

Michelle and the board had locked him out of the Heartbook network completely, so there was nothing he could do from home. Realising he was standing aimlessly in the lobby with more and more people funnelling past him, Blake set off towards a rotunda where he knew he would be okay to make a call.

A few women were glancing his way, but nobody was scowling at him like they wanted to poke his eyes out with the corner of a hardback. That was something, at least. Like he'd told Ellie, libraries always felt like a sanctuary to him. There was a quiet respect here, a kind of mutual understanding among people who valued ideas and stories.

He couldn't help thinking about Ellie, and the way her whole face lit up when she talked about books. It wasn't just a casual interest — she *felt* it, the same way he did. That connection had been unexpected and undeniable. For a moment, it had made him forget everything else.

He let out a slow breath, frustration simmering. They'd barely scratched the surface of that conversation before the night had gone to hell. He wished they'd had more time — just a little longer to dig into that shared love of stories, to see where it might lead.

But now, thanks to one angry barmaid and a viral video, any chance of that felt like a long shot.

Blake had no room for distractions now, not with everything that was on the line. Heartbook wasn't just his legacy — it was the livelihood of thousands of employees, people whose futures depended on the company staying afloat. If it collapsed, it wouldn't just be his reputation in ruins. It would ripple through countless lives.

84

However much Ellie lingered in his thoughts, however much she was beginning to mean to him, he couldn't afford to indulge in what-ifs. He needed to keep his head in the game, to lock his focus on what truly mattered: saving Heartbook.

There was no other option.

But what is truly important?

The voice belonged to his mum, and it made him want to pick up the phone and call her. How many times had she asked him that question when he was setting up his company, when he'd worked twenty-hour days and slept in his office? He'd stopped seeing his friends, he'd stopped dating, he'd even stopped speaking to her. All that had mattered was the company, but his mum had known that you can't fill your heart with business, and you can't feed your soul with shares. All she'd truly wanted for him was to be happy, to be loved, and it had made her sad to see him so emotionally devoted to something that gave nothing back.

Except it had given him something back. It had given him *everything*, hadn't it? The money, the houses, the cars, the clothes . . .

He shook his head as he made his way to the reading rooms on the first floor. You couldn't feed your soul with those things, either.

He weaved past the other library visitors and settled himself into a booth, checking his watch. It was only just nine. His plan was to find a quiet place and log in to Heartbook from a public IP address that hadn't been blocked. He still wouldn't be able to access his accounts, but he might be able to check the site for any other signs of hacking.

And, if all else failed, it was better than sitting at home on his own. If he couldn't do anything then at least he could lie on a window seat in the sun and lose himself in a good book.

But, for now, he needed a little outside help, and he knew exactly who to call.

He pulled out his phone and scrolled to Nathanial Parker's number. Nate was a founding member of the APEX

85

Billionaire Club and one of the most brilliant coders Blake had ever met. Nate had built a dating empire from the ground up, but Blake knew his proudest moment was when he was twelve and he'd hacked into his high school website to change the photos of all the teachers to cat memes. Nate had helped Blake and David build Heartbook, designing its intricate framework and — more importantly — installing a backdoor. A failsafe in case of emergencies.

And this was definitely an emergency.

Nate had texted Blake outside of the group chat last night and offered his help, and Blake was about to bite his hand off. He just hoped that Nate would have the skills to be able to find out what was going on in the depths of the Heartbook code. Blake hesitated, his thumb hovering over the call button. Then, with a sharp inhale, he pressed it.

The line rang twice before Nate picked up, his deep voice crackling through the speaker. "Blake, I'm glad you called." His West Coast American accent was like sunshine in a bottle.

"Nate," Blake said, keeping his voice low. "Thank you."

There was a pause, followed by the faint sound of typing. "What a mess, Blake. What a mess. I'm not, like, going to ask if you said those things because I know you better, man, but you must have right royally pissed someone off for them to target you so hard."

"Urgh." Blake scrubbed a hand down his face. "It's killing me, Nate. Heartbook is my life. Have you seen the news?"

"Who hasn't?" Nate replied, his tone laced with dry amusement. "Your name's trending worldwide. What can I do?"

"Literally no idea," Blake muttered, glancing around again. "The board's locked me out of the system. I can't even see what's going on. I need access, Nate. You're the only one who can give it to me."

"Locked out of your own company," Nate said with a low whistle. "That's brutal, even for Michelle."

"She's gunning for me — they all are. Well, nearly all of them," Blake said, his jaw tightening. "Can you help me or not?"

86

Nate chuckled softly. "Relax. I've still got the backdoor. But you know this is risky, right? If they find out I'm involved—"

"They won't," Blake interrupted, his tone firm. "I'll make sure of it."

Another pause. "Where are you?"

"Library," Blake said.

Nate snorted. "Classic Fielding. When the world's burning, hide out with the books."

Blake rolled his eyes. "Can you come and meet me?"

"Not yet," Nate said. "I'm in Switzerland, wrapping up a project. I'll catch the first flight back, but it'll be a few hours."

Blake cursed under his breath. "Fine. Text me when you're in the city. I'll come to your office."

"Deal," Nate said, his tone softening. "But listen, Blake. You're on thin ice. One wrong move could cost you everything."

"That seems to be the latest mantra of everyone I know," Blake said, his voice tight. "But I am not letting them take what I've built."

"That's the spirit," Nate said. "All right, I'll be in touch. And Blake?"

"Yeah?"

"Stay out of trouble. You're already in deep enough."

Blake smirked despite himself. "No promises."

"The girl from the bar, huh?" Nate's voice carried a smile that Blake didn't need to see to recognise.

"No comment," Blake replied.

Nate laughed. "Well, let's sort out this mess and then you can tell me all about her. I'll be in touch when I land."

As the call ended, Blake slipped the phone back into his pocket, his eyes scanning the room. The library was still quiet, but something felt off.

"Trouble in paradise?" a woman's voice said, cutting the silence like a knife.

Blake's heart jolted. He turned to see a woman sitting a few tables away, her sharp eyes fixed on him over the rim of her laptop. She was in her late thirties, her sleek black hair pulled into a tight bun.

"I'm sorry?" he said, forcing calm into his voice, while his whole body was screaming at him to run.

The woman tilted her head, her red lips curling into a smirk. "That sounded like a pretty intense call."

Blake's pulse raced, but he kept his expression neutral. "I think you've got the wrong idea."

"Do I?" she asked, her tone playful but her eyes sharp.

Blake's grip on the edge of the table tightened. "Just a work thing. Nothing exciting."

The woman chuckled, leaning back in her chair. "Right. Well, good luck with that."

As she returned her focus to her screen, Blake's instincts screamed at him to move. He stood, gathering his laptop and bag, and headed towards another section of the library. He would find a quieter spot — one of the reading rooms would work.

His mind raced. Who was she? A journalist? Someone working for the board? Or just a nosy library-goer who'd overheard too much?

Blake's stomach churned, as he tried to remember if he'd said Nate's name out loud. If this woman leaked anything, it could blow up Nate's involvement before they even had a chance to meet. And if the board found out he had a backdoor into Heartbook, that would snap the last sliver of trust they had left in him.

Taking a deep breath, he tried to refocus. He had work to do, and standing here panicking wouldn't help. He was muttering under his breath, reminding himself to stay calm, when a familiar voice called out his name.

CHAPTER 14

ELLIE

At first she wasn't sure if it was him. He looked different, his hair hidden by a cap, a pair of glasses perched on his nose. He was clean shaven, and his casual jeans and polo shirt didn't give much of a clue as to who he was.

But there was something about the way he carried himself, something unmistakable. She followed him across the floor of the library and halfway down the corridor to the reading rooms, her heart thudding harder with each step. When he turned his head slightly, that jawline gave him away, and she knew for certain.

"Blake?" She lightly touched his arm. There was nobody else around, but she spoke in almost a whisper so as not to give his identity away. He turned, his startled expression changing instantly to one of delight.

"Ellie!" he said, and he'd opened his arms before he even seemed to know he was doing it.

Ellie had to hold back from throwing herself at him, instead leaning in and kissing him on the cheek. His arms folded gently around her back for a moment, holding her tight. He smelled amazing, like sandalwood and citrus, and she let herself rest against the hardness of his chest. He let go too soon, and she took a reluctant step back. Her cheeks were on fire, and she waved a hand in front of her face.

"Really hot in here," she said, trying to cover her embarrassment. "Are you hot? I'm hot. Really hot."

Blake chuckled, his eyes sparkling behind the glasses. "It's definitely warm."

"Roasting." *Stop talking, Ellie.*

"What brings you here?" he asked, still smiling, and the way his voice softened made warmth pool in all the softness of her body.

You, she wanted to say, relief washing over her now that she'd found him. It had been a ridiculous long shot coming here, a spur-of-the-moment decision after last night. She hadn't been able to shake the image of him walking away, his shoulders weighed down by more than just the coffee-soaked hoodie.

"You know," she said, brushing a strand of hair behind her ear. "Work. LifeWrite stuff. Speaking with you last night motivated me, you know? I wanted to strike while the iron was hot and what better place to do so than a library?" She looked over her shoulder to make sure they were alone. "Are you okay, after . . . That barmaid never should have done that. She was way out of line."

Blake sighed, pulling off his glasses and dragging a hand down his face. When he slipped them back on, Ellie's breath hitched. The way the frames hugged his sharp features only emphasised the striking intensity of his eyes — eyes that burned with a quiet strength, yet carried a vulnerability that made her chest tighten. The contrast was intoxicating, a mix of control and rawness that had her pulse racing.

"She had every right to do it," he said. "If she believed I said the things on my Heartbook profile then she was actually entitled to do a lot worse."

"But you didn't do it," Ellie said, moving closer to him so that she could keep her voice low.

90

"I know that," he said. "But nobody else does. As far as the world is concerned, I'm a woman-hating monster."

"You're not," she said, her voice resolute. "I don't think you're a monster at all."

Blake managed a small, sad smile, but it didn't quite reach his eyes. "You're in the minority, then."

Ellie shook her head, wanting to scream from the roof-tops that this man wasn't what everyone thought he was. But she was in a library, and whispering was all she dared manage.

"Did you look at them?" he asked after a beat. "The posts?"

She hesitated, then nodded. "Some of them."

"Then I'm surprised you haven't thrown something at me yourself," he said. "I'm surprised you're even talking to me."

"Blake," she said, her voice soft but firm, "it doesn't take a genius to know when someone's lying. I've only known you a day, but I'd bet everything I own that you didn't write a single one of those posts. Not that I own a huge amount of stuff, but . . ."

He stared at her, his throat bobbing as he swallowed hard.

"I'd testify in court if I had to," she continued, her eyes locking with his. "I *know*."

Blake exhaled, his shoulders easing slightly, and for a moment, neither of them spoke. The faint hum of the library filled the space between them, punctuated with the distant sound of footsteps on polished floors.

He nodded.

"All we have to do now," Ellie said after a moment, "is figure out how to let the rest of the world know, too."

Blake's lips twitched — almost a smile — but there was still a heaviness in his expression. "Easier said than done."

"We'll figure it out," she said confidently, surprising even herself.

"You seem so sure of me," he said, his voice quiet, almost reverent.

"I am."

His eyes searched hers, and the weight of his gaze sent a shiver down her spine. There was so much vulnerability there, so much unspoken emotion, and she felt an overwhelming need to protect him. But it wasn't just that — she wanted to do more than protect him. She wanted to close the distance between them, to feel his breath against her skin, to trace the curve of his jaw with her fingertips. The thought of his lips on hers sent a rush of heat through her, and her heart raced, her body betraying her restraint.

"Thank you," he said.

"For what?" Ellie hoped he couldn't read her mind.

"For believing me." His hand twitched as if he wanted to reach for hers but thought better of it.

She smiled. "Let's just say I have a good gut instinct."

Blake chuckled, the sound low and warm, and for a brief moment, the tension between them eased.

"You know," she said, tilting her head, "you're pretty good at hiding, but the glasses don't fool me."

He laughed. "Yeah, I figured."

"Next time, maybe try a fake moustache," she teased, and the sound of his laughter was like a balm to her nerves.

"Noted." His smile lingered as he looked at her.

The air between them seemed to alter, the light-heartedness giving way to something heavier, more charged. Ellie's pulse quickened, but she didn't dare look away.

"We should find somewhere to sit," Blake said eventually, breaking the silence but not the tension. "Away from . . . people."

"Yeah," Ellie said, her voice a little breathless. "Good idea."

They walked along the corridor, peering in the reading rooms, and as they approached the room at the very end, away from all the prying eyes, Ellie couldn't shake the feeling that something between them had shifted again.

And she wasn't sure if she wanted it to shift back.

92

CHAPTER 15

BLAKE

Blake opened a door into the empty reading room and closed it softly behind them. The faint scent of old books and polished wood hung in the air, the soft glow of the desk lamps casting long shadows across the room. It was quiet, the kind of silence that heightened every sound — the rustle of clothing, the subtle hitch of Ellie's breath.

She stood just a few feet away, her gaze drifting around the room before landing back on him. The way the light caught in her hair made it shimmer, and the slight flush on her cheeks only added to her allure. She looked . . . irresistible.

Blake leaned back against the closed door, trying to keep his composure, but every part of him was hyperaware of her. The delicate curve of her neck, the way her fingers fidgeted with the strap of her bag, even the rise and fall of her chest as she breathed. It was maddening.

The tension between them felt thick enough to touch, and as she took a step closer, his pulse hammered in his ears. He could smell her faint perfume, something soft and sweet, but underneath it was the warmth of her — enticing, distracting.

He cleared his throat, his voice coming out lower than he intended. "It's quieter in here."

"Yeah," she said softly, her lips curving into a small, almost shy smile. "It's . . . peaceful."

Peaceful wasn't the word he'd use. Every nerve in his body was on edge, the quiet amplifying the rush of blood in his veins. Her presence filled the room and, for the life of him, he couldn't look away. Her yellow dress hung midway down her creamy thighs, hair the colour of hay pulled back into a messy ponytail. Behind her glasses her eyes glittered like a sun-soaked river.

She moved to one of the chairs by the window, the light brushing against her as she sat down. The way her dress shifted, revealing a hint more of her leg, made his throat go dry.

"You okay?" she asked, her eyes soft but searching.

Blake forced himself to nod, though he wasn't sure how truthful it was. "Yeah. Just . . . thinking."

About how much he wanted to cross the room. About how much he wanted to sink his hands into her hair, tilt her head back, and kiss her until he forgot everything — Heartbook, the board, the whole damn world.

But this wasn't the time. It wasn't the place.

Not that his body seemed to care.

He ran a hand through his hair, trying to ground himself. "I'm just glad you're here," he said finally.

Ellie gave him a small smile that almost undid him. "I'm glad, too," she said, her voice barely above a whisper.

She glanced at the chair beside her, as if inviting him to sit, but his legs wouldn't seem to work. If he got too close, he wasn't sure he'd be able to keep himself in check. Instead, he stayed where he was, his hands gripping the edge of the doorframe, his heart a riot in his chest.

She said that she believed him about the posts not being his words, but there must still have been a part of her that wasn't sure. He didn't want to do anything that she might take the wrong way — like telling her how she made him feel

94

while they were alone together in a room on the third floor of the public library.

Her gaze lingered on him, her teeth catching her bottom lip for the briefest moment. His eyes followed the movement, and he swallowed hard, imagining what it would feel like to taste her, to press his lips to hers in this quiet, hidden corner. The thought alone sent a pulse of heat through him, and he forced himself to take a slow, steadying breath.

"Blake?" she said, her voice drawing him out of his thoughts.

"Yeah?"

"You seem . . . distracted." Her lips quirked slightly.

He let out a low chuckle, shaking his head. "You could say that."

She laughed, the sound wrapping around him like a warm embrace. God, how was she doing this to him?

The silence stretched between them again, charged and heavy, and for a brief, reckless second, he imagined closing the distance, and capturing her mouth with his. The thought made his fingers tighten on the doorframe.

But he couldn't.

Not here. Not now.

"Ellie?" His voice sounded low and rough.

"Yeah?" she said, her cheeks flushing deeper as if she'd been thinking the same thing.

"Do you want to tell me more about LifeWrite?" he said, knowing it was a great excuse to keep her close to him for a little longer. "Seeing as we've got time and space and it's why you're here anyway."

Her eyes widened as she nodded briskly, her ponytail shaking irresistibly.

"Uh, great." He was fighting to organise his thoughts. He slid his glasses into his pocket, happy to be rid of them. "You want a coffee or anything?"

"No, not yet," she replied. "Are you sure you've got time? I mean, I know you must be really busy."

95

"Right now, I have nothing to do." He pulled out a chair that was at the opposite end of the table. "Literally nothing. I'm completely frozen out of everything."

"I'm so sorry," Ellie said.

He waved the apology away. "I'm not. It gives me a chance to be here with you. I mean, because of LifeWrite. Because it's such a great idea."

"I don't know," she said bashfully, pulling out her laptop and her notebook and throwing the bag to the floor. He scooted his chair a little closer so he could see as she switched on the ancient machine. "It was just a silly idea really, just some scatterbrained plan."

"You don't ever have to do that," Blake said. "You don't ever have to put yourself down. What you've got here is amazing, and what's even more special is that you did it in the first place. You found a passion, you fought to make it real. It's incredible. It's exactly what I did."

"Not quite," she said. "My idea isn't worth billions on the stock market."

"Neither's mine." He laughed. "Not today, anyway. And it wasn't when it started, either. You know, when I first had the idea for Heartbook I was working in Mum's restaurant as a dishwasher."

"I'd like to pretend I didn't know that," Ellie said, laughing too. It was contagious. "But I did a lot of research for my interview!"

"You'll know, then, that there was no place for me to work," he said, grinning. "So when I had a break I'd take my laptop into the toilet and lock myself in a cubicle."

"Didn't know that bit. That's disgusting."

"I know, right?" he replied. "But I'd sit there and write code whenever I could. I was in there so often the other staff started calling me Flusher."

A laugh escaped Ellie, and she clamped a hand over her mouth.

"Flusher! You do realise I'm going to have to call you that from now on."

96

"I deserve it," he said. "You know, after a while, because I was in there so often, Mum started charging me rent. Fiver a week."

"Harsh," said Ellie.

"Exactly," said Blake. "She was a ruthless landlord. I was young, not even twenty, and I didn't have any money at all. In fact, I couldn't even pay her that, I was so broke. I had pennies to my name at one point. But what I lacked in finances I made up for in passion. I never gave up, I never stopped believing. You shouldn't either. Let's see what you've got."

"Okay, Flusher," she said, and he laughed. "But I'm warning you, it's not much."

She opened up a folder on her laptop.

"I can't code. At least not very well. Not well enough for this. But the architecture is all here."

"LifeWrite," said Blake, reading from the screen. "*Write your own story*. That's good."

"Thanks." Ellie pushed her glasses back up her nose. "Like I said to you last night, stories are so powerful, they can unite us in so many ways."

Like our story, he thought.

He pushed that thought straight out of his head because this moment was about Ellie and what she was passionate about, not about him and his lustful dreams. Besides, her plan for LifeWrite seemed like a really good one.

"Show me more."

She did — she showed him everything. She gushed about her project, demonstrating how the accounts were called Pages, the groups called Chapters. It was laid out like a high street with nothing but book shops and cafés, libraries and parks, and as she flicked through designs and illustrations it felt almost as if she was showing him around her own private paradise.

"This part is based on my favourite book from childhood," she said, looking at him with huge pupils and pink cheeks. "*The Swiss Family Robinson*. Have you read it?"

97

Blake nodded. He'd taken a copy from his mum's shelves when he was a kid, intrigued by the premise of being stranded on a desert island. He must have read it a dozen times over the years, partly because of the story, but partly because the novel always reminded him of his mum.

"I had a copy," she said. "It wasn't a first edition, but it was old, like one of the first copies in English. I found it in a charity shop, back home, and I couldn't believe my luck."

"That's amazing," he said. "I'd love to see it."

"So would I," she replied with a sigh. "But it's long gone. Josh borrowed it. Left it on a plane. Didn't even read it. He bought me a cheap paperback to replace it and couldn't understand why I was so upset."

"I understand," Blake said, feeling as furious now as she must have then.

She smiled at him with gratitude, holding his eye for a beat. "Um, so, anyway, check this out."

She went on with the tour, showing him around a digitised island. He commented where she let him, telling her how much he loved this design, or that idea. Every time she moved to a different theme — each one based on a famous work of literature — he told her how much he loved the books she'd picked. He'd read almost all of them, and when there was one he hadn't, she detoured from the presentation to tell him all about it. She showed him how eventually LifeWrite would be able to use your computer camera to assess what kind of mood you were in, helping you out if you felt sad or lonely, reading poems and stories to you to cheer you up.

She was so animated, and so full of passion for her project. Her enthusiasm was contagious, and he found himself thinking about how easy it would be to make this a reality, and how popular it could be. The internet was full of negativity, social media drowning under the force of criticism and bile — Heartbook included. LifeWrite was refreshing, and such a good idea that he wondered why nobody had taken it seriously yet.

98

She reminded him most of all of his own excitement in the early days of Heartbook. Back then he had given everything to the company, but he hadn't minded because it had been his project. Ever since the company had gone public, and he'd had to answer to a board of directors and an army of shareholders, he'd enjoyed his role less and less. Nothing about Heartbook felt personal to him anymore.

"And that's kind of it," she said, sitting back. "That's my baby."

Blake nodded, emerging from the conversation the same way he emerged from dreams. He blinked, the room gradually reforming around him, noticing the muted sounds from the rest of the library, the sunlight filtering through the window.

"God, sorry, I really went on," Ellie said.

"No, not at all," Blake replied, feeling as if they had been talking for a matter of minutes. When he checked his watch his jaw almost hit the floor. Over two hours had passed since they'd entered the room. "Wait, is that right? Were we really talking all that time?"

"*You* weren't," she said. "I was. I don't know when to stop."

Never, thought Blake. *You never have to stop.*

"That was amazing," he said. "I mean, really. This is all your work?"

"Yeah. I've been working on it for ages. For *years*, really. It's where my heart has been."

"I can tell. It's so you, so naturally brilliant. It's like all those wonderful thoughts have just spilled out of your beautiful head and—"

Blake choked on his words. *Shut up, you idiot!* his brain yelled, and he gasped for a way to cover his tracks.

"I mean . . ." was as far as he got before Ellie started laughing.

"You're ridiculous," she said. "But thanks for being nice."

For what felt like a small eternity they looked at each other, their unspoken thoughts hanging between them like the little specks of dust floating in the sunlight.

99

Then his phone buzzed in his pocket, breaking the moment. He pulled it out, and a text from Nate lit up the screen: *Landed. Office in an hour. See you there.*

Blake felt the familiar pulse of adrenaline surge through him. This was it — his chance to get answers, to figure out who was behind the sabotage and how to clear his name. But as he glanced back at Ellie, the thought of leaving her here felt wrong.

She noticed the shift in his expression, her brow furrowing slightly. "Everything okay?"

"Yeah." He slipped the phone back into his pocket. "I've got a friend helping me with access to Heartbook. His plane's just landed. I need to meet him."

Her eyes widened slightly, and for a second, he thought he saw something like disappointment flicker across her face.

"Oh," she said, tucking a strand of hair behind her ear. "Then you should definitely go."

And it was true, which is why he was so surprised to hear himself say, "Will you come with me?"

CHAPTER 16

ELLIE

Ellie felt as if she was riding a roller coaster, with each new minute bringing an unexpected twist or a breathtaking loop-the-loop.

What is happening? she had to ask herself as she walked by Blake's side, down the sweeping staircase of the library and out of the main doors. She couldn't believe she'd talked his ear off for so long about LifeWrite, and that he'd listened to it all without looking at his watch, yawning dramatically and making an excuse to leave — which is what Josh had always done.

Most of all she couldn't believe he seemed genuinely interested, and it *had* been a genuine interest. His questions had all been intelligent and curious, his comments insightful. He'd heard every single word she had said. The whole thing had been literally unbelievable, yet here she was, walking out of her favourite building with her new favourite person.

Though she was certainly the *only* person in the Blake Fielding fan club at the moment.

Even with his glasses back on, subtly disguising his features, people were starting to notice him. Some of it was unavoidable — he exuded a quiet, commanding presence that naturally drew eyes.

But it wasn't the kind of brash confidence she'd come to expect from the few wealthy people she'd encountered in passing. Blake's aura felt . . . different. He carried himself with a calm, reassuring strength, the kind of energy that made you want to lean in, not shy away. Her mum had always said that truly kind people had a certain light about them, and Blake practically radiated.

It didn't hurt that he looked like he'd just stepped off the cover of *GQ*. Those broad shoulders, the way his fitted polo shirt hinted at the muscle beneath — yeah, he was bound to attract attention.

But some of the looks weren't admiring. Ellie caught a few sharp, disapproving glances as they stepped on to the pavement, and her stomach twisted. She could practically hear the judgement in their eyes.

How dare she walk with him?

It wasn't hard to guess what they were thinking. The viral bar video was everywhere, with over a million views when she'd checked that morning. At least some of the people around them must've recognised him — or worse, recognised her.

Her grip on her bag strap tightened as a couple of women shot her particularly sour glares. She wasn't used to being in the spotlight, and she definitely wasn't used to being on the receiving end of public scorn.

Blake, on the other hand, seemed unfazed. His pace was steady, his focus fixed ahead as though nothing could touch him. That calm confidence was like a shield, and Ellie found herself leaning into it, letting his presence ground her.

Luckily they didn't have to go far. A few seconds after leaving the building, a huge, shark-like Mercedes-Maybach purred to a halt in front of them. Blake opened the back door and gestured for her to get in. She hesitated for a split second, but the warmth of his small smile reassured her. Climbing inside, she was immediately hit by the rich scent of leather and polish.

The interior was unlike anything she'd ever experienced. It was like stepping into a mobile five-star suite, complete with plush quilted seats, soft ambient lighting, and an air of understated elegance. There were small crystal glasses tucked neatly into holders, a sleek control panel by her armrest, and even a perfectly fluffed cushion on her seat.

She ran her fingers over the buttery leather, marvelling at the attention to detail. She'd flown economy her entire life, and walking past business class on the way to her seat had always been the closest she'd got to this kind of luxury.

"It's a little much," said Blake, apologetically. He waited for her to sit down then closed her door, appearing a few seconds later on the other side of the car. A few people on the pavement had worked out who he was and Ellie could hear a few jeers which were abruptly cut off as he shut the door.

"Thanks, Alfie," Blake said to the young man at the wheel. "Better put your foot down before they start throwing bricks."

"Yes, sir," said Alfie, and the car moved off with so much power that Ellie felt her insides tumble.

Just another twist on the roller coaster, she thought.

The driver pulled smoothly into traffic, the city blurring past the tinted windows. Ellie stole a glance at Blake, her heart skipping as he adjusted his glasses and leaned his head back against the seat. Even in this moment of quiet, there was something magnetic about him, an unspoken tension that filled the space between them.

"So, where exactly are we going?" she asked, trying to keep her voice casual.

"To meet someone who can help. Someone I trust."

Ellie nodded, her curiosity piqued. "A secret mission, then?"

Blake chuckled, the sound low and rich. "Something like that."

She couldn't help but smile, the tension easing slightly. Despite everything — the viral scandal, the stares on the street

103

— this felt like an adventure, one she wasn't entirely sure she was ready for but couldn't resist joining.

The driver obviously knew where they were going, even if Ellie didn't. Blake stared at the crowds outside the window. After a moment he turned to her. "Thank you for coming," he said. "I didn't exactly plan to ask you — it just sort of slipped out."

Ellie smirked. "You make it sound like I'm doing you a huge favour."

"Aren't you?" He tilted his head.

"Maybe," she teased, leaning back. "But I'm also curious. You're like a walking mystery novel."

Blake chuckled. "Glad I'm keeping you entertained."

"Hey, it beats sitting at home," she said. "Besides, you've got me hooked now. I need to know how this story ends."

"Hopefully not with me in handcuffs," he quipped, though there was a shadow of seriousness behind his grin.

Ellie gave him a playful nudge with her elbow. "Well, if that happens, I'll be the first to smuggle you a file baked into a cake."

"Good to know I have someone in my corner," Blake said, his smile lingering as he studied her. "It's been a while since I've felt that."

She saw something flicker in his eyes — gratitude, maybe? Or relief? It was hard to tell, but whatever it was, it hit her square in the chest.

"Well, you've got me," she said lightly. "Just don't expect me to do anything illegal. I have my limits."

"Is smuggling tools into prison in a cake not illegal?" Blake laughed, shaking his head. "But, noted. No criminal activity unless it involves baking, right you are."

"I have been known to make an illegally good seven-layer gateau." Ellie turned her gaze to the window, ignoring the burning in her cheeks at the dad joke that had sprung from nowhere. "So," she said after a beat, "who's this mystery person we're meeting?"

104

"Nathanial Parker. Nate," Blake replied. "He's a genius coder and one of the original Heartbook team. He's helped me out of tight spots before. We go way back. He's a member of this . . . club I'm a part of and he's, well, what can I say? He's possibly going to save my bacon."

"A club?" Ellie asked. "Can anyone join? Or do you have to be blessed by the god of good genes to get a look in?"

Blake laughed. "If that were the only criteria, you'd be welcomed with open arms. It's an exclusive club for people with . . . let's say . . . a lot of money . . ."

"Billionaires," said Ellie. "I'm not naive, Blake. I know how much you and Heartbook are worth."

Blake smiled. "Not everyone is as genuine as you when they find out about the money. My friends I've made at APEX are all in the same boat, and so we all know the shit we have to deal with. We support one another."

Ellie was going to make a quip about using their piles of cash to keep Blake's company alive, but she'd had a glimpse of how money didn't really solve issues like this and decided now wasn't the time. "And Nate's okay with all of this?" she asked instead.

Blake shrugged. "Let's just say Nate doesn't scare easily."

Ellie raised an eyebrow. "Must be nice to have friends in high places."

Blake smirked. "It has its perks. But trust me, Nate's not the type to let me forget this favour."

Ellie couldn't help but grin. "Sounds like my kind of guy."

Blake's eyes flicked to hers, something playful sparking in their depths. "Careful. I might start getting jealous."

Ellie's heart did a little flip, but she kept her tone light. "Don't worry, Fielding. You're still the most intriguing billionaire I've met this week."

"High praise," Blake said with a laugh. "I'll take it."

The car slowed to a stop, and the driver turned in his seat. "We're here, sir."

Blake straightened, glancing out of the window before turning back to Ellie. "You don't have to come in, you know. This could get . . . technical."

Ellie shot him a look. "Do you want me to come in?"

"Yeah," he admitted after a moment. "I do."

"Then let's go," she said, her tone firm but teasing. "Just don't expect me to start speaking in code . . . or billionaire."

Blake chuckled, opening his door. "Deal."

Ellie followed, stepping on to the pavement. Blake appeared beside her almost instantly, his hand lightly brushing her elbow as he guided her around the car.

"Corporate secrets and all," he said with a wink as they approached the entrance to the building. "Mum's the word."

"Don't worry," Ellie said, matching his tone. "I'll take your secrets to the grave."

Blake paused at the door, glancing back at her, his expression momentarily serious. "I'm holding you to that."

Ellie gave him a playful salute, her smile easing the tension in his shoulders.

The doorman held the glass door open for them, and as they stepped inside Ellie took a quick breath, the cool air-conditioning a welcome contrast to the heat outside. She glanced at Blake, noticing the way his jaw tightened ever so slightly as they walked towards the bank of lifts.

"You okay?" she asked quietly.

"Yeah," he said, giving her a quick nod. "Just . . . a lot riding on this."

Ellie nudged him gently with her shoulder. "Good thing you've got me for moral support, then."

Blake's lips twitched into a grin. "Yeah, I think I'm in good hands."

The lift doors slid open and they stepped inside, the tension between them buzzing like static electricity. Ellie caught her reflection in the polished steel walls, her cheeks still faintly pink, her eyes brighter than usual. She felt alive, more alive than she had in years.

Blake pressed the button for the twelfth floor, and as the doors closed, their eyes met in the mirrored surface.

"You ready for this?" she asked, her voice low but steady.

"I am now."

The way he said it sent a thrill straight through her.

The lift hummed as it ascended, the city falling away below them. And as they stood there, side by side in the quiet, Ellie realised something: she wasn't just here to help Blake.

She was here because she wanted to be.

Because, for the first time in a long time, she felt like she was part of something bigger than herself.

And it was thrilling.

CHAPTER 17

BLAKE

Blake felt the subtle shift as they began their ascent. The polished steel walls reflected the two of them — Ellie standing beside him, her hands clasped in front of her, her expression a mix of curiosity and nerves.

"Nate's a bit . . . unconventional," he said, glancing at her reflection. "Just so you're prepared."

Ellie smirked, her shoulders relaxing slightly. "Unconventional how? Like, mad scientist vibes or eccentric artist?"

Blake chuckled softly. "Somewhere in between. Let's just say he doesn't exactly follow the corporate dress code."

"I think I can handle that." Her eyes sparkled with amusement.

He couldn't help but smile. She had a way of making even tense moments feel lighter.

"Are you sure it's okay for me to be here?" she asked, her voice softening. "I don't want to intrude."

"You're not intruding," Blake said firmly. "I want you here. Besides, you've already been dragged into this mess

108

— you might as well meet one of the few people who can help untangle it."

"Thanks." She gave him a small, reassuring nod, and Blake felt a flicker of calm in the storm of chaos swirling around him.

The lift slowed, the soft ding signalling their arrival. As the doors slid open, Blake stepped aside to let Ellie exit first, his hand hovering near the small of her back without quite touching. They walked into a short corridor lined with sleek, numbered doors.

The third door on the left was wide open, and Nathanial Parker was already leaning on the frame, one hand braced against the jamb. He looked every bit as Blake had described — barefoot, wearing a *Green Day* T-shirt and a pair of bright purple boxer shorts that left little to the imagination. His dark hair, incredible brown eyes and toned leg muscles shot a jealous streak through Blake that tore like fire, until he reminded himself that Nate was going to help him, not steal Ellie out from under him.

"Blake!" Nate's voice boomed, his LA accent unmistakable. "Dude, you should've given me a heads up you were bringing royalty with you. I'd have put on pants!"

Ellie spluttered as Blake led her to the door.

"Please don't bother on my account," she said, and Blake's jealous streak stepped up a notch.

"Nate, this is Ellie. Ellie, Nate. Don't say I didn't warn you."

"I'm hardly royalty," Ellie said.

Nate offered his hand, pumping Ellie's with almost painful enthusiasm. "Hey, I say what I see," he said. "And I see a queen. Come on in, coffee's already on."

The space was bright and inviting, with floor-to-ceiling windows flooding the room with light. With a cosy mix of tech chaos and homey touches, it was clear this was Nate's kingdom — an eclectic blend of cutting-edge gadgets and quirky decor.

109

On one of the oversized sofas sat a woman with a colourful silk scarf wrapped around her head. She looked up as they entered, her face lighting up with warmth and affection. Standing slowly, she crossed the room and wrapped Blake in a gentle, motherly hug.

"Darling Blake," she said, her voice soft. "It's so good to see you."

"It's good to see you too, Sophie," Blake said, his voice losing some of its usual tension. "How are you feeling?"

"Wonderful," Sophie said, her smile crinkling the corners of her eyes. "Thank you."

"Still free and clear," Nate chimed in, stepping behind his mum and wrapping an arm around her shoulder.

Blake beamed. "That's great news."

Sophie turned her attention to Ellie, her smile widening. "And who's this lovely young woman?"

Blake's lips twitched into a smile. "Sophie, meet Ellie. She's been keeping me sane the last couple of days."

"Sounds like a full-time job," Sophie teased, extending a hand to Ellie. "It's a pleasure to meet you."

"Likewise," Ellie said, her tone warm but slightly shy.

"Right—" Nate clapped his hands together — "let's get down to business. Coffee, water, or straight to the good stuff?"

"Just water for me," Blake said, sliding a glance at Ellie.

"Coffee for me, please," she said, her lips twitching into a grin. "But thanks for the offer."

"Suit yourselves." Nate grabbed a bottle of water from the fridge and tossed it to Blake before pouring Ellie a supersized mug of coffee. "Let's head to the lair. Time to fix this mess."

Blake nodded, his jaw tightening. This was the moment he'd been waiting for — the first step towards reclaiming everything that had been taken from him.

And somehow, having Ellie by his side made it feel just a little less daunting.

He led them into a large office where three huge screens were sitting on a curved beech desk. Nate's boxers were

110

threadbare and the rear view of them left even less to the imagination. Ellie gave a little giggle and threw her attention deliberately in the other direction, which Blake was glad of.

"Sorry," he whispered, and Ellie gave him a little grimace in return.

"Please, sit," said Nate. "Make yourselves at home. I'll be right back."

He scampered from the room, and Ellie perched on an office chair. Blake sat next to her, running a hand through his mass of thick, dark hair. He looked almost pained.

"I forgot just how weird he was," he said.

"They're lovely," Ellie replied. "Good people, you can tell."

"The best," said Blake. "Even though they don't always wear trousers."

"Good people without trousers are still good people," Ellie said, laughing.

"Pants are overrated," he said. Fortunately, he was now wearing some — green combat slacks with bulging pockets. He slid into his chair, spinning it around so that he was facing Blake and Ellie. His smile had vanished, and he looked dead serious. "You're in trouble, Blake. This whole business smells rotten."

"It is," Blake said. "You know it wasn't me who—"

Nate held up a hand. "I know, I know. Nothing in the universe would ever convince me that you had anything to do with this. I've seen few people in my life who treat women — who treat anyone — with the respect that you do. God bless your parents, they brought you up right."

"Thank you," said Blake.

"Which is why I was so surprised to discover that you did it," Nate said.

Blake's heart lurched, and Ellie gasped. Somehow, his hand found its way into hers and she held it tight.

"No," said Blake.

"Not you, but your computers," said Nate.

111

"That's impossible," said Blake. "The hack has to have come from outside. David says he's looking at Eastern Europe, maybe Russia. Maybe even a fledgling social network looking to take down Heartbook. Maybe even some crazy . . ."

Nate was holding his hand up again, and Blake's words petered out. Nate wheeled his chair to one side, showing them the TV-sized flatscreen. On it was a bunch of code, and Ellie scrolled through it. Some of it was familiar PHP and XHP, but most was too advanced for her to make any sense of.

"I got started as soon as I got on the plane," said Nate. "I still have the old backdoor — Agnes and Maurice never knew about it. The servers record every post, every tiny piece of data entered into Heartbook — even data that you write and delete without posting."

Blake nodded.

"Each post has a whole tranche of data attached to it. The date, obviously, the IP address, information about the device used to post, plus everything that Heartbook already associates with that information. It knows who you are, where you are, *everything.*"

"Scary," said Ellie.

"Seriously scary," said Nate. "But useful. Look, every single one of those horrific posts on your page came from you."

Blake leaned in, feeling the colour draining from his face.

"From your phone, from your laptop at work, from your desktop at home. The devices match, the passwords match, the IP addresses match. Most importantly, the dates match. The first post is from eight months ago. The last was yesterday morning."

"But it's all fake — the dates have to have been manipulated," said Blake. Ellie was still holding his hand, and he wasn't making any effort to pull free.

Nate shook his head. "That's impossible. Whoever did this was smart. The time stamp on these posts is cast iron — it can't be changed, not even by somebody with a Heartbook master admin account. They're real. They were posted in real

112

time over the last few months, but kept private so that nobody could see them. You probably never noticed them because nobody ever commented."

"And I never really used the site," said Blake. "It was just for show."

"Exactly," said Nate. "They were like bombs which somebody left there, ticking away, and yesterday they set them all to public and lit the fuse. Kaboom."

Blake pulled free, stood and paced down the office. "So, whoever did this was playing the long game," he said. "They've been planning this for a while. But what about the addresses? They can't have come from my devices."

"They did," said Nate. "I looked at them all. There is no way that information could have been hacked. Somebody used your machines to make these posts. But I did spot something interesting, something weird. Look at this one — uh, hang on."

He scrolled through the code for a few seconds, then jabbed the screen so hard it wobbled on the desk. "I quote, *Women should not hold positions of power. It diminishes the integrity of our democracy and undermines everything that generations of great leaders have built. Leadership is, and always has been, a man's duty.*'"

Blake felt his fury rising, hot and unrelenting, as he clenched his fists at his sides. It wasn't just the humiliation of the fabricated remark, it was the calculated malice behind it — someone working to paint him as a man he wasn't. The thought twisted like a knife in his gut.

A quick glance at Ellie only stoked the fire. Her eyes burned with a righteous anger, her lips pressed into a tight line. He knew she didn't believe it, not for a second, and yet someone out there wanted the world to. The injustice of it made his jaw tighten, and the muscles in his arms coiled like springs ready to snap.

"According to our data, you made this comment on the fourth of January this year, at 3.03 p.m., using your mobile from your office."

113

Blake chewed over the thought, then looked up, frowning. "But I wasn't there."

"You weren't," Nate confirmed. "You were with me, in the hospital, waiting for Mom to come out of surgery."

"That's right," said Blake. "I left my phone in the office. I completely forgot to take it because the call for surgery was so quick. I remember thinking I should go back for it, but I didn't because I wanted to be there when she went in."

"You were," said Nate. "And you never left my side. Not for twelve hours."

The room fell into an uneasy silence as the weight of the information settled over Blake like a fog. He kept his gaze fixed on the floor for a moment, his jaw tight, his breathing steady but shallow.

"That means somebody used my phone," he said. "While I was with you, somebody went into my office, unlocked my phone, wrote this post and set it to private."

Nate nodded sadly.

"All of these posts — somebody used my computers, my phone, when I wasn't in the room."

Blake sank back into his chair as if the air had been knocked out of him.

Ellie reached for his hand, her fingers instinctively wrapping around his in a firm, grounding grip. She could feel the faint tremor running through him, a physical manifestation of the storm brewing beneath his calm exterior.

Nate's voice dropped lower, each word landing like a hammer. "These hacks came from inside your own building, Blake. From someone you know."

114

CHAPTER 18

BLAKE

It couldn't be true.

It just *could not* be true.

Blake literally felt the warmth drain out of him, his skin breaking into goosebumps, his scalp shrivelling. He was shaking like he'd fallen into ice water. It was only Ellie's touch that kept him from sinking into the cold, dark depths completely.

He forced himself to take a long, shuddering breath, fighting the dizziness that threatened to pull him under. The room swayed, and he squeezed his eyes shut for a moment before opening them again to find Ellie's face.

Her expression mirrored his own turmoil, her brows knitted together, her lips pressed tight. She wasn't just sympathetic — she *felt* this pain with him. That understanding, that fierce empathy, was like a lifeline.

Blake managed a weak smile, and Ellie responded by squeezing his hand tighter before reluctantly letting go. The absence of her touch was like losing a tether, and the chill rushed back. He pushed himself upright and strode to the window, his hands gripping the ledge as he stared out at the city below.

"It's somebody I know," he said. "Somebody at Heartbook has done this to me."

"Without a shadow of a doubt," Nate said. "I'm so sorry, man."

But who?

Maurice was a snake, and Agnes he was surprised at, given how she was like a mother figure to him, but they were loyal to him and to David, he was sure of it. They were old-school businesspeople, interested only in the bottom line. They'd never do something to sink the ship. Even though Mike could be a loose cannon, he wasn't the kind of guy who would orchestrate such a cruel and dangerous plan. There were thousands of people who worked for the company, of course, but none of those would have had access to his office, or the passwords for his computer and his phone.

Which left only one possibility.

"Michelle," he growled.

Nate leaned against the desk, arms crossed. "You think she'd go that far?"

Blake turned, his fists clenched. "You didn't know her like I did. She hated how much attention I got, and when I ended things, she was furious. This—" he gestured vaguely to the room, to the weight of their conversation — "this is exactly her kind of revenge."

Ellie's eyes widened, her lips parting slightly as if she wanted to speak but wasn't sure what to say.

"But," Blake added, the thought striking him like a blow, "the timeline doesn't fit. These posts started appearing months before we broke up. Why would she start sabotaging me while we were still together?"

"Good point," Nate said, rubbing the back of his neck. "But it doesn't rule her out completely. Maybe she had her reasons. People like Michelle? They don't need logic to justify their actions."

Blake paced, the floorboards creaking under his weight. "I don't have time to guess, Nate. I need answers."

116

"I'm working on it," Nate said. "But it's not going to be easy. The posts are gone, but the damage is done. The metadata's out there, screenshotted and saved by thousands of people. Your profile is down, but that doesn't clear your name. Unless you've got security footage of your office proving someone else was at your desk . . ."

"No such luck," said Blake. "The cameras cover every corner of the building, except our private offices."

Nate sighed. "Even the one post you couldn't have made, because you were with me, would only be my word, and who's going to believe a coder with a hatred for trousers?"

"There *has* to be something we can do." Ellie stepped forward, her voice laced with determination. "Is there anyone else who can vouch for how awful Michelle is?"

"Yeah, David. He hates her as much as I do." Blake looked from Ellie to Nate.

"I'll pull every string I've got," Nate said. "But you need to prepare for the fact that clearing your name isn't going to happen overnight."

Blake clenched his teeth, his frustration bubbling over. He hated feeling powerless, hated that someone had taken everything he'd built and twisted it into a weapon.

A soft clink of china interrupted his thoughts and he turned to see Sophie standing in the doorway, a tray of steaming mugs in her hands.

"Tea," she said with a gentle smile. "It won't fix anything, but it helps."

Blake took a mug, the warmth seeping into his cold fingers. "Thank you, Sophie. You're an angel."

Ellie took a mug as well, cradling it in both hands as if drawing strength from its heat. The four of them stood in silence, sipping their tea, the room heavy with unspoken thoughts.

Finally, Blake set his cup back on the tray. "Thank you," he said, his voice steadier now. "But I can't stay. I have to figure this out."

117

"Go," Sophie said softly, her eyes filled with compassion. "And remember, you're not alone."

Blake nodded, then pulled Nate into a quick hug. "Thanks for everything, man. Let me know if you find anything."

Nate clapped him on the back. "I will. Stay sharp, Blake. We'll get through this."

Blake glanced at Ellie, her presence still grounding him. Whatever came next, he was glad she was by his side.

"Let's go," he said, a flicker of determination lighting his heart.

Blake's jaw was still clenched as they left Nate's apartment, his mind cycling through every possible betrayal, every moment where he might have let his guard down around Michelle. His shoes hit the floor hard as he strode down the corridor towards the lifts, Ellie keeping pace beside him. She didn't say anything, but her presence grounded him in a way he hadn't expected, like an anchor in the middle of a storm.

At the end of the hallway, he jabbed the button to call the lift, the glowing circle dimming under the force of his thumb. The metallic buzz of the lift's approach filled the silence, but the noise barely registered over the thrum of his blood pounding in his ears.

"Blake," Ellie said softly, breaking through the haze of anger clouding his thoughts.

He turned to her, his expression tense, his chest rising and falling in shallow breaths. "What?"

She didn't flinch at the roughness of his tone, just stepped closer, her eyes steady and filled with something he wasn't sure he deserved. "We'll get through this," she said. "Together. Nate and Sophie were right, you're not in this alone."

Her words stopped him cold, hitting him like a punch to the gut. He stared at her, the power of her gaze pulling him out of his spiral for a moment. The air between them seemed to thicken, the charged silence suddenly electric.

He felt his anger still simmering just beneath the surface, but now it was twisting into something else, something he wasn't entirely prepared for. His pulse quickened as her hand lightly

118

brushed his forearm, her touch sending a jolt through him. The tension wasn't just from his frustration or the betrayal they'd uncovered — it was deeper, messier, a dangerous blend of his heightened emotions and the undeniable pull he felt towards her.

Blake gritted his teeth, trying to shove it all down, but the energy between them crackled, almost tangible. He didn't want to let his anger manifest as something he couldn't control, something charged with arousal. Yet as he stood there, inches from her, the temptation was undeniable.

Her eyes flicked to his mouth for the briefest second, and he felt the shift like a spark igniting a fuse. His heart slammed against his ribs, his breath shallowing as the tension wrapped tighter around them.

"Ellie . . ." he said, his voice low, rough around the edges.

Her fingers tightened on his arm, her lips parting as if she might say something, but no words came. She didn't move away, didn't break the connection, and that only made the moment more volatile.

Blake's hand hovered at his side, the urge to close the gap between them almost overpowering. Every muscle in his body was coiled, his self-control fraying. He knew better than to lean in to this kind of intensity, not when everything in his life was already on the verge of collapse, but with Ellie standing there, looking at him like that, it was damn near impossible to think straight.

And then, a door creaked open.

The sound cut through the moment like a blade, and Blake jerked back, his head snapping towards the source. A man emerged from one of the neighbouring apartments, balancing a stack of cardboard boxes, oblivious to the charged atmosphere he'd just disrupted.

Ellie dropped her hand, her cheeks flushed, and Blake took a step towards the lift, running a hand through his hair as if that would somehow clear the heat still buzzing in his veins.

"Let's go," he muttered again, his voice harder than he intended.

Ellie nodded, her eyes wide, and followed him in.

CHAPTER 19

ELLIE

The lift doors slid shut, and Ellie was suddenly hyperaware of how small the space felt. The hum of the machinery and the faint click of the floor numbers were the only sounds, but the tension between her and Blake filled the silence like a living thing.

He stood beside her, hands in his pockets, his jaw tight and his gaze fixed on the metallic doors. The faint reflection of his face in the elevator's sheen revealed just how hard he was trying to hold it together.

Ellie wanted to say something, to comfort him, but the words wouldn't come. She shifted her weight, glancing at him out of the corner of her eye. His face was pale, his shoulders taut beneath the fabric of his polo shirt. He looked like he was carrying the weight of the world — and maybe he was.

"Blake," she said softly, unsure of what else to do.

He turned his head, his eyes locking on to hers. The intensity of his gaze hit her like a lightning bolt — deep, blue, and full of emotion. There was anger there, frustration, but beneath it all was something raw and unguarded that made her pulse stutter.

"You don't have to—" she began, but her words were cut off as Blake took a step towards her, closing the small distance between them.

Without hesitation, he reached up, his hand cradling the side of her face, his thumb brushing lightly against her cheek. Ellie's breath caught in her throat, her heart rate leaping as he leaned in.

His eyes, dark and smouldering, flicked to her lips before meeting hers again. His voice was low and sent a thrill cascading through her body to the electric spot between her legs.

"Ellie," he growled softly, his fingers tightening slightly against her skin. "Tell me if this is okay . . . if I can kiss you."

Her throat constricted, the words catching before they could form. She couldn't speak, couldn't think past the way his hand felt on her, the way his gaze seared into her. All she could do was nod, a small, shaky movement that sent a silent yes between them.

And then his lips were on hers.

The kiss started slow, but within seconds it had deepened, Blake's lips claiming hers with a hunger that stole her breath. His hand found her waist, pulling her against him. She could feel the tension in his body, his arousal pressed firmly against her stomach.

Blake broke the kiss only long enough to reach behind him and slam the emergency stop button. The lift lurched to a halt with a sharp jolt, the overhead light flickering as the machinery groaned into silence.

And when he turned back to Ellie, everything had shifted. He was done holding back. His hands were on her in seconds, skimming her hips and sliding beneath the hem of her dress to grip the bare skin on her thighs. Ellie gasped as he lifted her effortlessly, pressing her back against the cool metal wall. Her legs wrapped around his waist instinctively, the friction between her legs drawing a moan from deep within her throat.

Blake's mouth moved to her neck. Kissing, sucking, biting marks she knew she'd feel later. His hands squeezed her

121

thighs as he ground against her, and she could feel exactly how big and hard he was through his jeans.

"I've been trying," he growled against her skin, "to take this slow, but when you look at me like that — like you want me . . . Fuck, Ellie."

Her fingers tangled in his hair, pulling him closer. "Don't stop," she breathed, her voice thick.

"I wasn't planning to."

He kissed her again, bruising her lips with his own, his fingers sliding up the undersides of her thighs. He hooked beneath the edge of her underwear, slipping inside, and the low sound he made when he felt her wetness made her tremble.

"Fuck, Ellie," he murmured. "You're so—"

Suddenly a harsh crackle filled the air as the emergency intercom sprang to life.

"Hello?" A voice called. "Is everything okay in there? We've received notice that the emergency stop has been activated. Please advise which emergency service you need."

Ellie froze. Blake dropped his head to her shoulder and let out a strangled laugh.

"You've got to be kidding me." He cleared his throat and gently lowered Ellie to the ground, adjusting her dress as she went. He pressed a thumb a little too hard into the intercom button. "Uh, yeah, just a technical issue."

"Copy that," the voice crackled back. "I'll get someone to reset the system. Shouldn't be long at all. Sit tight."

The line clicked off and silence fell over the lift again. Ellie looked up at Blake, wide-eyed and aching from where he'd touched her. Neither of them spoke and when the lift jolted back to life moments later, she almost reached out to hit the stop button again so they could finish what they'd started.

But then the lift doors dinged open and the concierge stared at them with wide eyes. Ellie's cheeks flushed, but Blake only chuckled softly, running a hand through his hair. "Well," he said, his voice a little rough. "That's one way to kill the mood."

122

Ellie couldn't help but laugh, the sound bubbling up and breaking the last of the tension between them.

"Yeah," she said, breathlessly. "Definitely effective."

Blake caught her hand as they stepped out of the lift, his grip firm and reassuring. She felt the warmth of his touch radiate up her arm and tickle the skin on her neck.

As they walked through the lobby, Ellie couldn't help but glance up at him. His posture was straighter now, his expression lighter, but there was still a fire in his eyes when he looked at her.

The doorman held open the door for them and they stepped out of the cool interior into the heat of the day. The car was waiting for them, its engine purring, but Blake halted before he reached it. He looked like he was wrestling with something inside his head.

"I didn't plan that," he said quickly, the words spilling out. "It just . . ."

Blake's gaze snapped to hers, sharp and focused, and the rest of his sentence evaporated.

"Don't," she told him, expecting the worst. "Don't apologise."

He closed his eyes, taking a breath. Ellie studied his lips, wanting nothing more than to kiss him again. She forced the thought away. It felt as if her heart was running away with her, and if she didn't try to stop it now then it was going to carry her right over the edge of a cliff. If there was one thing Ellie Mae Woodward was good at, it was getting her heart broken.

"I want you, Ellie," he said, his tone ragged, almost like he was forcing the words through a knot in his throat. "That kiss . . ." His jaw clenched, and his grip strengthened slightly. "Never mind the lift, I'd stop the damn world to touch you like that again."

For a moment, she thought he was going to kiss her again. She wanted him to, so badly it was almost painful, but then his expression shifted — became cautious, guarded.

123

He sighed, and she could hear the 'but' before he said it. She braced herself.

"But I can't right now," he said, quietly. "As much as I want to. As much as I want you, I'm a mess, and you deserve more than that. You deserve more than someone whose life is currently a train wreck."

He shook his head as if he couldn't believe he was saying it.

Ellie swallowed, her throat dry. "Blake, you don't—"

"I do," he cut her off. "I don't want to drag you into this storm. I need to figure it out on my own. And I need to go after Michelle — that's not going to be pretty."

There was a finality in his voice that made her stomach drop. He was putting up a wall, a solid one, but she could still see the cracks.

"It's not about you," he said softly, his thumb brushing her knuckles. "You've been . . . incredible. Since the moment we met. I don't know who sent you, but if I let myself fall into this right now, I don't know how I'd ever pull myself back out, and you deserve someone who can show up for you completely."

Ellie felt her heart sink, but she refused to let him see it. She'd already given away too much. She nodded, forcing herself to keep her voice steady. "I get it. You need space."

Blake's hand lifted to her face, his fingers grazing her cheek, and she leaned into the touch despite herself. For a second, everything else fell away — the noise of the city, the heat of the sun, the ache of what he'd just said. It was just him and her, suspended in a fragile, fleeting moment.

"I'm sorry," he said, his voice barely above a whisper.

She shook her head, her lips curving into the faintest smile. "Don't be."

She placed her hand on his for a moment, holding it tight to her cheek, then she stepped away.

He turned to the car, Alfie rolling down the window as Blake gave the driver his instructions. Then he faced Ellie

124

again. "Alfie will take you home." His tone was firm, leaving no room for argument. "I'll find another way back."

"That's ridiculous," Ellie protested. "I'm not kicking you out of your own car."

"You're not kicking me out," Blake said with a ghost of a smirk. "I'm offering."

Before she could argue further, he stepped away, nodding at Alfie, who tipped his cap in response. Blake's gaze lingered on her for a heartbeat longer than it should have, his eyes dark and unreadable. Then, without another word, he turned and walked down the street.

Ellie watched him go, her chest tightening with every step he took. She told herself to look away, to let him go, but her eyes refused to obey. Even as the distance between them grew, even as he disappeared into the crowd, she stood there, rooted to the spot, her heart racing like she'd just run a marathon.

She finally forced herself to turn away, her hands trembling slightly as she shut the car door. Alfie glanced at her in the rearview mirror but said nothing, pulling smoothly away into the traffic.

CHAPTER 20

ELLIE

They drove in silence, but Ellie's mind was an orchestra of noise. The tune was a chaotic one, every thought playing out of time:

He kissed me.
I kissed him back.
He touched me.
I gave myself to him.
He told me he couldn't do this.
What the hell just happened?

She exhaled sharply, pressing her fingertips to her temples in a futile attempt to calm the chaos. The urge to open the window was overwhelming, and when she finally did, the hot, heavy air from outside hit her like a slap. But at least it was real — she needed real right now.

"You okay back there?" asked Alfie. She nodded at his concerned expression in the rearview mirror. It was a lie, of course. She wasn't okay at all. She was about as far from okay as it was possible to be. This had to be a world record, even for Ellie Mae: falling for someone and getting her heart broken, all in the space of twenty-four hours.

126

Pull yourself together, she told herself, staring at the blur of the city as it whizzed past. She couldn't let herself spiral. Not over this.

Not over him.

Sure, what they'd done in the lift had felt like something out of a movie, all-consuming and impossibly perfect. But it didn't mean anything — did it? Kisses like that didn't guarantee a happy ending. They didn't erase all the obstacles between them. Blake had said as much. He'd made it clear that his life was a mess and that now wasn't the time for . . . whatever this was.

Maybe what had happened had been a result of emotions boiling over. The secrets, the tension, the adrenaline from Nate's revelation. Maybe all it had been was a crack in the dam, a release they both needed.

Ellie leaned her head back against the seat, closing her eyes briefly. She couldn't let herself get carried away. She had never believed in love at first sight. She'd always been methodical and reasonable when it came to feelings. You had to take the time to make sure you were compatible, otherwise there could only be disaster ahead when you realised you had absolutely nothing in common.

No. She wouldn't make the same mistake again.

But Blake wasn't Josh.

That thought landed like a stone in her chest. It was true. Blake didn't pretend to be anything he wasn't. He didn't talk down to her or try to make her feel small. If anything, he'd done the opposite — he'd listened to her, really listened. He'd made her feel seen in a way that she hadn't felt in years.

But that didn't change the facts.

Blake Fielding was on a whole other planet compared to her. They came from such different worlds, it could never, ever work. He was rich, he was famous — *infamous*, now. He travelled the world in private jets and in cars like these. He lived for his work, gave everything to Heartbook. And as for her? She was perpetually broke, she waited tables in a coffee

127

bar, she was hopeless at relationships, and she was cursed. Her dreams would never be anything more than dreams.

Ellie had not always believed she was cursed, but when disaster kept following her around like a shadow, her friends had teased her about it so much that they'd given it a name. The Ellie Mae Curse. She always seemed to miss the bus by seconds, and when she took a biscuit from a pack, it was always broken. Her queues were always the slowest and her tables always seemed to be wonky. Then came the bigger things: the landlord who sold her flat just as she was getting settled, the dream job as a magazine columnist that she had been *this close* to landing, only for them to go with someone else at the last minute. And, of course, Josh — the biggest mistake of them all. Every time she let herself believe that something good was finally happening, the rug was yanked from under her feet. And now, just when she had started to believe things could be different, Blake had kissed her . . . and then walked away. The Ellie Mae Curse had struck again. She should have known it was going to. It always did.

She opened her eyes, catching her reflection in the window. Her hair was slightly mussed, and her glasses sat slightly askew on her nose. She looked as frazzled as she felt.

"Get a grip, Ellie," she muttered under her breath.

"Say something?" Alfie glanced back at her again.

"Nope," she said quickly, managing a small smile. "Just talking to myself."

He nodded but didn't press further, and Ellie was grateful. She sighed. Despite the sunshine that poured into the car, the world seemed a whole lot darker than it had twenty minutes ago.

When Blake had kissed her, it felt like the universe had shattered into a million stars, a supernova of emotion detonating inside her. She'd never experienced anything like it — not even close. With her exes, there had always been hesitation, second-guessing. *Should I be kissing him? Am I doing this right? Does he even like me as much as I like him?*

128

But with Blake, there had been no hesitation, no self-doubt. Her mind had gone blissfully quiet, filled only with the sheer intensity of him. The moment their lips met, everything else had evaporated — the chaos of what was unfolding at Heartbook, even the lift itself. There was just him. His lips and roaming hands had made her melt. It had felt so real.

But he'd pulled away. And who could blame him? His entire world was crumbling around him, and she was just . . . Ellie. Ellie Mae Woodward, a woman who had spent the last twenty-four hours falling for a man she had no business falling for.

She shook her head, forcing herself to focus on the present. She needed to get her head out of the clouds and back on solid ground. Daydreaming about Blake wouldn't solve anything.

The car slowed as they neared her street and Ellie felt a pang of relief. She needed to be home, to decompress, to sort through the mess in her head.

As Alfie pulled up to the kerb, she gathered her bag, pausing for a moment before opening the door. "Thanks for the ride."

"No problem," Alfie replied. "Take care of yourself, yeah?"

She nodded, stepping out of the car and into the warm evening air. The sound of the Maybach pulling away lingered in her ears as she made her way up the steps to her building.

She pushed through the stairwell door and headed into her flat, knowing as soon as she smelled coffee brewing that she wasn't on her own. Seeing Josh was the last thing she felt like doing, but where else was she supposed to go? At least here she could disappear into her room and cry away the rest of the day. If she was quick, she might even get there before he spotted her.

"Ellie?"

No such luck.

She closed the door behind her. Josh was standing in the living room, by the window, his arms folded over his chest.

129

"Oh my God, Josh, can you just leave?" Ellie felt her nose sting.

"It's my flat too, remember," Josh huffed. "In fact, whose name is first on our lease? Mine. And, by the way, whose car was that?"

"Are you spying on me?" She walked into the kitchen area, poured a glass of water and took a deep drink, but it did little to make her feel better.

"You wish," he spluttered. "I was just admiring the view when that monstrosity pulled up. Let me guess, it's something to do with that Blake person? I knew there was something going on there."

"That's none of your business, Josh," she said. "Blake's just a friend."

"Sure," he sneered. "You looked pretty cosy for friends. Ask me, he got what was coming to him when that drink was poured over his head."

"Nobody asked you," she shot back, slamming her glass on the counter. "For your information, he was interested in LifeWrite. He thinks it has potential. That's why we were meeting."

It was a lie, of sorts, but at least it would stop Josh's stupid questions. He unfolded his arms, his face wrinkling.

"He's interested in *that*?" he said. "Your half-baked social media idea? Come on, Ellie. I know you're naive, but just think about it. Haven't you heard the news, haven't you seen the things he posted? He's just using you."

Ellie felt her blood boiling, her head whistling like there was steam coming out of her ears. She was so angry her fists were clenched, and she had to force herself to relax them.

"Why don't you think he would be interested?" she asked, meeting Josh's eye and holding it. She thought of Blake, of the way he had spoken to her as an equal, of the way he had praised her ideas. It gave her the strength to continue. "You never believed in me, never thought it would work. But I'm

130

smart, Josh. You did your best to convince me otherwise, but you know it as well as I do. I'm smarter than you."

He snorted, sneering at her like she was a madwoman.

"Blake told me it could work. He even said he could help me make it happen. And no, not because he had another agenda, thank you very much, but because he saw what I see — he saw how important this could be."

Josh held out his hands like she was a runaway horse. "Whoa," he said. "Don't get your knickers in a twist, Ellie. He really said that?"

Ellie took a breath and nodded.

"He really said he would help you?" Josh said, licking his lips. "Like, give you the money?"

"No," she said. "Not like that."

And not at all, now, she thought. Blake had enough on his plate. She doubted he'd have the time to help her launch LifeWrite.

"We should do it, then," Josh said, walking to the other side of the counter. "I helped you with the original plans. We should try to make it happen."

It was Ellie's turn to snort. "You *helped*? All you did was criticise."

"Exactly," he replied, smiling. "That's how good teams work. If I'd told you how great everything was, you would never have tried to make it better. I was criticising you for your own good, the same as with your hair, your physique. That's what a good man does. He pushes a girl up to her full height, and makes her the best she can be."

Ellie screamed inside her head, walking out of the kitchen. She barged past Josh, heading for the bathroom. What she really needed was a glass of wine and a bath — preferably together.

"What?" said Josh. "Don't you dare cut me out of this, Ellie. I was there for you all those years when you were making LifeWrite. It's as much mine as yours."

131

She walked into the bathroom, ready to slam the door behind her. Josh was standing in the kitchen, looking at her with an expression of pity. "Poor Ellie," he said. "Don't you see it? You're nothing without me. I made you, and I was always there for you, even now. You might think you can do better than me, but I promise you there's nobody else out there who will love you like I do. Nobody else who will stick by your side like I will. Blake Fielding might be a billionaire, but he's no Josh Bigsby. And deep down, Josh Bigsby is the man you love." He smiled that arrogant smile of his. "Go have a wash, then we'll talk about the future. Because a future with me is what you deserve. Nobody else will be there for you."

Ellie shut the door on him, leaning against it and doing her best to hold back the tears — tears of anger, yes, but tears of sadness too, and tears of resignation. Because if today had told her anything, it was that Josh was probably right.

CHAPTER 21

BLAKE

Blake stared into the river, lost in the gently meandering water. The sun shimmered on its surface like liquid fire as it was stirred by the breeze blowing upstream. The trees rustled, the birds sang, and if he really tried, he could convince himself that he was back home, a kid again, ready to ride his bike down the hill with his friends.

His phone buzzed against his leg, reminding him he was an adult with responsibilities. He ran a hand through his hair, waiting for the stomach-swooping hit of angry emails or messages from the board. But when he unlocked the screen, he was relieved to see it was his friends blowing up the group chat again. He dropped a quick greeting.

Devlin: *How's life, Blake?*

Blake: *Business is a car crash. Life's not much better.*

Devlin: *Someone tell me why Blake is brooding like the lead in a depressing indie film.*

Nate: *Life isn't shit, mate. It's actually looking pretty damn good. And I've met her.*

Christian: *Met who?*

Devlin: *Wait. YOU met her? Since when did you get involved?*

Nate: *Since Blake showed up at my place with her. She's smart, funny and, let's be real, way too good for him.*

Ruairidh: *I'm literally on the other side of the world, but I don't even need context. He's in deep.*

Nate: *Also, not to make it weird, but the lift in my building mysteriously stopped working when you guys left.*

Nate: *For twenty minutes.*

Nate: *With no mechanical fault noted.*

Nate: *Blake, just asking, is it safe to touch the buttons or will I be taking the stairs from now on?*

Devlin: *I'm dead.*

Christian: *Classic.*

Devlin: *Standard Fielding.*

Christian: *Someone take his phone before he self-sabotages.*

Ruairidh: *Probably too late.*
Blake has left the chat.

Blake locked his phone and exhaled sharply, staring out at the water. They weren't wrong. But that didn't mean they understood why he'd done it. Wanting something didn't mean you got to keep it. Wanting something didn't mean you wouldn't end up wrecking it. He didn't want to think about what had happened in the lift. The way Ellie had tasted on his lips and felt beneath his hands.

He heard voices and glanced over his shoulder to see a group of people walking up the path, talking excitedly about

134

something. He pulled his cap down, adjusted his glasses and watched the river until he was sure they were gone. He'd been lucky so far — the taxi had carried him through a throng of reporters right to the main car park, and he'd made it to the river without being identified. It wouldn't be long before somebody worked out it was him, but he couldn't quite face the thought of walking into the building yet.

Because somebody in there was his mortal enemy and they were going to destroy him.

Not just his reputation — though that was shredded enough — but everything he'd spent his life building. His company. His people. His vision. Someone was behind the attacks, and he needed to figure out whether it actually was Michelle or someone else altogether before they finished him off completely.

He closed his eyes, blocking out everything around him. But, instead of darkness, there she was. Ellie. Her wide eyes, the curve of her lips as she'd parted them for him.

Oh man, that kiss.

Blake exhaled slowly, trying to hold on to that fleeting surge of hope she'd given him. It had been the most unlikely moment for something like that to happen. He'd been at his lowest, his world falling apart, and yet she'd managed to cut through the chaos with nothing more than her presence and those incredible lips.

I don't know who sent you, he'd told her. And he still didn't. It felt too serendipitous, like a cosmic force had thrown Ellie Mae Woodward into his path at the exact moment he'd needed her most.

Then why did you let her go, you idiot?

Blake rubbed his jaw, the tension coiled tight in his chest. He knew why. Because the timing was all wrong. His head was a warzone, his life a disaster. There was no room for anything else, no matter how much he wanted it — wanted her. He had to save Heartbook. His friends were right about him, even if they did say it with the tact of a high-speed train.

Just then his phone buzzed in his hand. He ignored it at first, still lost in his own head, but when it wouldn't stop, he sighed and glanced at the screen.

Devlin added Blake to the group chat.

Devlin: *All right, all right. Maybe we went a bit hard.*

Christian: *A BIT?*

Nate: *What we meant to say is — you're not alone in this, mate.*

Ruairidh: *Yeah. You've got us, whether you like it or not.*

Devlin: *And we won't even say WE TOLD YOU SO when you sort this out.*

Christian: *Except we definitely will.*

Blake: *Appreciate it. Now piss off.*

He smirked, shaking his head as he locked his phone. He turned his gaze back to the water, willing the peace of the river to seep into him. But it didn't come. Not while the memory of Ellie's touch still lingered on his skin, a quiet ache inside reminding him of what he'd walked away from.

Besides, outside of his tight circle of friends, he was now public enemy number one. Even if he managed to find out who had done this to him, and prove his innocence, he would always be tainted. The damage had been done. The internet was a harsh place, and people didn't forgive easily.

And by pushing Ellie away, he had saved her from being tainted by association. She had something good in LifeWrite, brilliant even, and he was sure it would succeed. But not if she was seen with him.

Blake's jaw tightened as he resolved to help her in the only way he could. He'd ask David to support her vision, to make sure her dreams took flight.

136

But as he turned away from the river to stop himself thinking about her, he knew it was because of more than that. Ellie was extraordinary. She was kind and intelligent. And beautiful. The only thing he had to offer was chaos. She didn't deserve to be dragged into his storm. So he needed to walk away while he still could.

Gathering as much strength as he was able, he marched down the path towards the main building. A few people were clustered outside, and they pointed at him, whispering to one another as he entered through the large doors. The reception desk was still frantically fielding calls, oblivious to him, and the security guard did a double take before letting him through the barriers.

"Hey, Billy, is Michelle in?" Blake asked.

The guard nodded, jerking his thumb to the upper floors. "They all are," he replied. "They called a meeting for this afternoon."

Blake's heart sank. He thanked the man and ran for the lifts. The ride up to the tenth floor took an eternity and when the doors finally opened he was greeted with an eerie silence, a stark contrast to the turbulence below. Most of the senior staff were likely on the fourth floor, putting out fires with the customer service team.

He stepped up to the boardroom and scanned the empty chairs. Good. It gave him a moment to regroup. But his reprieve was short-lived as he could hear voices drifting from the corner office, low but unmistakably heated.

Blake moved closer, his own footsteps muffled by the thick carpet, straining to catch the conversation.

"...can't do this," came David's voice, urgent and strained. "We have to at least let him know. He deserves to be here to fight his corner."

"He had his chance and he blew it," said Michelle in the haughty sneer that Blake had come to hate. "Agnes has made her decision. We're not here to babysit. The company

137

is bleeding and it's on him. He committed a grave offence, a stupid one, and now he has to pay. He's a liability."

Blake clenched his fists. His pulse pounded in his ears, but he wouldn't give Michelle the satisfaction of seeing him rattled. He pushed open the door and stepped inside.

Michelle leaned back in her oversized leather chair, her eyes cold. David was standing in front of her, both hands planted on the desk, his expression desperate.

"Thank God," David said, crossing the room in two strides and pulling Blake into a fierce hug, patting his back like a coach rallying a player. "You're here."

Blake stepped back, shaking his head. "What's going on? Why has Agnes called a meeting?"

"Why do you think?" Michelle said in a tone as sharp as her features, her arms folded as she leaned forward. "Shares are down another twelve percent, and over a hundred thousand users jumped ship after that little spectacle last night. You're a sinking ship, Blake, and you're taking us down with you."

He didn't flinch. Instead, he levelled his gaze at her, his voice edged with steel. "And your solution is what? To throw me overboard and hope the sharks get bored?"

Michelle just smirked, her own eyes as dark as a shark's.

"Well, what about the hack? Any news on that?" he asked, and she laughed.

"There was no hack," she said. "You're not fooling anyone with that. You're a sexist pig, Blake. Just accept it. Stop pretending otherwise and take the punishment like the big man you proclaim to be."

Blake looked at David, who shrugged. "Nothing," he said. "We had the team work through any possible breach of the network from here or from Russia. There's no evidence the system was ever hacked. I don't know what to say, Blake, but every shred of evidence points to the posts coming from your own machines."

"Because they did," Blake said.

"What?" David frowned.

138

"Blake?" said Michelle, standing up. "You're admitting it? You did write those posts."

"No." He kept his tone as calm as he was able. "They came from my machines, but I didn't write them."

"What are you saying?" David asked. "Somebody else used your phone? Your computer?"

"Exactly," said Blake, not taking his eyes off Michelle. "Somebody who knew the passwords. Someone who barely left my side."

"Be very careful what you say next," said Michelle, her expression carved from ice. She pointed a long, thin finger at him. "You are in dangerous territory."

Blake took a step closer. "I know it was you, Michelle. I have proof. I saw Nate, and he showed me the metadata. I couldn't have written some of those posts, and you know it."

"The words of a desperate man," Michelle said.

"Desperate men are dangerous," Blake replied. "The post on the fourth of January, this year. I was in hospital with Nate while his mum was in surgery. No phone, no laptop. I couldn't have made that post. David, you remember that?"

David nodded, his expression brightening. "Sure, you left your phone here. I was trying to call it all morning, and when I came to your office I found it on your desk. You weren't back until the next day. You think . . . ?" David looked at Michelle as if he couldn't believe what he was hearing.

"I don't think," said Blake. "I know. Michelle knew all of my passwords — she regularly accessed my accounts for work. She planted the posts there, then activated them yesterday morning. Nate will back me up, and we can convince the board."

Michelle stared at him, then her mouth curved up into a cruel smile. "You think that will convince them? You think that even matters? The world has spoken — you're as guilty as they come."

"Did you do this?" David asked, his eyes blazing.

Michelle didn't reply, but everything in her expression told Blake the truth.

"Why?" Blake asked.

"Why do people do anything?" she said. "Money, power, love. You thought I loved you? You were wrong. It wasn't you I loved. It was this." She waved her hands around, indicating the plush office.

"You did all this to get your hands on Heartbook?" Blake spat. "It's my life, Michelle. My whole life."

Michelle turned to the window, staring out at the flawless blue sky. "It's too late to change it, Blake. It's business, and I win."

How could she do this to him? She had to be a genuine sociopath to have planned his downfall with such precision. The sudden rush of anger made his vision blur, but David's voice cut through the haze.

"This ends now," he said, stepping between them. "We're calling Agnes and Maurice. Today. Right now."

He pulled out his phone and shot Blake a determined look. "We're not letting her get away with this." His hand gripped Blake's shoulder like a lifeline. His voice was resolute, each word a promise. "It's going to be okay, Blake. We're going to fix this."

Blake's breath hitched, the weight on his chest easing slightly. For the first time in what felt like for ever, he allowed himself to believe it.

"Let's do this," he said, his voice steady, filled with a renewed sense of purpose.

140

CHAPTER 22

ELLIE

"Come on, it will do you good. Fresh air, sunshine, clear your lungs of that city smoke."

Ellie stretched one leg out of the water, letting it cool. The bathroom was thick with steam, the water so hot it was almost uncomfortable. It felt good, though, hot enough to ease some of her aches and pains, and to sweat the disappointment of the day out of her. The only alcohol in the flat had been an ancient bottle of prosecco in the fridge, and she'd just poured herself a second glass. The feeling of gently melting into the water was a pleasant one. At least it had been, until her mum called.

"I'm really busy," she said, tilting her head back and almost dropping the phone into the water.

"I can hear that," her mum said, her voice full of sarcasm. "Be sure to wash behind your ears."

"I mean in life," Ellie said. "Things might be happening and I might need to be here."

"Lissa will give you some time," said her mum. She must have been feeding the chickens because there was a sudden

141

flurry of clucks and squawks. "It sounds like you could do with a break from work, or from whatever else is bothering you."

The 'whatever else' was probably sitting right outside the bathroom door, eavesdropping on her conversation. Ellie pulled her leg back into the water, a current of warmth running up her body.

"Tell you what," her mum went on. "Just come for the weekend. I'll transfer you the money for the train tickets. One weekend, recharge those batteries."

The honest truth was it *would* be good to get away for a bit. Mum's farm was an island of peace and tranquillity, a haven where she had always felt better about herself and the world. True, Mum would fuss about her hair and complain about her diet and lecture her on her love life and tell her what she should be doing to improve her business plan, but she would also put extra pillows on her bed and plait her hair and give her plenty of cuddles.

"I'll make banoffee pie," teased her mum, and Ellie laughed.

"Okay, okay," she said. "I'll come. I've got this weekend off anyway. I'm fine for money." She hoped her mum wouldn't hear the lie. "I'll travel down tonight. You're right, it will be good to get away from it all. From work, from you know who."

And from Blake, she thought. Here in the city there was no way she'd be able to shake him from her thoughts. She could still feel him on her lips, taste him on her tongue. She could still remember the heat of his hands on her skin, his fingers winding through her hair.

"Can you pick me up from the station?" she asked, hoping her mum wouldn't be able to feel the heat of her cheeks through the phone. She sat up, water sloshing.

"Of course, dear. I'll be there. Just text me your train times."

"I will," Ellie said. "Thank you."

"You know you're always welcome," said her mum, a twinkle in her voice. "And you know you're also always welcome to bring a guest. Like the man you were out with last night."

"Goodbye, Mum." Ellie jabbed a wet finger on the 'end call' icon. She threw the phone on to her dressing gown and took a big gulp of her prosecco. She could almost feel the countryside wind on her skin, the fresh, woodland-scented air in her lungs, Blake's hand in hers as they strolled through the trees . . .

Stop it!

Why had her mum planted that image in her head? Ellie downed the rest of the glass then rinsed her hair and climbed out of the bath. Wrapping herself in her dressing gown, she opened the door and nearly jumped out of her skin. Josh was leaning against the wall, waiting for her. He looked her up and down, a sly smile appearing on his face.

"Nice," he said.

Behind him, the TV was tuned to the news. The anchors were dissecting the fallout of Blake's scandal, and Ellie's heart clenched at the sight of his picture on the screen, what must be the members of the board standing with him. But suddenly Ellie felt her brain itch with a warning as she looked at them all.

"Get out of my way, Josh," she snapped, heading for the bedroom.

"You never used to put a dressing gown on," he said as she slammed the door behind her.

Her skin crawled. He was such a creep. Why wouldn't he just get the hint? At least she didn't have to take him home to the farm anymore. He'd always put Ellie down in front of Mum, making cheap shots at her lack of domesticity at the dining table, or laughing at her attempts to saddle the horses — even though he'd never set foot on a farm in his life.

To her credit, Mum had always put him in his place and come to Ellie's defence, but it made her sad to think that her mum had needed to do that. What kind of man belittled his girlfriend everywhere they went?

Maybe she could go home and never come back. There were plenty of coffee shops there, after all, and Josh would never come looking for her.

143

"By the way," he said from right outside the door, his voice making her shudder. "I thought you should know, that idiot is on the TV again. Blake Whatshisname."

"I saw," she heard herself say. "And?"

"Just thought you might want to know what kind of trouble he's got himself into now," said Josh. "That guy is toast. A fraud. And he's heading straight for the scrap heap."

Ellie saw red — literally, her vision darkening with the force of her rage. She wrenched open the door so hard it crunched into the wall. Josh stood there, an expression of surprise on his round face. Ellie took a step towards him, jabbing a finger in his direction.

"He's not a fraud," she said, her voice low and dangerous. "In fact, I only know one fraud, and I'm looking right at him."

Josh's wet lips parted as he tried to object, but Ellie cut him off. "You, Josh. You're a fraud. Just look at yourself, you're so desperate, so pathetic. You hang around me like there's a hope I might come back to you. But I never will. It's not just that you're weak, it's not just that you treated me like shit. It's not even that you lied to me every single day we were together, because YOU ARE A FRAUD. It's that you believed it — you believed you were better than me, and that you were doing me a favour by deigning to be with me."

She had to stop so that she could claw in a breath. "I'm never going to be with you, do you understand? I'm never going to say yes. You make my skin crawl, Josh. You make me feel ill. Is that clear enough? You can spend every single day hanging out here or at my work, but nothing will make me like you, nothing will make me care for you, and even if you were the last man on Earth, I wouldn't be with you."

Josh's eyes looked like they were about to roll out of their sockets. Ellie took another breath. "You're the one heading for the scrap heap, Josh. Because you have lost me. For ever."

Josh's mouth gaped like a landed fish. He clutched at his chest as if her words had actually pierced his heart. Then, just as she knew he would, he got angry. His face creased, his

144

eyes growing dark. He sneered at her. "Well, thank goodness for that. You don't know how relieved I am. All this time I've been hanging around you because I was worried that you were losing your mind. I was worried that you were going insane. And I think you are. But now I don't have to worry anymore. I don't have to look after you. I'm free."

He folded his arms over his chest and made no sign of moving.

"Go on then," said Ellie. "Go be free. Get out of here."

"If I leave, I'm never coming back."

It was a threat, but to Ellie it sounded like the most wonderful promise in the world. She didn't reply, and she didn't break eye contact. After a few more seconds he stamped his foot like a toddler, then wheeled around and strode towards the door.

"You'll regret this," he shouted over his shoulder. "And I won't."

Only when the door had slammed shut behind him did Ellie let herself smile. It spread over her face like sunshine, impossible to stop. Had she really done that? Had those words really just come out of her mouth? It felt like a dream. Ellie Mae Woodward just wasn't capable of standing up for herself like that. But somehow she had done it — she had finally told Josh to leave her alone.

Not *somehow*. It wasn't luck, and it wasn't anyone else. It was her.

Ellie had finally realised that she wasn't someone to be pushed around. She was valuable and deserved to take up the space that she did, without apologising for it. And she was done letting Josh, or anyone else, make her feel otherwise.

Thank you, Ellie Mae, she thought. Then the smile vanished from her face as she remembered the niggling worry she had when she'd seen the image of Blake and his board on TV. The feature had finished, so she dashed back into the bedroom and opened the news app on her phone.

Three articles down was a post on Blake, and Ellie felt a rush of guilt as she noticed the photograph attached to the piece

145

was him recoiling as the waitress poured the drink on his head. Thankfully, Ellie had been cropped out of it. She clicked the link, clicking her tongue impatiently as she waited for it to load.

Heartbook press conference imminent — Blake Fielding expected to address shareholders and users of the floundering social media giant.

She scanned the article, shaking her head. It was full of the posts that somebody had made on Blake's account and laden with accusations against him. It was so unfair that even the press had decided on his guilt. Ellie rested a finger against another photograph of him, this one taken at an IT conference, and he was beaming with happiness. She couldn't imagine how hard it would be for him to step out in front of a group of people who had already made up their minds about him.

And then, as she scrolled down, a live feed flickered into place: a video of the Heartbook board members arriving for the upcoming meeting, their names flashing on the screen as the camera panned around the familiar glass building. Figures stepped out of luxury cars, buttoning suit jackets and striding towards the entrance.

Ellie's breath caught in her throat at the sight of two of them.

A man and a woman walking side by side.

Something tugged at the back of her mind, her fingers tightening around the phone. She knew them. Not from a newspaper or the internet. Not from anything to do with Blake. But from somewhere else — somewhere real.

Her head snapped up, heart pounding as the image clicked into place.

No. It couldn't be. It didn't make sense.

She swallowed hard, her hands suddenly clammy as her pulse thundered. A sick, twisting feeling settled deep in her stomach, one that sent her bolting for her coat and keys.

She had to get to Heartbook.

Blake needed to know.

146

CHAPTER 23

BLAKE

The board members filed into the room like it was a funeral procession, and Blake couldn't help feeling like he was the guy in the coffin. He stood at the head of the table — a table that he himself had bought for the company when he'd made his first million — waiting for them to take their seats.

Agnes was first, dressed all in black. She sat opposite Blake, shuffling her papers into a pile and looking sad. Maurice groaned wearily as he descended into his chair, Mike dropping into his like he was completing a wrestling move. David came next, offering Blake a smile and a reassuring nod. For a moment it looked as if Michelle wasn't coming, and Blake prayed that she'd had the sense to remove herself quietly from the situation rather than stay here and face him. Then she strolled past the window and through the door, smiling as if this was Christmas Day. She had the audacity to wink at Blake, and he had to look away to keep the rage from boiling over.

"Good afternoon, everyone," said Agnes. "Thank you very much for coming. Blake, how are you?"

The question took Blake by surprise, and he cleared his throat. "Better now that I know who did this," he said, glancing at Michelle.

If she was worried, she wasn't showing any sign of it. She was perfectly calm, her features icy. She drummed her long nails on the desk as if she was bored.

"Thank you for giving me the opportunity to present my case," Blake continued.

"This meeting will give you the chance to do exactly that," said Agnes. "But I should warn you, Blake, we will be making a decision about your future in the next ten minutes. We are at a tipping point for Heartbook. If we do not act now, then everything is lost. We have a press conference scheduled for three sharp. We will either be telling them your story, or telling them that you've decided to leave the company."

"She means it," said Mike, popping gum. "I'm not going to let you strip my bank account. My ex-wife does enough of that. Either you convince us, or you're gone."

Blake felt a tremor of fear run through him. He was ten minutes away from losing everything that he had spent his life building. He could practically feel the colour drain from his face as everyone looked at him, scrutinised him.

"Easy, Mike," said David. "Let's give Blake a chance to explain himself."

Mike threw his hands in the air dramatically. Maurice adjusted his glasses, then nodded at Blake. "Please, go ahead," the old man said.

Blake took a moment to compose himself. This was probably the most important speech he would ever have to make, and he couldn't afford to mess it up. He looked each of the board members in the eye, ending with Michelle. She gave him another cold smile and he knew for sure that she was guilty.

"I have proof that it wasn't me who made those posts," he said. Michelle scoffed, but the other board members studied him with grave expressions. "I had my own expert look

148

into it, and he found that somebody else used my devices to upload the posts, setting them to private with the intention of activating them later on. This person wasn't acting on behalf of the government, or another company, or another country. The person who did this is sitting in this very room."

Agnes gasped. "That is a very strong accusation."

Blake nodded. "I know, Agnes. I've been facing the same accusations for two days now. But it's the truth. If you look at the time stamps for each post you will see that they were written at a time when I was either away from my desk, or away from my phone. I haven't had time to look at them all yet, but I can guarantee this. My expert — you all know him, but his name is embargoed — discovered one instance where a post was made and I was inside the hospital with him waiting for his mum to come out of surgery. There is no way I could have posted to Heartbook at that time."

Maurice and Agnes shared a look. A flicker of concern passed over Michelle's face, but only for an instant. David threw him another smile, urging him to go on.

"You all knew my Heartbook security details — it was part of the deal we made. I had to be untouchable, so everyone here had the ability to log in to my account and vet it. But only one person was with me during work hours *and* home hours."

He looked at Michelle, and for once she didn't meet his eye.

"I spoke to Michelle earlier, and she all but admitted that it was her who hacked my account. This is her doing."

There was silence in the boardroom, other than the hammer blows of Blake's pulse in his ears. He wasn't sure how much later it was that Agnes spoke.

"Michelle? This can't be true."

Michelle looked at Blake, and he thought there might be tears in her eyes. The wave of relief that passed over him felt strong enough to knock him over. She was going to confess — it was going to be okay.

149

Michelle turned to Agnes and clasped a hand over her mouth to contain the sobs that were spilling out of her.

"Michelle?" said Maurice. "We need to hear your response immediately."

"I . . ." she started. "I don't know what he's talking about."

Blake slammed a hand on the table. "You admitted it!"

"I did no such thing," she replied, smudging away the tears. "He's lying. I know we were together for a while, and it didn't end well, but I would never do that to anyone, even you, Blake, and I would never jeopardise a company that I love with all my heart. It's financial suicide — it wouldn't make any sense."

"It makes perfect sense," Blake said. "You were always looking for a way to hurt me after I broke it off with you."

"You broke it off with *me*?" To her credit, she could have been an Oscar-winning actor. "Another lie. I ended it with you because of your views on women, because of the way you treated me."

"That's insane," said Blake. "*You're* insane."

"No, it's true," she said, throwing pleading looks to all of the board members. "You were horrible. In the public eye you were Mr Charming, but behind closed doors you thought women were inferior in every way. Your views made me sick."

"What?" He couldn't believe this was happening. He couldn't believe she was doing this to him.

"These posts were written when we were still together," she said. "That's proof enough that it wasn't me."

"You planned it," he said. "You were only with me to force my downfall. You knew from the start what you wanted and it certainly wasn't me. It was my office."

Even as he said it, he heard how crazy it sounded. Michelle was an expert — she'd planned this perfectly. But there was one thing she hadn't planned for. Blake turned to David, his best friend and right-hand man. "David, you were there when Michelle confessed. Tell them."

150

"I was there," David said. "I was there when Blake confronted Michelle earlier."

"And?" said Agnes.

"And I totally agree," David said. "Michelle is innocent."

CHAPTER 24

ELLIE

Ellie stood across the street from Heartbook's headquarters, her fingers gripping the strap of her bag as if it were a lifeline. She'd expected chaos, but this was on another level. A wall of reporters clustered around the building's main entrance, cameras flashing like angry fireflies. Security guards were frantically trying to hold them back, and above the din, Ellie could hear shouted questions about Blake. There were plenty of spectators there too. The atmosphere felt intimidating, almost hostile.

Her stomach clenched. The whole scene felt volatile, like a powder keg on the verge of detonation. But she didn't have time for hesitation. Blake was in there, alone, and she had information that could change everything. The realisation of who she'd seen had sent a surge of determination through her veins. She had to get to him.

But how?

Ellie's gaze darted to the front doors, where the press had gathered like piranhas in a feeding frenzy. The rest of the building was impenetrable, a fortress of steel and glass, so she was going to have to go through the front doors if she was getting inside. Then it struck her — maybe she could use the infamy of the last few hours to help her get to Blake. If the press loved anything, it was a good story, regardless of the truth of it.

"Excuse me!" She pushed her way between a man with his phone held in the air, trying to get video of the doors, and a woman using hers as a Dictaphone. "I need to get through. Blake's expecting me."

As she'd predicted, the noise around her rose to deafening levels as the reporters got wind of what she was saying. Soon the cries of recognition filled the air.

"It's the girl from the video," one shouted.

"She's not his new girlfriend, surely," called another, as though Ellie wasn't standing right next to him.

"Well, she's an idiot if she is," cried a third. "Hope he treats her better than he does the women in his family."

Ellie wondered if this was how Blake felt all the time. As though he was fair game for people to talk about as they wished. She didn't like it. And she didn't like the idea of Blake having to deal with it, either. The reporters crowded her, shoving their phones and mics into her face.

"Hey, you. Does Blake make you do all his washing?"

"Does he chain you to the kitchen sink?"

"Are you his sex slave?"

Sex slave? Seriously? The idea burrowed a little too deep in Ellie's mind and she felt her cheeks heat. Might not be such a bad thing. Right?

She shoved her chin down and pushed her way through the throng. *No comment* was on the tip of her tongue, but she didn't know if that was something real people said, not just TV people, so she stayed quiet. Reaching the doors to the lobby, Ellie looked up at one of the burly doormen that hadn't been here when she'd arrived for her interview, and gave him a pleading smile.

"Blake's expecting me," she said, sternly.

153

The doorman raised a brow at her and shrugged his shoulders, which was surprising, given how muscular they were. Ellie half expected them to push up his cheeks at the same time. His equally muscular mate smacked him on the chest with sausage-shaped fingers and laughed. "It's Blake's new girl," he shouted over the chaos. "I recognise her from the press. Let her in."

"Welcome to the fun house." The doorman waved Ellie inside. "They're in the boardroom."

The crowds were thinner in the lobby, most of the press being unable to get past the bouncers. The ones who had been allowed in were better behaved, although the receptionist still looked like she was being harassed from every angle possible. Her neatly piled hair had drooped to straggles around her face.

Ellie approached the desk, her heart pounding, but her voice steady. "Hi, I'm here to see Blake Fielding."

The receptionist glanced up briefly from her computer, and carried on typing and talking to someone on the phone at the same time. "He's in a meeting. Do you have an appointment?"

Ellie hesitated, not sure if that was directed at her or the person on the other end of the phone conversation. "He's expecting me."

The lie slipped off her tongue a little easier this time.

The receptionist just rolled her eyes and went back to shouting "No comment" down her headset.

"Oh," Ellie said, her surprise that it was actually a thing overshadowing the rudeness of the receptionist. "Don't worry, I'll make my own way up."

Ellie's trainers padded softly on the tiled floor as she walked, her eyes scanning for any indication as to where she might find the boardroom. A few steps later, she spotted a glass-mounted map of the building posted on the wall.

"Perfect," she muttered, stepping closer. Her finger traced the layout of the floors, her pulse quickening when she spotted the boardroom was on the tenth floor. That had to be

154

where the meeting was happening. She'd just have to figure out how to get there without running into too much trouble.

She followed the corridor until she reached a stairwell. The lift was too risky — someone might stop her if she was stuck in a confined space and had to talk to them for long. Taking a deep breath, Ellie started climbing.

At about floor five, the doubt started to creep in. What exactly was her plan? Was she just going to burst into the board meeting and start shouting? Demand they listen to her? Tell them what she knew?

What if Blake didn't want her there?

She gritted her teeth, gripping the cool metal railing as she pushed forward. She had spent too long second-guessing herself, waiting for the right moment, *playing it safe*. Not this time.

Blake had helped her when she needed it most. Now, she was going to help him.

She picked up her pace.

By the time Ellie reached the tenth floor, her legs were burning, her breath coming in short, sharp gasps. She pressed her back against the wall, willing herself to calm down. The corridor was quieter here, the thick carpet swallowing every sound, but tension crackled in the air like static before a storm.

She edged forward, her eyes locking on to the glass-walled conference room at the end of the hall. The blinds were partially drawn, offering glimpses of movement inside — shifting silhouettes, sharp gestures. She crept closer, pulse hammering, straining to hear.

A man's voice, clipped and precise. Blake's deeper tone, steady but tight.

She couldn't make out the words, but the slow, suffocating energy in the room was unmistakable.

A sudden laugh echoed from further down the corridor, making Ellie jolt. She turned to see a group of employees chatting as they headed towards the lifts, oblivious to her presence.

155

Pressing herself against the wall, she held her breath until they passed.

When the corridor was empty again, she inched closer to the conference room. Through a small gap in the blinds, she caught sight of Blake. He was standing at the head of the table, his hands planted firmly on the polished wood. His expression was intense, his jaw tight as he spoke. Ellie felt a rush of admiration. Even in the midst of this storm, he looked completely in control.

Then her gaze flicked to the woman standing opposite him.

Ellie stiffened.

The woman had the kind of carefully curated appearance that screamed wealth — glossy hair, tailored clothes, a smile sharp enough to cut glass. Even without being able to hear her, Ellie knew exactly who she was.

Michelle.

The woman who had betrayed Blake. And the man who had helped her was right there too.

Ellie's blood boiled as she watched Michelle lift a hand in a dismissive wave, as if swatting away an inconvenience. David was seated beside her. He wasn't as obviously smug as Michelle, but there was still something cold about him. His movements were precise, controlled. His fingers tapped against the table once, twice, then he spoke.

Blake flinched.

Whatever David was saying, it wasn't good, and Ellie could see the way his jaw was grinding even from out in the corridor. His words seemed to hit Blake like a physical blow.

Ellie's stomach twisted as she watched Blake stagger slightly, his grip tightening on the chair. Then, as if the weight of the room had finally crushed him, he sank heavily into the seat, his head dropping into his hands.

Michelle's lips curled into a knowing smirk and David leaned in just slightly, the two of them together a condescending pile of crap that she had recognised the moment she'd seen them on the TV. Because she'd been on the end of their

156

derision before, when they'd swanned into the Bookworm Café and made ridiculous demands. Blake had said David hated Michelle, but David was lying. Because David and Michelle weren't just colleagues. They weren't even enemies pretending to tolerate each other.

They were a couple. And Blake had no idea.

Steeling herself, Ellie stepped forward and went to open the door. She barely had time to grip the handle before the sound of a throat clearing behind her made her freeze.

"Excuse me," said a security guard, less built than the one she'd sneaked past at the front door, but ten times more intimidating. "This area is restricted. I'm going to have to ask you to leave."

Ellie turned, her cheeks heating. "I need to get in there, I'm—"

"I know who you are." The guard's gaze was impassive, but his words hit like a punch to the gut. "You're Blake Fielding's . . . friend."

Before she could respond, two more guards appeared, flanking her ominously.

"Blake Fielding no longer has clearance to be in this building," the first guard continued. "And neither do his guests."

"This is really important. Please, I have to—"

The guard raised a hand to stop her. "Miss, please don't make this harder than it needs to be."

Her heart plummeted as they escorted her, not gently, towards the lifts. She tried to look back, hoping for one last glimpse of Blake, but the guards were careful to keep her moving forward.

"He'll be leaving the building soon, too," he said, his voice softening. "There's a press conference arranged for three p.m. You can meet him once he's spoken to the crowds."

But that would be too late. The damage would already be done.

157

CHAPTER 25

BLAKE

It was as if the floor had opened up beneath his feet. Blake felt so dizzy he had to sit down, and even then the sense of vertigo was overwhelming. He looked at David, at the way his friend's face was masked with sadness.

"What?" he asked him in little more than a whisper.

"I'm afraid there is no evidence to show that Michelle tampered with Blake's account," said David. "As she says, the posts were made when they were still together. Blake's accusations don't make any sense. And from my own research, the posts were made when Blake *did* have access to his devices."

"David, why are you saying this?" Blake asked, but it was as if he had lost his voice.

"As for the claim that he was at the hospital without his phone, that is a lie," David went on. "I remember that occasion well. Blake called me from a hospital phone after he arrived and asked me to bring his over so that he could work while they were waiting for news." He turned to Blake and sighed dramatically. "I can't cover for you anymore. I've put up with it for too long. Michelle is right, Blake has always

158

been this type of man. Even when we were at university. I've kept it to myself because we were friends and we were building Heartbook, but this is too much. Blake, it's time for you to leave."

Blake opened his mouth to reply, but what good would it do? Michelle and David were working together, and Blake understood that this wasn't just a random hack, or a revenge plan. It was a coup. They were trying to take over his company.

And they had won.

"Is there anything you want to say?" Agnes asked, a look of disgust on her wrinkled face. They were all staring at him with the same expression, and it broke his heart to see it.

"These are lies," Blake said. "I'm innocent. But I don't have any way to prove it."

"Then you leave us no choice," said Maurice. "I hereby call a vote to terminate Blake Fielding's contract with Heartbook PLC, to strip him of his rights as a board member, to begin efforts to reclaim his shares in the company, and to permanently ban him from the network. Please raise your hand if you agree."

Agnes hesitated, and Blake loved her for it, but eventually her shaking hand rose. Even Mike didn't seem too keen to swing the axe for the executioner's blow. This was a huge moment — they were about to assassinate the king. There was no going back. All the same, after a few seconds, his hand shot up too.

"I'm going to abstain," said David. "Out of respect for our friendship."

The hypocrisy lit a fire of rage inside Blake, but he stamped down on it. One more vote and he was out, and it didn't take a genius to know where it would come from.

"I agree," said Michelle, and even though Blake couldn't bear to look at her, he could hear the smile in her voice. "He needs to go."

"Then we have it," said Maurice. "The motion is passed. Blake, for the record, I am truly sorry that your behaviour has

159

led to this. Your family will be heartbroken. You will address the press conference now, and then you will be escorted from the site. I hereby formally terminate your contract with Heartbook."

Blake watched them stand and drift out of the room.

"Be outside the main doors in five minutes, please," said Agnes. "We expect you to do this quickly, Blake. This is about Heartbook shares and Heartbook jobs. If you don't go quickly and quietly then it's lost. Do the right thing, Blake."

She left, and only David and Michelle remained.

Blake stared at them, his anger a live wire sparking dangerously. "This isn't over."

Michelle laughed, a sound like shattered glass. "Oh, Blake. It's over. You're over."

And then, as if to twist the knife, she leaned towards David, pressing her lips to his. It was a slow, deliberate kiss, a final declaration of their alliance.

Blake's heart thundered in his chest, but he refused to give them the satisfaction of a reaction.

They walked out, the door swinging shut behind them and plunging Blake into a silence worthy of the grave.

CHAPTER 26

ELLIE

The trip back to the ground floor was awkward and warm. Too many egos shoved into a small space. And when the security guards finally dropped her off at the front doors, they gave her a little shove to make sure she understood which way she was supposed to go.

Ellie scowled at them as she made her way down the steps outside and huddled next to a TV news crew as they geared up ready for action. It seemed impossible that only yesterday she had been sitting inside reception waiting for a job interview. And it seemed impossible that, then, she hadn't even met Blake. How could a life change so suddenly in such a short space of time?

To her left was a small, raised stage, a lectern set up there with a microphone perched on top. All Ellie wanted to do was run up to it and scream that Blake was innocent, he was being framed, that he was the nicest guy she'd ever met and that the world would see this if they just gave him a chance. But of course she didn't. That would probably do more harm than good. Instead, she stood her ground as people pushed and shoved their way as close to the front of the crowd as they were able.

She checked her phone. Seven minutes until three. There was no sign of Blake anywhere through the big glass windows, just a wall of security guards. The crowd spoke in hushed whispers, the constant click of camera shutters sounding like rain. Several of the reporters were broadcasting live, one hand pressed to their ear as they spoke about "this day of judgement". The crush of the crowd and the relentless noise made Ellie feel like she was drowning, but she couldn't leave, not when she'd come this far.

"Look!" somebody yelled.

Ellie did, squinting through the windows to see the lift doors open. At first she wasn't sure if the man who stepped out of it was Blake, because he looked broken. His back was bent beneath the pressure, his head bowed low. He looked like a man on the way to the gallows. But it was him.

Blake joined a group of people by the door — the same people who had torn him apart in the meeting room — and they stepped out into the late afternoon heat. The crowd launched into a chorus of boos and jeers as they emerged, some women chanting "Blake out!" on the far side of the crowd. The group stopped at the base of the platform, leaving Blake to climb the stairs alone. The noise seemed to swell as he did so, and Ellie couldn't even hear herself think.

Quiet! she wanted to scream. *Let him talk!*

Blake held up a hand, and after a while the noise faded into almost total silence. All eyes were on him, and Ellie suddenly wondered if the quiet was worse than the deafening roar of the crowd. Blake was pale, and he looked frightened. Ellie lifted a hand to wave to him, but she was so short and the crowd was so big, he didn't see her. She tried to project her strength to him. It sounded stupid, but she couldn't do anything else.

You can do this, she said. *Just tell them the truth.*

Blake hesitated, frowning. His eyes scanned the crowd and for a moment she thought he saw her. He took a deep

162

breath, his back straightening. "Good afternoon," he said, the slightest of tremors in his voice. "Thank you all for coming today. As you know, I have been accused of posting some horrific comments on my Heartbook page. Comments that insult and denigrate women."

"Yeah, you suck!" shouted a man from the middle of the crowd.

Blake's head dropped, then he looked behind him to the group of people that he had walked out with. The old woman nodded her head to him, her expression stern.

He turned back to the crowd. "I've asked you all here to explain what happened," he went on. "I . . ."

Just say it, Ellie pleaded. *Just tell them you're innocent. The rest we can work out once you know the whole truth.*

Blake balled his hand into a fist, resting it on top of the lectern. He seemed to make a decision, nodding to himself. "I am hereby announcing that I will be leaving the company with immediate effect, and will no longer be involved in any way with Heartbook or its subsidiaries," he said.

The crowd started to murmur, cries of anger rising into the air.

"I do so with a heavy heart. But whatever you think of me, and whatever you think I have done, this is a good company that believes in equality and diversity. I will continue to protest my innocence in this matter, but it seems there is no way to prove it. For that reason and to save the reputation of this company, I am stepping down."

"Get out!" somebody yelled.

"I want to apologise to everyone who took offence at what was posted on my page," he said, barely audible now. "Thank you."

He stepped off the platform to a roar of boos and angry shouts. The reporters were all yelling the same thing: "Blake, did you do it?" But he obviously wasn't answering any questions.

Ellie stood in stunned silence. Blake had pretty much given up, but why? She *knew* he was innocent — he had

163

evidence, or at least testimony from a trusted source. Why wouldn't he fight to clear his name? Whatever had just happened, whatever had driven him to give up so easily, it didn't make sense.

Ellie bit her lip, watching as Blake headed towards the building, the crowd still jeering behind him. She pushed her way through the crowd, thankful this time to be as small as she was.

"Blake!" she shouted, but everyone else was calling his name, too, and hurling insults his way. She apologised as she rammed past a news reporter, struggled through one last camera crew and a group of women with anger twisted on their faces, and finally reached the front. Blake was less than a dozen yards away from her, but another ogre of a security guard planted a hand on her shoulder.

"That's far enough," he growled.

"Blake!" she shouted past the man. But her voice was lost in the chants. Blake was striding back through the doors and Ellie had the sudden terror that if he went, she would never see him again. He would vanish into the ether, he would spend the rest of his life in hiding, and all she would have of him was the memory of his smile, and the fading touch of his kiss.

"Blake, please!" she shouted. Then, remembering what he had told her about the early days of the company, she called, "Flusher! Flusher!"

Blake paused, his head cocked to one side. Ellie called his nickname again and he turned around. The old woman who he had been standing next to the stage was right behind him, trying to usher him inside the building, but he steered her gently to the side and scanned the crowd.

"Here!" Ellie shouted. "Here, behind Shrek!"

He found her, and a sad smile appeared on his face.

"Billy, I'll be out of your hair soon. Can you please just let me past?" he said, and the security guard stood to one side.

Blake strode up to her, stopping when they were merely inches apart, a great smile crinkling his eyes. It took all her strength to not throw herself on him and start kissing him, but that would be a mistake, especially in front of this crowd.

"Hi," he said, fighting to make himself heard, his smile growing bigger.

"I had to find you," she said, breathless. "Blake, I know who did this. Michelle and David—" She took his arm, gripping it as if she could physically keep him from walking away. "They're together."

Blake blinked, his forehead creasing. "I know. They were kind enough to show me."

"And that means . . ."

"That David's been lying to me from the start," Blake finished.

"Yes," Ellie confirmed, her voice thick with frustration. "I saw them together at the café, the day your posts went viral. He must have been with her this whole time. And that means he set you up too. Blake, you don't have to do this. You don't have to step down. You can fight."

"I can't." His gaze flicked past her, towards the crowd pressing in around them, security struggling to hold them back. His expression was unreadable, warring emotions flickering across his face.

"Why, Blake? Why didn't you just tell the truth to the reporters?"

"Because I made a decision." Tears glistened in his eyes. "I could either save myself, or I could save Heartbook. I chose the company. I chose the people."

Something exploded on the ground by Blake's feet, what might have been strawberry milkshake splattering both of them. He looked up, alarmed, and the security guards started closing in. One took Blake's arm, but he shrugged them away, his eyes locked on Ellie's. "I'm sorry," he said, his voice raw.

"You don't have to apologise for being a good person," Ellie said, her voice steady even though her heart raced with everything unsaid between them. She hesitated for a second, then the thought hit her like a flash of lightning. Before she

165

could overthink it, the words spilled out. "Come away with me. Right now. Let's just get away."

"What?" Blake's brow furrowed, the surprise clear in his eyes. "Where?"

"I'm going to my mum's farm tonight. It's in Devon," she said, her words rushing out like a flood. "The fresh air will do us both good. Forget about all this, just for a little while. You need to breathe, Blake. I want you to come with me. We can escape together."

For a brief, breathtaking moment, his face softened. The light returned to his eyes, and Ellie thought he might actually say yes. She held her breath as the silence stretched between them, the chaos of the crowd fading into the background.

But then another object whizzed past, smashing on to the pavement a few feet away. This time it was a cup of coffee, the dark liquid splattering dangerously close.

Blake flinched, instinctively pulling back, and the fleeting hope in his expression dissolved. "I can't," he said, shaking his head. "I won't do that to you. You mean too much to me to be dragged through the dirt. This is what I meant when I said I can't see you anymore. Don't you understand? It's not because I don't want to, it's because of what happens to the people around me."

"Blake . . ." Ellie's voice wavered, her hand still outstretched. She wanted to grab him, to shake him, to make him understand that she didn't care about the dirt or the chaos or the crowd. All she cared about was him.

She opened her mouth to say something else but another security guard appeared and between them they dragged Blake through the doors. Blake looked back once, his face barely visible between the men. His eyes met Ellie's and they were the saddest eyes she had ever seen.

Then the doors closed, the men steered Blake around a corner, and he was gone.

166

CHAPTER 27

BLAKE

"You did the right thing, Blake."

Agnes hovered in the corner of Blake's office, pretending to study the books that lined his extensive shelves.

"It's the first rule of business," she went on. "The company must come first. Today may have been the result of your blatant stupidity. I mean, why anyone would make their innermost feelings public is a mystery to me, let alone somebody whose innermost feelings are as unpopular as yours. But you saved Heartbook. The share price is already recovering. Because of what you did today, seventeen hundred people will most likely keep their jobs. Including me, I should say. So, I'm sorry it has come to this, but thank you."

Blake didn't reply. He was staring out of the window at the campus that stretched as far as the eye could see, right up to the glittering, sun-drenched river. It was a landscape of memories, and each one hurt like a wasp sting. He felt as if he'd built this place with his own two hands, brick by brick, and now Michelle and David had led a rebellion against him. He grieved for the loss, calm on the outside, but a hurricane of anger raging within.

167

His phone buzzed in his pocket, breaking the heavy silence. His first instinct was to ignore it, but old habits die hard. There was still a part of him that expected a last-minute reprieve, a message from someone — anyone — telling him that this was all some kind of mistake, that they could fix it.

He pulled it out and glanced at the screen.

Devlin: *Just seen the news. That's brutal, mate. What are you going to do?*

Christian: *Yeah. We're here for you, man. Just say the word and we'll do anything you need us to.*

Devlin: *Anything legal!*

Ruairidh: *It's your company. Doesn't matter who signs the papers now — everyone knows you built it.*

Devlin: *And let's be real, does anyone actually believe that crap?*

Blake: *Yeah, hordes of people. Wouldn't change anything though. It's done.*

Nate: *Maybe that's not a bad thing.*

Christian: *Bold take, considering he just lost everything.*

Nate: *DID he, though?*

Devlin: *All right, just say it already.*

Nate: *Ellie?*

Christian: *Knew it.*

Ruairidh: *There it is.*

Blake: *Not the time, Nate.*

Nate: *Maybe it is.*

Blake: *...*

Christian: *He's ignoring it. That means we're on to something.*

168

Devlin: *Blake?*

Nate: *What do you want to do?*

Blake: *I don't know.*

Nate: *Yeah, you do.*

Blake: *I'm signing off.*

Devlin: *FIELDING.*

"Maurice is with the lawyers now." As Agnes interrupted him, he pocketed his phone. "They're drawing up the paperwork. It will be ready by tonight, tomorrow at the latest. You should really seek your own legal counsel, Blake."

"I'm fine." He turned away from the window, blinking the sunshine from his eyes. "Do what you have to."

Agnes sighed, pulled a book off the shelf and flicked through it. Blake did a double take when he saw what it was.

It was his copy of *The Swiss Family Robinson*, the one that he had read when he was a child. What were the chances that out of all the books here, she would pick that one? He thought of Ellie and how it was one of her favourite books, and had influenced her designs for LifeWrite. Seeing it made him smile, and Agnes frowned at him.

"You seem almost happy," the old woman said. "Why? Has it not sunk in yet? It can't be easy all of this. Losing everything."

She was right. Practically his whole adult life had been spent building Heartbook, and in one moment it was over. He never thought in a million years that he wouldn't be part of this company.

Thankfully, he still had savings and most of his wealth was in shares. Michelle and David couldn't take those.

And, after all, he still had his books and — he checked his watch — if he was quick, maybe he still had Ellie.

"Blake, are you okay?" Agnes said again. "Are you hearing what I'm saying?"

169

"Yes," he said. "I'm listening. But you're wrong, I haven't lost everything. My friends are right. They're so right."

"What?" Agnes uttered, one eyebrow shooting skyward.

Blake grabbed his suit jacket from the back of the chair, then walked over to Agnes and took the copy of *The Swiss Family Robinson* straight out of her hands.

He clutched it to his chest. "I have this," he said. "And, right now, that's all I need."

Agnes looked at him as if he was mad, and he almost felt it. But it wasn't a scary madness, it was an exciting one, like the rush just before a skydive. He didn't feel afraid of what might happen, he felt strangely free. It was as if he'd been wearing a weighted coat for decades, and had only just taken it off.

He had spoken the truth. The book *was* all he needed. Not because of what it was, but because of what it meant.

"Excuse me, Agnes." He leaned over and kissed the old woman on the forehead. "I have somewhere I need to be."

"But you can't leave," she protested as he walked past her. "The paperwork, we need you to sign it."

"Email it to me," he replied over his shoulder.

"But I don't know where you're going," she said. "Blake? Blake!"

He stopped at the door and took one last look at his office.

"I'm going to Devon," he said.

170

CHAPTER 28

ELLIE

Ellie scrambled through the heaving train station, struggling with the weight of the bag on her shoulder. There were people everywhere and muffled Tannoys going off every few seconds, and it gave her the same sense of claustrophobia as the crowd had back at the Heartbook HQ. She couldn't wait for the moment she disembarked the train in Exeter and drove out of the station in her mum's car, heading for the hills where their family farm was based.

At this rate, though, she wasn't going to make it. Her mum had booked her on to the seven o'clock service, and thanks to the heavy traffic around Heartbook and an accident on the motorway, she was cutting it way too fine.

"Come on," she muttered to herself. "Where are you?"

She pressed her phone to the ticket barrier, the e-ticket opening the gate. Her bag slid off her shoulder as she walked through, snagging on the gate and pulling her back. She heaved it back up, apologising to the woman behind her, and looked around for the right platform. It had to be around here somewhere. Spotting a map on the wall, she walked towards it

171

only to jump back as an electric transport buggy zoomed past, its horn blaring. She checked that the coast was clear, then ran to the map, seeing that she was in completely the wrong place.

"This isn't happening," she said, panic starting to set in. If she missed this train then she couldn't exactly afford to buy another ticket herself, and she didn't have the heart to ask her mum. She'd end up slinking home and spending the weekend in her flat, probably sobbing into a tub of ice cream.

She understood why Blake had done what he did, but it still broke her heart. No, it hadn't just broken it. It had *shattered* it — partly because she knew how hard it had been for him to stand there and admit to something he hadn't done, and partly because she had seen in his eyes the simple fact that he would withdraw himself from everything now, including her. Even though he hadn't said goodbye, that's exactly what it meant.

"Move it," said an elderly woman who was walking surprisingly fast. Ellie apologised again, breaking into a jog as she headed back the way she'd come. It had just gone five to seven and they'd already made an announcement that the train would be leaving imminently.

Ellie flew through the station, towards the correct platform as quickly as she could. She skidded to a halt in front of the train, reading *Exeter St Davids* on the departures board. She'd made it. Just.

Hoicking her bag up, she made to run to the nearest door and jump on. Even if it was first class, she could walk down the train to find her seat.

As she reached the nearest entry point a shrill whistle sounded down the platform and the train hissed and juddered to life.

"No!" she shouted. "Let me on."

There was nobody in sight other than the guard standing there, *Shelby* written on her name badge. She shook her head sadly. "I'm really sorry, hon. It's too late."

"Please," said Ellie, panting for breath. "I got lost. The train's still there, can't you let me on?"

172

Shelby glanced at it as it slowly moved on the tracks, then she shook her head.

"Would it help if I told you I'd just lost the love of my life?" Ellie said, thrusting her ticket at Shelby.

"I really can't." Shelby glanced at the ticket before handing it back. "I could lose my job. You could lose a leg. Or worse."

It was official. This was the worst day of her entire existence. Ellie scrunched up her ticket and sat on the nearest seat, putting her head in her hands.

"Hey, honey?" said Shelby.

Ellie looked up.

"I'm gonna make a call, see if I can get you on the next train, okay? Just sit tight."

She walked away, and Ellie was suddenly alone in a pool of quiet. She fished in her bag, pulling out her phone. Mum wouldn't be angry, she'd just be disappointed. And so was Ellie. Disappointed in her life, disappointed in herself. The Ellie Mae Curse seemed to have doubled in power, and she wondered how much worse it would get.

The Tannoy squealed again, a muffled voice spilling out of it. Ellie half listened, watching the trains come and go on the vast platforms. She couldn't believe how close to escape she'd come, only to be denied it at the last hurdle.

Something in the announcement caught her ear, and she cocked her head, listening.

"*That's Ellie Woodward to the main desk. Thank you.*"

Were they talking about her? She stood up, wishing she'd been paying more attention. Where was the main desk? She scanned the station and spotted it right in the middle.

She raced over and hovered impatiently in the queue until she was called forward. It was the same girl she'd spoken to before, Shelby, and she smiled at Ellie.

"Hi," Ellie said, sliding her bag up on to her shoulder again. "I'm Ellie Woodward. I think you just called for me."

"I did," said Shelby.

173

With any luck they'd let her on to the next train. She could text Mum and ask her to pick her up an hour later.

The girl typed something into her computer, frowning. "I'm really sorry, but the next train to Devon doesn't leave for another three hours."

Ellie's heart crashed into her shoes. Why had she called her over just to give her bad news?

"But that's not why I need you. You've been requested. Hang on."

Requested?

"Yeah, it's definitely you. Come on, I'll take you."

"Take me where?" Ellie asked, pushing her glasses back up her nose. "I don't understand."

"You will." Shelby slipped out from behind the desk, climbed on to an electric trolley and patted the seat next to her. Ellie got on, clutching her bag to her chest. They drove away, weaving through the crowds and heading out of the main station. Ellie's mind was a whirlwind of confusion. She couldn't understand what was happening to her.

"You say the love of your life broke up with you today?" Shelby asked.

"Yeah." Ellie held on tight as they went around a corner. "Well, kind of. Um, not really. I mean, no. We weren't even together. I just knew there was something special about him. I felt it. It's never happened before. I've never met anyone I clicked with so easily."

"He sounds amazing," said Shelby.

"Yeah," said Ellie. "But no. It wasn't to be. Too much going on in his life. He pretty much said he would never be able to see me again. There aren't any happy endings for me."

"I wouldn't be so sure about that," Shelby said with a grin. She steered them around the back of the train station and on to a large patch of tarmac, where a few small planes sat in a row.

Where were they? Were they going to throw her in a cargo plane and parachute her out over Devon?

174

"Come on." Shelby climbed off the trolley and led the way through the gate. Ellie followed her down a set of stairs then out into the warm, still evening. There were three planes in sight, and all of them looked like the kind of private jets you saw in the movies. The one right in front of her had its engines running. The pulse of it trembled through the tarmac and into her feet. The door was open, a small staircase leading into it. Somewhere deep inside her sparked the smallest flame of hope.

"Whose plane is that?" she asked, and Shelby smiled again.

"You don't need me to tell you that."

As if on cue, Blake appeared in the plane's doorway. He was backlit by the warm glow of the cabin, his tall frame cutting a striking silhouette against the sleek lines of the plane. He looked different, somehow. He looked younger. He looked stronger, but softer too, as if part of his stony facade had melted away.

Blake's eyes found hers, and his entire expression transformed. His smile wasn't just a curve of his lips, it was a revelation, a pure, unapologetic display of joy. And those eyes — warm and alive — held her captive, drawing her in with a magnetic pull she couldn't resist.

Ellie's heart thudded painfully in her chest, the kind of ache that came from too much emotion all at once.

"From what he was telling us, he feels exactly the same for you as you do for him," Shelby said. "So go get him. Go get that happy ending."

She didn't need to be told twice. Her legs moved before her brain had a chance to second-guess, her steps quickening until she was sprinting towards the plane.

Blake didn't hesitate either. He clattered down the steps, taking them two at a time, and by the time his feet hit the tarmac, they were both running.

Ellie threw herself into him with all the momentum of her sprint, her arms locking around his neck. Blake caught her effortlessly, his arms strong and unyielding as they encircled

175

her waist, pulling her tight against him. The heat of his body was a tonic against the stress of the day, and Ellie clung to him like she never wanted to let go.

"Ellie," he breathed.

She barely had time to register his words before he dipped his head, his mouth finding hers. The kiss was urgent, blazing, and everything she hadn't realised she'd been waiting for. There was no hesitation, just the intoxicating pressure of his lips and the perfect angle of his head that deepened the kiss. Her fingers slid into his hair, tugging gently, and she felt the low growl rumble through his chest as he pulled her closer still.

The hum of the engines faded, the world around them dissolving into nothing. It was just him, just her, and the undeniable heat between them. When they finally broke apart, both of them breathing hard, Blake pressed his forehead to hers, his hand cradling the back of her head like she was something precious.

"You came," he said, his voice low and hoarse.

"I couldn't not," she replied, her words spilling out in a rush. "Blake, I— Well, actually I literally couldn't not. Shelby here bundled me on to the buggy."

Blake burst out laughing and wrapped his arms around her, squeezing her tight. Ellie melted into the embrace, her hands sliding up his back and feeling the taut strength beneath his shirt.

But then she pulled back. Not far, just enough to look up at him. She needed to see his face, to confirm that this wasn't some cruel dream. Her fingertips brushed his jaw, tracing the sharp lines and the warmth of his skin. His eyes, impossibly blue, locked on hers, and in them, she saw everything she had hoped for: relief, desire, affection, and something deeper she dared not name.

"It's really you," she whispered.

"Yup," he replied softly, his own hand lifting to cup her cheek. "In the flesh."

176

She smiled as she shook her head. "You look . . . different."

"I feel different." His thumb grazed her skin in a way that sent shivers cascading down her spine. "I feel free. Like I can breathe again. And it's because of you."

Her heart flipped at his words, her pulse skittering out of control. "What about your company? What about everything you worked so hard for?"

Blake's eyes darkened, his gaze dropping to her lips for a heartbeat before meeting her eyes again. "None of it matters. Not at this moment in time." His hand slid into her hair, fingers tangling at the base of her neck. "You're all I want to think about."

He leaned in, and her breath hitched as she waited for the inevitable kiss. But he hesitated, his lips a whisper away from hers, his expression turning playful. "But, um . . . maybe we should get on the plane. Looks like we've drawn a crowd."

Ellie looked over at the buggy where she'd been dropped off. Shelby was there, three more women in uniforms standing by her side. Even from here she could hear them cheering, and Shelby grinned at her, raising her thumb in celebration. Ellie grinned back — a smile so wide it hurt her cheeks — and both she and Blake were laughing as they climbed the stairs and entered the jet.

CHAPTER 29

BLAKE

Blake's head was spinning, and it had nothing to do with the plane accelerating down the runway.

He gripped the armrest with his right hand and held tightly to Ellie's with his left. She was sitting next to him in one of the ten plush leather seats on the company jet, her head resting on his shoulder as she stared out of the window. The runway lights streaked by, but he barely noticed them. He only had eyes for her — he literally couldn't look away.

Ellie's beauty was effortless, unfiltered and magnetic. She had a kind of presence that drew you in, like a quiet flame that radiated warmth and lit up everything around her. Including him.

The plane bumped, Blake's stomach lurching as they soared into the evening. Ellie clutched at his hand, a small gasp escaping her. He pried his fingers free and wrapped his arm around her shoulders instead, pulling her close. He'd never been a great flier, but once again there was something about Ellie that was giving him a courage he'd never had before. When he was with her, he felt as if he could do anything. He

178

hadn't lied to her. He really did feel like a new man, and it was her doing.

The world below began to blur as they ascended into the darkening sky. Ellie's gaze stayed fixed on the window, watching the rolling hills and weaving highways grow smaller, the lights twinkling like scattered stars. But Blake? Blake watched her. The curve of her jaw, the delicate line of her neck, the way the evening glow caught in the unruly strands of her hair — it was all more captivating than any view outside.

Her dress certainly wasn't helping. The flowing sunflower-print fabric skimmed her figure in all the right ways, baring her shoulders and leaving her skin tantalisingly exposed. His eyes lingered on the smooth dip of her collarbone, the curve of her bare arm, the way the light caught on her skin. She exuded natural elegance, a quiet sensuality that was impossible to ignore. Each small movement she made — a shift in her seat, the brush of her head against his shoulder — set his senses on fire. Heat coiled low in his stomach, his pulse pounding in rhythm with every tiny adjustment she made, his body responding in ways he wasn't sure he could control much longer. She had no idea of the effect she had on him, and that made it even harder to breathe.

Part of him still couldn't believe he'd dropped everything and run for the station, but when he saw Ellie miss her train, he knew it had been the right thing to do. Even if she'd not wanted anything to do with him after how he'd left her — twice now — he could still help her get to where she needed to be.

He might have lost everything he'd worked so hard to build, but in doing so he'd managed to find the one thing his life had been missing. He held Ellie more tightly, and she pressed herself into him. He swore he could almost hear her purring.

And then she turned her face up to his, her lips slightly parted as if about to speak. Her amber eyes locked on to his, wide with unspoken emotion, and the connection between

179

them sparked. His gaze dropped to her mouth, and for a moment, all he could think about was how soft it had felt under his in the lift and outside on the tarmac, how perfectly they'd fit together.

"Blake." Her voice was barely audible over the hum of the engines, but it hit him like a thunderclap.

"Ellie," he replied, his tone rougher than he intended. His fingers, almost of their own accord, brushed a stray strand of hair from her cheek, lingering at the corner of her jaw. Her skin was warm and impossibly soft under his touch, and the slight hitch in her breath sent a fresh wave of heat pooling low in his stomach.

The tension between them thickened, charged with something primal and magnetic. Blake's heart was pounding, his thoughts clouded by the sheer pull of her. He wanted nothing more than to close the small space between them, to taste her again, to feel her melt into him like she had before. Every nerve in his body screamed for it.

"Do you . . . " he began, his voice barely a whisper as his thumb traced slow, light circles at the edge of her jawline. He inclined his forehead, almost brushing hers, her breath mingling with his.

Just then, the captain's voice broke through the speakers, announcing their ascent and the evening's short flight details, shattering the spell.

Ellie blinked, her lips twitching into a small, almost bashful smile as she turned back towards the window. "I thought you were going to disappear," she said, her words misting the glass. "After what you said to me earlier."

"I thought I might," he admitted. His gaze flickered to the window as the plane trembled slightly, cutting through a thin layer of clouds. "I didn't want you caught in the fallout. The idea of you suffering because of me, of you being dragged down just because you were near me — it felt unbearable."

She turned and settled her hand gently on his chest, the warmth of her touch cutting through the haze of doubt and

180

exhaustion. Without thinking, his hand covered hers, his heartbeat hammering beneath her palm like a racing engine.

"What changed your mind?" she asked.

"*You* did," he replied. "You made me realise something I couldn't see before. Even though this wasn't how I wanted it to happen, maybe it was time. Time to pass the reins to someone else and step back."

Her brow furrowed, but she waited, letting him find the words.

"Don't get me wrong," he continued, leaning back but not letting go of her hand. "I didn't want to lose Heartbook, not like this. It's everything to me. I created it. I nurtured it. It was my life's work. But somewhere along the way, I started feeling . . . trapped by it. Like it was no longer my company, but I was its."

"You mean you'd been thinking about stepping back?" she asked, surprised.

"Not entirely. I was still holding on, convincing myself I was the only one who could steer it. But maybe, deep down, I knew I was ready to let someone else take over the day-to-day. To be there as an advisor, to guide it from the sidelines. Just not like this."

Her expression softened, and he saw something in her eyes that made the tightness in his chest ease — understanding, maybe even a flicker of admiration.

"It wasn't supposed to be this way," he said, his voice quieter now. "Being forced out — it feels wrong, like they've taken a part of me. But maybe losing it like this has shown me that I was holding on too tightly. I was afraid to let go. Afraid that if I wasn't Heartbook, I didn't know who I was."

Ellie squeezed his hand gently, her presence as steady as an anchor in a storm. "Heartbook will always be yours," she said. "No one can take that away."

"I know." His voice sounded rough with emotion. "But it doesn't make it easier. Seeing it go, knowing I can't even stay to watch over it — it feels like I've lost a part of myself."

181

"But maybe now you can find the other parts of yourself," she said. "The parts you've been ignoring because you were so busy holding everything together."

Blake stared at her, her words settling into him like stones in still water, rippling out to places he hadn't considered in years. When she finally pulled her hand away, the loss was almost unbearable. He reached towards her without thinking, his body reacting to the absence of her touch. He craved her like she was air and he was a man underwater.

His skin was still humming where her hand had rested moments ago. Blake caught himself, forcing a measured breath as he steadied his thoughts. Was he reading too much into her smiles, her laughter, the way she leaned towards him? All the signs seemed to scream that she felt it too, this intense connection, but he couldn't risk rushing things and misjudging her feelings.

He unclipped his seatbelt and stood, stretching his arms overhead. It wasn't just the tension of the flight — it was the tension of being this close to her, knowing she could undo him with a single word or glance.

He stepped away, giving her space. He didn't want her to think he was crowding her or pushing too hard. Besides, he needed a moment to cool the fire raging through him.

Ellie tilted her head, her eyes sparkling with mischief as she watched him move. When he turned back, she was pouting playfully, her lips plump and teasing. A soft giggle escaped her, and she quickly covered her mouth with her hand, her cheeks flushing in a way that only made her more captivating.

"Sorry, I'm not laughing at you," she said. "This is all just . . ."

"Insane," he replied. "I know. But it feels good, doesn't it?"

Ellie nodded. "A hundred percent right."

"I just hope your mother likes me," he said.

"She will," said Ellie. "She met my last boyfriend. To be honest, if I went home and told her I was dating a turkey she'd think it was an improvement."

182

"Er . . . thanks?"

She laughed. "That was supposed to be a compliment. It came out wrong. But don't worry, you're whisking me to her in a private jet — she'll be impressed. Oh, wait, I should tell her that I'm arriving at a different time and a different place in a different mode of transport. And with a guest. She'll be thrilled."

"I hope she doesn't mind," he said. "There's a car waiting for us at the airfield ready to take us to your mum's farm. We shouldn't be too much longer."

"Really?" she said. "That's great. I guess money really can buy anything."

"Not for much longer," Blake said. "This is a company jet. The only reason I'm on it is because they haven't stripped all my credentials yet. I can't even guarantee we'll be able to fly it back. From now on, I might not have a lot to my name. Certainly not a lot to offer. Though, I do have this for you."

He opened the overhead compartment and pulled out his dog-eared copy of *The Swiss Family Robinson*.

He handed it to her. "It's a little used," he said. "It was my mum's, and it's not an early edition like the one you lost, but it's a rare print. I want you to have it."

Ellie stared at the book, her lips parted in surprise, her fingers brushing over the cover as though it was made of spun gold. She glanced up at him, her eyes shimmering. "You remembered," she said, her voice almost a whisper.

"Of course I remembered." His gaze locked with hers. "I remember everything you—"

Before he could finish, Ellie was on her feet, closing the space between them in a heartbeat. She grabbed his shirt, pushing him back against the table opposite with a force that knocked the breath out of him. Then her lips crashed against his, and the world around him dissolved.

The kiss was fire and electricity, igniting something in him. His hands found her waist, pulling her flush against him as if the mere inches of space between them were unbearable. Her fingers tangled in his hair, tugging slightly, and a low

183

growl rumbled in his throat in response. Every nerve in his body surged to life, his senses overwhelmed by the softness of her lips, the sweet, faint scent of her, the way her body pressed so perfectly against his.

Blake had never felt anything like it. He wasn't just kissing her. He was unravelling, every guarded piece of him falling away as her warmth consumed him. The pressure of her mouth, the way she sighed against him, sent a jolt of raw need straight to his groin.

When she finally pulled back, her breathing ragged, her cheeks flushed, Blake could barely think straight. Her hands rested on his chest, her fingers splayed as if she needed to steady herself. He stared at her, dazed, his body humming with energy and craving more.

Ellie met his gaze, her eyes darker than he'd ever seen them, her expression somewhere between astonished and hungry. For a moment, neither of them said anything, their heavy breaths filling the charged space between them.

Then she pushed him down onto one of the leather seats and straddled him in one fluid movement. The moment her hips ground down onto his, Blake nearly lost his mind. She tugged at his shirt, pulling it free from his waistband and ripping open the buttons, her hands hot and urgent on his skin.

He was already hard, straining against his suit trousers, and when her hand cupped him through the fabric he had no idea how he didn't come right there and then.

"Fuck, Ellie," he groaned, his head falling back against the seat, his jaw clenched tight.

She popped the button on his trousers, dragged down the zip, and wrapped her fingers around his cock.

He hissed through his teeth, hips bucking at her touch. "You're going to kill me."

Her grip tightened, stroking him with a maddening rhythm. He closed his eyes, his breath coming in short, ragged bursts. He was dangerously close, teetering on the edge, but he needed to be inside her. Now.

184

Pulling her hips, he slid a hand under her dress and tugged her panties to the side, releasing himself from her hand and guiding his tip to her core. She was hot and wet, and he felt her tremble on his lap.

"Wait," he said, breathlessly. "Do you have a condom?"

"No," Ellie let out a sigh. "I wasn't exactly expecting this. Don't you?"

"Shit," he muttered. "Not on me. Packed away in the hold."

Ellie collapsed onto his chest, laughing, her body still wrapped around his. "For a billionaire, your plane isn't very well stocked, is it?"

"You're making fun of me while I'm suffering," he joked.

She glanced down at where he was still hard, twitching against her thigh. "You're not suffering that badly, from what I can see."

He tightened his grip on her thighs, feeling her wetness stick to his skin. "I'm not leaving you like this, not again."

Before she could reply, he lifted her off him and set her down gently on the seat opposite. Her dress rode up her thighs, her underwear gone with one quick tug, then he knelt in front of her and spread her legs open like a man starving.

His mouth was on her in seconds. Licking through her folds, groaning as the taste of her wrecked him. Then his tongue circled her clit with purpose, flicking and sucking until her hips lifted from the seat and she gave a sharp cry.

"Blake, don't stop."

He didn't stop. Groaning in response, his hands gripped her thighs, pulling her taut as he devoured her. When he slid two fingers inside her, curling them just right, he felt her start to contract around them as she bucked on his face. Her moans echoed around the cabin.

"Come for me, Ellie," he breathed against her. "I want to feel you fall apart."

And she did. Hard. Thighs trembling, breath stuttering, her hands fisted in his hair as her body locked tight around his fingers and mouth. He didn't stop until she was quiet, her

185

skin slick with heat. Only then did he pull back and kiss the inside of her thigh before meeting her eye.

And at the way she smiled back at him — a wicked, teasing curve of her lips — Blake knew he was utterly and completely undone.

CHAPTER 30

ELLIE

"Wow!"

Her mum had only just opened the door, and that was the first word out of her mouth. She looked Blake up and down with her twinkling eyes, then flashed Ellie a smile.

"Really, *wow!*"

"Mum!" Ellie exclaimed, feeling the heat creep into her cheeks. "Could you be any more embarrassing?"

Blake chuckled, and Ellie slapped him lightly on the arm, trying to stifle her own laugh. He feigned injury, clutching his side dramatically, which only made her laugh harder.

"Mum, this is Blake," Ellie said, leaving out his last name for now. "Blake, Mum."

"Call me Isla, dear," she said, taking his hand. "You can call me Mum if you like, but that might be weird."

"It's a pleasure," said Blake. "I can see where Ellie gets her smile from."

"Oh, shush," Isla said, blushing. "You two had better come in before you swoon all over my porch. I've only just hosed it down. Come on."

187

Ellie tutted, following her mum into the house. It was past ten, and the farm was drenched in darkness. Her mum didn't have a lot of livestock, and the goats and chickens and horses she did own were quiet. A few birds still hurled their calls into the night, but the peace of the countryside was almost absolute. Ellie closed her eyes for a moment and listened to it, remembering how much she had loved that absence of noise when she was little. The city never stopped shouting, and right now she would be happy to never go back.

The door closed behind them and Ellie opened her eyes. The farmhouse wasn't huge — it was probably tiny compared to wherever Blake lived — but it was cosy, and it was loved. Bookcases sat against almost every wall, stuffed with old novels and coffee-table art books and various trinkets her mum had collected over the years. There were also dozens of framed photographs, and Blake made his way towards one on the other side of the room.

"Oh, God, no!" Ellie exclaimed as she recognised which one it was. She ran after him, but she was too slow. He had picked up the frame, already laughing. "That isn't me!" she said. "That definitely, absolutely, one hundred percent isn't me."

"Well whoever she is, she's adorable," Blake said, admiring the picture of a thirteen-year-old Ellie standing with a group of people outside the school gates, wearing a pair of huge red glasses and a pink shell suit. She was holding a book, grinning with happiness and showing off her braces.

"Reading club," she said, blushing. "Man, I was so uncool."

"I think you were the coolest." He replaced the photograph. "I think you still are."

"She hasn't changed a bit." Isla was watching them both from the other side of the room, her eyes crinkled with kindness.

"I have!" Ellie said. "I'm completely different. Don't you dare gang up on me."

"Come through to the kitchen," her mum replied, leading the way. "I wasn't sure if you'd be hungry, so I made French toast."

188

Ellie was so excited she almost started jumping up and down. Managing to contain herself, she took Blake's arm and walked him through to the kitchen. The smell of fresh bread and cinnamon filled the air, making her feel truly at home.

"It's amazing," she said to Blake. "You have to try it."

"And if you don't like that, I whipped up a batch of brownies earlier," Isla said. "And there's banoffee pie too, Ellie's favourite."

Blake grinned. "Why do I feel like I've died and gone to heaven?"

He pulled out a seat for Ellie and she took it. Then he unbuttoned his jacket and sat next to her.

"A true gentleman as well," said Isla. "How refreshing."

"Completely and utterly." Ellie grinned at Blake, the sparkle in his eyes telling her he was also thinking about the journey here.

"Are you okay?" Blake took her hand and rubbed the inside of her wrist with his thumb. The touch sent a bolt of longing to the soft, warm places Ellie had been trying to ignore.

"I'm more than okay," she said.

How had she got so lucky? Even the thought of it, that this might just be luck, made her panic.

Slow down, she told herself. *You're still cursed, Ellie Mae. Don't let this fool you.*

What if she was reading it wrong? What if Blake was just here because he felt sorry for her, or because he knew it was a good place to hide from the world? What if he didn't care at all? A million doubts circled her mind like a cloud of squawking crows and she pulled her hand away, pretending to fiddle with her cutlery.

Isla served up French toast with crème brulée and lashings of freshly whipped cream. She warmed the brownies in the oven before putting down a plate of them along with a cake stand replete with banoffee pie. Ellie realised that she was right — that Blake didn't just have eyes for her, because he looked at the food like he was in love with it. He devoured two brownies, a slice of French toast, and a piece of pie in almost as many minutes before crashing back in his chair and putting a hand over his stomach.

"That was amazing," he said. "But I think I might have overdone it."

Isla laughed, fixing up coffee for her and Blake, and tea for Ellie. They chatted while they drank, Isla asking Blake a hundred and one questions, all of which he answered with candour and humour. He spoke about his own upbringing, about his father and mother running the restaurant. He spoke about how he hadn't seen them in a while and Ellie could see the sadness wash over him. Isla laughed and nodded and gave her sad face in all the right places. Ellie could tell instantly how much her mum liked him. It made her relax a little, because her mum had always been a great judge of character.

It was only when Blake reached the end of his teenage years that Ellie started to worry.

"And what do you do now?" Isla asked, the question that Ellie had been dreading. But there was no escaping it. If she and Blake were going to be . . . whatever they were — friends? A couple? Ellie didn't know, but either way her mum would find out the stories about him.

Ellie took her glasses off and cleaned them on her dress, replacing them with a sigh. She shared a look with Blake.

"I work in IT," he said. "A company called Heartbook."

"Oh, yeah, sure," Isla said, nodding. "The social whatsit thing. Ellie tried to get me to create an account once, so we could Hearttime or whatever, but I could never get the hang of it. What's wrong with a good old-fashioned telephone?"

"Absolutely nothing," said Blake.

"What do you do for them?" Isla asked. "IT? Wasn't there some kind of scandal yesterday? Some inappropriate comments or something? I saw it on the news. What was the guy's name . . . uh . . . Burt, or Bryant, or . . ."

190

Ellie saw the moment it clicked. Her mum's eyes widened and she looked at Blake, then at Ellie, then back at Blake.

"Or Blake," Blake said, and the air seemed to deflate out of him. "Look, I'm sorry, I—"

"It's not true." Ellie grabbed his hand and pulled it on to her lap. "It's all a lie. Blake didn't say the things they accused him of."

To her surprise, her mum reached over and took Blake's other hand, holding it tight between her own. He looked at her, and for all his handsomeness and strength he looked nervous, as if her mum's opinion really mattered.

"Blake, my Ellie Mae is one of the most decent and most wonderful human beings on this entire planet."

"I know," he said, but she hushed him.

"What I'm saying is that she sees people — she sees them for exactly who they are. Even with Josh, at heart she knew what kind of person he was. She just didn't admit it to herself."

Tears stung her eyes at her mum's words. For so long, she'd carried the quiet fear that her mum had judged her for her disastrous choice in Josh. But hearing those words of pride now was like a balm to her soul, washing away the lingering doubts. Deep down, she'd known her mum believed in her — she just hadn't been ready to trust it. And somehow, her mum had always understood that too.

"Ellie can look into a person's eyes and read their soul, and if she has looked into your eyes, and if she has read your soul and understood what kind of man you are, then I trust her completely. If she tells me you are kind and you are decent, then I believe it. I can almost see it myself. Here, in my house, nothing matters but happiness. So forget about it all while you're here."

"Thank you," Blake said. "I can't tell you what that means to me. I hope I live up to what she sees, what you both see. There are things I've done that I feel ashamed of. I'm not perfect. I'm a long way from that."

191

Ellie wasn't sure if that last part was true, but his words made her pause. She had known Blake for less than two days — who knew what kind of secrets lay behind that smile?

Isla let go of him, and he scrubbed at his face with his free hand. He looked at Ellie, and she could see the war waging inside his thoughts. He wanted to do the right thing, she knew. And for him, the right thing was leaving her so that she wouldn't be associated with his alleged crimes. But he felt something for her, she was sure of it, something powerful and something right.

"Thank you," he said again. "But now I've got you here safely, maybe I should go. I can—"

"I want you to stay," Ellie said. "I want to escape, and I want you to escape with me. It's just a weekend. Whatever happens on Monday, I just want the next two days to be about us. I want us to be free."

Blake nodded, but the sadness was still there. Ellie looked at her mum, and her mum sighed.

"It's late," Isla said, standing up. "Why don't you two go to bed. I made you up separate rooms in the main house." She smiled at Ellie, the twinkle in her eye growing brighter. "But they're right next door to each other."

"Mum!" Ellie said, and they both laughed.

Blake relaxed a little. "That's really kind of you," he said. "But I'm going to have to ask you for one huge favour."

He sounded deadly serious, but then he smiled and reached for the plate of brownies. "I'm going to have to insist that you let me take these up with me."

CHAPTER 31

ELLIE

Ellie lay in the same bed she'd slept in when she was fifteen, staring at the faded pop band posters on the wall. She was back in a world that felt impossibly familiar and yet distant, a place she hadn't thought about enough lately. The room smelled faintly of sweets and old books, a comforting blend that wrapped around her like a warm hug. She felt more at peace than she had in years and she vowed to come back more often. It wasn't that far away, really, even if she didn't travel by private jet.

Blake had been given the guest room next door. It had been her parents' room at one point, before her mum had moved down to the annex at the back of the house so she could be nearer the livestock. They'd exchanged goodnights at the top of the stairs, standing awkwardly close in the dim hallway. Neither of them had made a move to leave, lingering in the charged silence that said everything they didn't. When she'd finally stepped into her room, she'd glanced back to find him watching her, something unreadable and magnetic in his expression. It was as if neither of them had wanted to break the moment, but neither had dared to cross the invisible line.

Now, stretched out on the slightly-too-small bed, Ellie couldn't stop replaying it all. Her body felt too awake, too aware, every nerve charged as though he were still nearby. She shifted against the sheets, but it didn't help. The ache he stirred in her refused to be ignored.

The muffled sound of water running from the bathroom across the hall only made it worse. Her mind betrayed her, painting vivid pictures she had no right to imagine: the steam curling around his sharp jawline, droplets trailing over the hard lines of his chest, his hands pushing back his damp hair. And then there was the way he'd felt in her hands — hard, thick, so hot it burned her skin. She could still see the hunger in his eyes and the tension in his jaw as he'd sworn through gritted teeth. Heat flowed urgently through her, making her press her thighs together as if that would somehow contain the longing that was surging there.

She'd felt desire before — at least, she thought she had. But Blake had rewritten that definition. This was on another level entirely. Her skin seemed to hum at the memory of his hands on her, the way his tongue had circled as his fingers had explored her. Every inch of her ached to feel him closer again.

Ellie sat up abruptly, her pulse thrumming in her ears. This wasn't her. She wasn't the type to lose herself like this, to let her thoughts spiral out of control. She'd always been cautious, measured, even in her past relationships. But Blake had torn through those defences with a single look, with the way he made her feel like she was the only person in the room, the only person who mattered.

She pressed her hands to her face, the coolness grounding her for a moment. Was she really falling for him? The thought sent a wave of panic rushing through her, but it was followed by something even more unsettling: a flicker of hope. Maybe, just maybe, this wasn't as crazy as it seemed. Maybe it could work.

Ellie lifted her pillow and scrunched it over her face, yelling her frustrations into the duck feathers. It did little to satisfy

194

her longing, but her chest felt less constricted. Her glasses ached on her face so she took them off, placing them on the bedside table. She was wearing a pair of floral pyjamas that her mum had kept for her. They were a little tight now, and smelled almost pleasantly musty, but they were still comfortable.

Something bleeped from inside her bag and she walked across the room to fish out her phone. Reception up here was sketchy at best and a voicemail from Josh had just come through, even though the time stamp told her it had been left nearly two hours ago. Her face wrinkled in disgust. What did he want? It would be a desperate plea to win her back, probably by insulting her in some way. That's what he had always done, tried to make her feel so insecure that she'd fall back into his arms.

But what if he'd messaged to tell her their flat had burned down or something like that? It was just a message, it wasn't like she had to speak to him. She dialled her voicemail, straining through the static to hear Josh's whiny voice. The signal kept coming and going, so she could only make out a handful of words.

"... think you could just leave me ... not fair ... you'll wish you hadn't ..."

Typical. He sounded so pathetic. Once upon a time she'd thought he was a strong guy, but he was a weakling in body and soul. He was a child. His words faded out and Ellie paced the room, opening the door to try to find a better signal.

"... didn't think I knew but now you'll see," Josh went on as she walked out into the corridor. "... make something of myself, so you come crawling back ..."

He faded out again and she checked the phone as she walked, tapping the screen.

"You stupid—" she started, then she collided with something big and the phone spilled from her hands. "Oh!" she said. "I'm so ..."

Blake stood in front of her, completely naked apart from the incredibly small towel around his waist.

195

"Oh!" Ellie said again, feeling her eyes wander without permission.

She'd seen him like this before, yes. But freshly showered was a whole new level of torture. Her body reacted instantly, heat blooming low in her stomach. The memory of his mouth on her hit like a sucker punch, and the trail of water running languorously from his chest down to the deep V of his hips was not helping.

"We *really* should stop meeting like this," Blake said, a wicked glint in his eye.

Ellie froze, her pulse pounding in her ears as her eyes locked on Blake's. Her breath hitched, and suddenly, the corridor seemed much smaller, the air charged with something electric and undeniable.

"I . . . Uh . . ." she stammered, her mouth dry as he stepped closer, his towering frame filling her vision. She could barely think, barely breathe, as the fire in his gaze pinned her to the spot.

"Ellie," he murmured, his voice low and rough, sending shivers down her spine. "I told myself to behave while I was here as a guest."

"And how's that going?" she whispered, though she already knew the answer.

A muscle twitched in his jaw. "Fucking terribly."

Before she could respond, before her brain could catch up with her body, Blake closed the distance between them. His hands came to her waist, firm and possessive, and then he was lifting her as if she weighed nothing at all. Instinctively, her legs wrapped around his torso, her arms looping around his neck to steady herself. The towel around him slipped slightly, teasing her with the idea that it could fall at any second.

"Blake . . ." she started, but her protest dissolved into a gasp as his lips found hers.

The kiss was a storm, fierce and consuming, his mouth moving against hers with an urgency that stole her breath. Her fingers tangled in his damp hair, her body arching into

196

his as his hands slid lower, gripping her thighs and holding her against him. Every inch of her was pressed to him, and she could feel the strength of him beneath the towel, his sheer physical power making her head spin.

"Tell me to stop," he murmured against her lips, his voice strained, as if he was fighting to hold himself back.

"Don't you dare," she replied, her own voice certain.

That was all it took. Blake turned, carrying her the short distance to her room. The door was already ajar, and he nudged it open with his foot before stepping inside. The light from the hallway cast a soft glow over the bed, and he crossed the room in two strides, his lips never leaving hers.

Ellie barely registered the world around her until she heard the door click shut behind them and her back hit the mattress. She let out a soft gasp as Blake hovered over her, his strong arms braced on either side of her body. His towel had loosened further, barely clinging to his hips, and the sight of him above her stole the last remnants of her breath.

His gaze roamed over her, hot and keen, and she felt the weight of it everywhere. She reached up, her fingers brushing against the hard lines of his chest, tracing the curve of his muscles. His skin was warm and smooth, and the feel of him beneath her hands sent a wave of fire through her.

"Ellie," he said, her name like a prayer on his lips. He leaned down, his mouth finding the curve of her neck, his teeth grazing her skin just enough to make her shiver.

She arched beneath him, her hands moving to his waist. His breath was hot against her collarbone as he kissed her skin through the fabric of her pyjamas, the weight of him pressing her into the mattress. Every nerve in her body was alive, her skin burning everywhere he touched.

"Blake," she whispered, her voice trembling with both need and disbelief. She'd never felt anything like this before, this complete and total surrender to someone else, this over-whelming desire to be consumed by him.

197

His lips found hers again, and she felt him smile against her mouth, a low growl rumbling in his chest as if he could sense just how much she wanted him.

"Tell me if I need to stop," he murmured again, his hand sliding to the hem of her shirt.

"Don't stop." She tugged at the edges of his towel. "Don't ever stop."

CHAPTER 32

BLAKE

Blake's hands trembled as they found the buttons of the softest pair of floral pyjamas he'd ever seen. Not from hesitation, but from the sheer weight of everything he was feeling. His fingertips brushed against the fabric, and beneath it, her warmth called to him like gravity. He wasn't sure if it was the sound of her breath catching or the way her body arched ever so slightly towards him, but every nerve in his body ignited with need.

He took his time, undoing the first button slowly, his eyes fixed on her face. Ellie's lips were parted, her cheeks flushed, her chest rising and falling with shallow breaths. She looked up at him with a mix of trust and desire that made his pulse thunder in his ears. His thumb pushed the second button, and as it slipped free, the fabric parted to reveal the smooth, pale curve of her collarbone. He couldn't resist leaning down to kiss it, his lips caressing her skin as she let out a soft, breathy sigh. His cock sprang to attention and the towel that had been trying its hardest to stay tight around his waist fell on to the bed between them.

199

"You're incredible," he murmured against her, his voice rough. His fingers worked their way down the row of buttons until the floral print slid open to reveal the swell of her breasts, her body glowing in the faint light of the room, her nipples taut and too delicious not to taste.

He shifted back on top of her and Ellie shivered beneath the swirl of his tongue. She slid her hands up his back, her nails grazing his shoulders just enough to make him groan. She wasn't holding back, wasn't shy, and it made him want her even more. He flicked his tongue over one nipple, then the other, his hands lifting the curve of her breasts to his mouth. She tasted like warmth and sweetness, like everything he hadn't realised he'd been craving.

She was utterly breathtaking.

"You're perfect," he said, his voice raw with emotion, and Ellie moaned quietly as she urged him up her body to kiss him.

"And I'm in your debt," she whispered. "Lie back."

She pushed at his chest. Blake blinked for a second, stunned, then did as he was told, easing onto the pillows as Ellie shifted on top of him. Straddling his waist, she dragged her nails down his chest, her eyes dark with intent as she reached his rock-hard cock.

"God, you're so hard." Her fingers wrapped around him and began stroking.

Blake's breath caught. "That's not helping me stay composed."

Ellie gave him a wicked smile. "Then don't."

Her touch was confident and slow, and she eased her way down his body, teasing the sensitive underside of his cock with her thumb before she took him deep in her mouth.

Blake swore, loudly, his hands flying to her hair as the heat of her mouth wrapped around him.

"Fuck, Ellie!"

Taking her time, she drew him deeper, using her tongue to flick against the head as she withdrew, pumping his base with her grip. His hips flexed involuntarily. The sight of her was too much.

200

"You keep doing that," he groaned, "and this is going to be over embarrassingly fast."

She pulled back slowly, licking his length with her tongue. "Do you want me to stop?"

"Only if you're planning on climbing on top of me next."

"Your wish," she whispered as she moved back up his body, "is my command."

His hands gripped her hips, holding her still. They looked at each other, realisation flooding them.

"Condoms," they said in unison.

Ellie laughed, arched a brow, and looked around. "This is my childhood bedroom. You think I've got condoms stashed behind my teddies? Where are yours?"

Blake was breathless, still barely holding it together. "Oh, man. Don't go anywhere."

He kissed her and pulled back with a groan, lifting her from on top of him and sliding off the bed. Grabbing the towel to cover himself, he sprinted out of the room, rummaged through his suitcase, and back again with surprising speed given how Ellie had turned his legs to jelly.

He stalked towards the bed, his eyes locked onto Ellie's, the foil packet already torn open between his teeth. Rolling the condom on with practised ease, he climbed onto the bed on top of her.

"Look at you." He ran a hand up the inside of her legs, spreading her wider as he settled between them. "You're so wet."

His fingers dipped into her, just enough to make her gasp, then he lined himself up at her entrance, the head of his thick cock teasing her folds, and pushed into her slowly, groaning deep in his throat as he filled her inch by inch. Her body stretched around him, tight and hot and slick and perfect. They both stilled, breathless, letting the sensations wash over them. Then he began to move.

Slow, deep thrusts that had her hands clawing at his back, pulling him deeper. He held her hips, angling her so they fit perfectly together, as he built her up, thrust by thrust.

Ellie dragged her hands up his chest, her nails grazing over the skin until she reached his chin, cupping it and forcing him to look at her. "Lie down, let me."

Blake stilled, almost shooting his load with her words. He took a deep, ragged breath, trying to focus his attention anywhere but her amazing body to stop himself coming. He pulled out, easing onto his elbows then his back as Ellie rose to her knees. She straddled him again, this time lowering herself back onto him, taking his full length with a moan that hit him square in the gut.

"Ellie!"

She started to move. Slowly at first, grinding her hips with meticulous precision. Her confidence wrecked him, the sight of her almost too much. Slipping a hand between them, his thumb found her slick, swollen bundle of nerves at her centre. He circled it slowly, then pressed harder making her gasp. Her eyes fluttered closed, hips jerking reflexively.

"Keep going." His thumb moved rhythmically, matching her hips. "Come on me."

She let out a broken moan. The more he circled her clit, the more erratic her movements. Blake couldn't take his eyes off her. Her mouth parted, her body trembling, every motion of her hips sending sparks up his spine.

"Come for me, Ellie." His thumb flicked faster and faster. "I want to feel you fall apart on my cock."

She cried out as she came, the walls of her pussy clenching his cock. Blake lost it then, thrusting into her one final time before he came mere seconds after Ellie with a guttural groan. She collapsed forward onto his chest, thighs trembling. He felt her still pulsing around him, felt the heat of her breath against his neck. They lay there, tangled in each other as Blake exhaled a shaky breath.

"Holy shit," Ellie murmured, and Blake could do nothing but agree.

* * *

Blake stirred, stretching out his legs and feeling the cold, hard end of a bed against his feet. He opened his eyes, seeing an unfamiliar room around him — cheesy posters on the walls, and a pink duvet cover on the bed. It took only a second for it all to come rushing back, and when it did, a slow smile spread across his face.

Ellie.

He sat up, the little bed creaking beneath him as he ran a hand through his tousled hair. The memory of her was everywhere — in the faint scent of her perfume lingering on the pillow, in the warmth still clinging to the sheets. He glanced around the room, his chest tightening when he realised she wasn't there.

For a fleeting moment, he felt a pang of panic. Had she regretted it? Had he crossed a line? No, he'd made sure she wanted it too. But more than consent, Ellie had done things to his body that made him twitch even at the memory.

He climbed off the bed, walking to the window. The curtains were obviously blackout ones because when he pulled them back a shaft of sunshine punched into the room. He whisked them open, then grabbed his discarded towel, made his way out of Ellie's room and into the one that her mum had made up for him.

His phone lay on his neatly folded clothes and he picked it up. There were twenty-seven missed calls, all from various members of the board. Eight voicemail messages waited for him but he couldn't bring himself to check them. There was also a news alert announcing that he had stepped down from Heartbook. Gritting his teeth, he opened it up and scrolled through it. There was a photograph of him from the press conference and he barely recognised himself — he looked like a shadow of the man he had once been. There was also a photograph of Michelle and David standing side by side, smiling smugly. According to the article, they had both been appointed the joint CEOs of the company.

He couldn't bear to read any more, and he tossed the phone on to the bed. He only picked it up again when he

203

remembered that he hadn't checked the time, and when he did he couldn't believe it. It was nearly nine — later than he had slept in years. He had no intention of ever wearing his suit again, so he opened his travel bag and pulled out a pair of Levi's and a plain grey T-shirt instead.

After a pit stop to wash his face and brush his teeth, he headed downstairs, a little tentative about why Ellie had left him alone in her room. Blake hoped he'd not done anything stupid in his sleep or that Ellie regretted what they'd done. He headed to the kitchen where they'd eaten the previous night, following the delicious smells of coffee and pastries.

"Morning, sleepyhead," Ellie said, as he poked his head around the door. She was working on her laptop, a dozen piles of paper stacked around it and several notepads open to the side. A fresh mug of coffee sat in front of her and Blake licked his lips in anticipation. "I would ask you how you slept, but I don't need to."

"I didn't mean to sleep for so long," he said.

"It's the fresh country air." Isla held a mug out for him.

"Thank you," he said, grateful for the coffee and the distance Isla's room was from Ellie's.

"I hope you don't mind that I didn't wake you?" Ellie said. "I woke early and my mind was buzzing."

"Not at all." He kissed her head and sat down next to her. "I was a bit worried when I saw you were gone, but we're okay, yes?"

Ellie nodded, her eyes sparkling and her cheeks an adorable pink.

"Anyone for eggs and bacon?" came Isla's voice from by the stove.

"Yeah, sure. Thanks, Mum," Ellie called back.

"Count me in too, please," Blake replied, his stomach growling.

Isla set a plate of scrambled eggs, bacon, sausages, tomatoes, and toast in front of both of them and made a retreat.

204

"Anything fun?" Blake nodded at the laptop. The world felt weird after the intensity of the last few days, and he took a sip of coffee to remind himself this was real.

"Kind of," Ellie said, frowning and turning her screen so he could see. "Do you want to look?"

He did. On the laptop screen was a page of code and he scanned through it, whistling. "That's impressive. Tell me you didn't write all that in one morning."

"No way." Ellie laughed. "Just half of it. It's something I've been working on for a while now, a thing I want to try with LifeWrite. You inspired me to get back to it."

Blake's smile widened, the pride in his expression unmistakable. "Ellie, this is brilliant. Honestly. I've seen a lot of pitches and ideas over the years, and this . . . this has real potential."

"You think so?" she asked, her voice soft with vulnerability.

"I know so." He turned to face her. "Look, I may not be in a position to throw financial backing your way right now, but that doesn't mean I can't help. I can look over the code, give you feedback, connect you with people who can guide you, whatever you need. You've got something special here, and I want to see it succeed."

Her eyes lit up, and she took his hand, her grip warm and reassuring. "You really mean that?"

"Absolutely," he said, squeezing her hand back. "This is your vision, Ellie, but I'm here to help in any way I can. Just tell me what you need."

She smiled, her confidence blooming in his presence. Using her free hand, she scrolled down the page, showing him more of her work. "Okay then, Mr Fielding, tell me what you think of this. So, the whole thing about LifeWrite is that I want it to be a positive experience. I want it to make people feel good about themselves and about the world."

He nodded. He'd wanted exactly the same thing for Heartbook, it just hadn't quite worked out that way. When the

205

company had gone public, and Michelle and Mike had come on board, the emphasis had gone from social good to making money, and the network just hadn't been the same since.

"And I want it to help people," Ellie went on. "Heal people. You know, if you're down, or sad, or depressed, or angry. This piece of code is designed to study your facial expression and work out how you're feeling."

"That's amazing," said Blake.

"It's a little rusty, but try it," she said. "Hang on."

She opened the LifeWrite interface on the laptop, activating the camera, and their faces appeared side by side on the screen. Blake caught their reflection and couldn't help a flicker of surprise — how natural they looked together, like they belonged in the same frame. She angled the laptop slightly so that only he filled the shot, her fingers skimming the keyboard with practised ease.

"All right, superstar," she said with a small smirk. "You're on. It's capturing footage, so don't say anything you might regret."

The old computer clunked and whirred, struggling with the complexity of the code. On-screen he saw a series of whorls and lines appear on his face, then the computer beeped. A crudely animated cartoon avatar appeared, and Ellie's voice drifted from the speakers.

"Good evening," it said.

"Urgh, I've got to work on the time stamps," she said. "Pretend it said morning."

"You look . . . flustered," said the avatar, and a laugh escaped Blake's lips. He probably *did* look flustered, but only because his mind kept taking him back to last night. "Please relax, take a deep breath, and listen to this poem."

On the computer, Ellie's voice began to narrate a calm and soothing poem.

"Wordsworth," he said, recognising it. "That's nice."

"You really do know your books," she replied. "So, yeah, the idea is that there is a response for every mood, and a huge

206

database of writing to choose from. Eventually, when the network is up and running, LifeWrite will analyse your mood and do other things too, like connect you to family members, or just find someone for you to talk to."

"United by stories," he said. "It's brilliant."

Ellie's cheeks flushed pink, and she tucked a strand of hair behind her ear, avoiding his gaze. Her fingers toyed with the edge of the laptop, and when she finally glanced up at him, a small, shy smile played on her lips. "I don't know about that."

"It's brilliant," he said again. "I mean it. Look, I know I can't offer you much, but let me at least be your cheerleader. LifeWrite *has* to exist. I think it can really help the world. I'll help where I can, where you want me to. *If* you want me to."

"I want you to," Ellie said. She patted the laptop. "And there's no backing out now, I've got it all on film."

Blake looked at his face on the screen and laughed.

"I hereby declare that my only purpose in life from now on will be to help and support Ellie Mae Woodward, because she is the most wonderful, intelligent, beautiful person I know."

Ellie gently slapped his arm, but she was laughing. Blake turned to her, ready to tell her that he had fallen totally head over heels for her, but at that moment Isla came crashing through the farmhouse's front door, a look of alarm on her face.

"I'm sorry to interrupt," she said breathlessly. "But you must come quickly. It's an emergency."

CHAPTER 33

ELLIE

"An emergency?" Ellie stood so fast her chair almost toppled over behind her. "What's happened?"

Isla stood red-faced and panting in the doorway, like she'd just run a marathon. Sweat dampened her brow, her wild hair sticking up in all directions. She waved them over. "Hurry." She ran out the door again.

Ellie started after her, Blake at her side. They ran down the porch steps and across the large, neatly kept yard towards the small barn where the animals lived. Blake charged ahead, his strides long and powerful despite his bare feet. Isla had stopped by the open barn door, her hands on her knees as she fought for breath.

"What is it?" Ellie said as she reached her. She breathed in the scent of livestock, the smell reminding her of her childhood. "What's going on?"

From the way her mum was acting there had to be a fire somewhere, an animal in distress, or maybe even a murder. Her stomach twisted in knots as she scanned the yard, but Isla just pointed through the barn door.

"The goats," she cried. "They've escaped."

"*What*?" Ellie held a hand to her chest. "Mum, that's hardly an emergency. I thought something was really wrong."

"Something is really wrong," her mum answered. "Something must have spooked them. They're in the vegetables. If I don't get them back in the barn then everything will be eaten."

Ellie blinked incredulously, and turned to share a look with Blake.

"The goats have escaped," she said.

Blake's lips twitched, his amusement clear, though he was trying hard to hide it.

"Well, we'd better go get them," he replied, deadpan. "Where are they?"

"Through here."

Isla led them into the barn and out of a door on the other side. The farm's impressive vegetable beds lay ahead, bigger than Ellie remembered because her mum had dug up another couple of potato patches since last time she'd been home. It was an ocean of leafy greens, sweet peas and potatoes, cabbages and lettuces, courgettes and pumpkins, strawberries and gooseberries, and just about everything else you could imagine. Currently five goats were tearing their way through the garden like children in a sweet shop, bleating with delight.

"Hurry!" cried her mum.

"I'm coming!" Ellie said, running through the gate. Blake was right next to her, slipping in the freshly watered earth.

"Is there a trick to this?" he asked, hesitating as he approached the group of wayward goats.

"Just grab them by the horns," Ellie called back to him. "And try not to get butted. They are stronger than they look."

Blake nodded slowly. "Noted," he said, the word dripping with scepticism. He scanned the unruly group, eyes narrowing at a large, stubborn-looking white goat chomping on a patch of lettuce with alarming determination.

"I'll go for the white one," he announced.

209

"Bob," Ellie said, barely hiding her amusement.

"Bob?" Blake turned to her with a questioning look.

"Bob," she repeated.

"Hmm."

"He reminded mum of her uncle," she said. "He's pretty angry. You sure you want Bob?"

Blake studied the goat, tilting his head as if assessing his opponent. Bob lifted his head and stared back, chewing slowly, his horns gleaming in the sunlight.

"How bad can he be?" Blake asked, his tone more confident than his expression.

Ellie burst out laughing, shaking her head. "Bad," she said. "Really bad. Don't say I didn't warn you."

Blake set off, careful not to step on any of the plants. Ellie ran the other way, clucking gently as she approached the little grey goat known as Dolly. She was fairly docile and let Ellie steer her away, happily chewing on some rhubarb stalks. Ellie led her into the barn where her mum was waiting, and together they wrangled the goat into her pen. She bleated mournfully and Ellie laughed. "Sorry, Dolly."

She ran back outside. Blake looked almost like he was wrestling with Bob, one hand on one of the goat's horns, the other on his neck. But Bob wasn't having any of it, and with a sudden lurch he broke free. Blake yelped, slipping in the dirt and falling on his face.

Ellie couldn't help it — she burst out laughing. And when Blake stood up with mud smeared over his T-shirt and face, she laughed twice as hard. She had to slap her hands to her knees to stop herself falling over.

"I told you he was angry," she called to him when she could speak again.

"I didn't even know goats got angry," he replied. He rubbed his hands down his T-shirt, making it even more filthy, then set off again, his arms outstretched as he chased down the goat.

Ellie left him to it, her sides aching. Betty was just up ahead and she led her back into the barn. Petunia was just as easy, and even Sir Ronald didn't put up too much of a fight.

210

By the time she walked out of the barn again, Blake was struggling down the path between the beetroot plants, Bob's horns grasped firmly in his hands. The goat was resisting, and Blake's arms bulged impressively as he fought to keep control. He was covered in mud, his hair rucked up, his skin slick with sweat. But he was grinning like an idiot, and when he saw her looking at him, he laughed. "Why didn't you tell me this would be so hard?"

"Pretty sure I did?" she reminded him. She took one horn from him, both of them gently coaxing the old goat through the door and back into the pen. Her mum closed the gate and locked it, clapping her hands together.

"Thank you," she said, smiling. "Thank you both so much. They would have torn through my crops in a heartbeat. And it's not like they don't have enough delicious grass to get through in their pens, and I give them all my kitchen scraps too. Ungrateful buggers."

She looked Blake up and down, then winked at Ellie. "If I didn't know any better, I'd have said he enjoyed it," she went on. "You're suited to this life, Blake."

"I don't know about that." He looked at his mud-streaked clothes.

But he *was* suited to it — Ellie could tell by the way his cheeks glowed, the way his eyes seemed brighter. She waited until her mum had left the barn, then she took his hand.

"Sorry about your clothes," she said. "I'll wash them."

He laughed. "It's nothing. Honestly, I think it's a good look. I always hated formal wear anyway."

"Clean clothes aren't exactly formal," she teased, squeezing his hand. "But Mum was right, you do look like you're suited to this."

"The farm?" he asked, tilting his head as if considering it seriously. He nodded, the smile on his face deepening. "Yeah. I never would've thought it, but there's something about it. The air, the freedom . . . it's like I can actually breathe out here."

He paused, his gaze softening as it lingered on her. "And maybe it's not just the farm," he added, his thumb tracing lazy circles over her knuckles. "Maybe it's the company."

211

Ellie felt her cheeks heat, the flutter in her chest impossible to ignore. She looked down at their joined hands, a smile playing at her lips.

Blake shifted closer, his free hand lifting to tuck a strand of hair behind her ear. His touch was warm, and she shivered at the sensation. "I like this side of you," he murmured. "Here, out of the city. You're . . . glowing."

"Glowing?" she repeated, laughing softly.

"Yes," he said, his tone serious despite the teasing smile on his lips. "Glowing. And it's the most beautiful thing I've ever seen."

Her breath caught, and for a moment, the barn seemed to shrink around them, the air between them charged and electric. She leaned into him slightly, her pulse racing as she caught the look in his eyes — a look that made her feel like she was the only thing in the world that mattered.

"And you," she whispered, her voice trembling with honesty. "You're not so bad yourself, city boy."

Blake chuckled, the sound low and warm, then tilted his head towards her, his lips hovering just inches away. "I could afford a nice place," he murmured, his voice rough as he pulled her closer, their bodies barely a breath apart. "Maybe something nearby. A few acres, some animals . . ." His fingers brushed against hers, their warmth igniting tiny sparks along her skin. His lips quirked into a teasing smile. "But there's just one condition."

"What?"

"No goats."

Ellie burst into laughter. "No goats," she agreed, her hand sliding up his muddy chest.

Blake leaned in, capturing her lips in another kiss that was anything but gentle. It was hard and possessive, filled with every ounce of desire. Ellie melted into him, her arms wrapping around his neck as she kissed him back with equal intensity.

"And one more thing," Blake whispered against her lips, his voice ragged with need.

212

"Anything," she breathed.

"I want you to be there with me."

Her heart raced, her pulse thrumming in her ears as she tilted her head up and kissed him again. This time it was slower, deeper, her body pressing against his like she wanted to memorise every line, every contour of him. Blake groaned softly, his fingers tangling in her hair as he pulled her even closer.

"Deal," she whispered against his lips. "We could leave the city, leave the smoke and the noise."

It sounded like the best idea in the world, and she couldn't believe it when he nodded.

"We could live out here," he said. "Not just live, but *live*."

She held him close, her head on his chest. His heart pounded, and she knew it was only partly to do with the fact that he'd just wrestled a goat. That was the drum beat of somebody who genuinely felt excited. She could have listened to it all day.

Except there was something else on the edge of her hearing, a strange thumping noise coming from outside the barn. She pulled away, cocking her head to hear it better.

"It's back," Isla said, storming into the barn. "That pesky thing is what spooked the goats."

"What is it?" Ellie asked.

Blake pulled away, his expression dark. "It's a helicopter."

"It flew past a while ago," Isla said. "It's obviously looking for something."

"Yeah." Blake looked up to the sky. "It's looking for me."

213

CHAPTER 34

BLAKE

By the time Blake had walked out of the barn, the helicopter was closing in. It was a powerful, black Eurocopter, and even before he saw the Heartbook logo plastered on the door, he knew who it belonged to. He had ridden in that very same helicopter countless times, and even though he hadn't always liked flying, he'd always loved the feeling of being airborne, of soaring over the streets and buildings below. Whenever he'd taken the chopper, he'd felt free.

Now, though, the sight of it made his heart tumble into his stomach. He was a prisoner on the run, finally being cornered by the police. The helicopter spun lazily above the large yard, kicking up a storm of dirt. Through the window he could see David in sunglasses and headphones making the signal to land, and sure enough, the chopper slowly descended, bumping gracefully on to the grass. The noise of it thumped through him, the wind buffeting his clothes and ruffling his hair, drying the mud on his skin, but he stood tall. He may have lost his crown, but he would not bow to the monsters inside the helicopter.

A hand found its way into his and he looked to see Ellie there. Her hair streamed behind her, but her expression was defiant and brave, her eyes fierce. Even dressed in her pink joggers and T-shirt she looked like royalty. She met Blake's eyes and nodded, and he nodded back. Even though they didn't speak, the message was clear: whatever happened next, they would face it together.

The thrum of the helicopter grew quieter as the throttle eased off. The doors opened and David hopped out, tossing his headphones on to the seat. He waited by the door, offering his hand to Michelle as she appeared behind him. She was wearing a ridiculous pair of heels, and her nose wrinkled with disgust as she dropped gracefully on to the dirt. When she looked at Blake, though, her expression turned into one of delight. She threaded her arm through David's and they ducked under the spinning rotors, walking briskly across the yard.

Now somebody else was climbing out of the chopper, seemingly forgotten by the other two. He was a short, plump, balding guy in faded jeans and a baggy, lime-green T-shirt, a cheap all-weather jacket thrown on top. Blake frowned. He wasn't anyone he recognised from the company, and he certainly wasn't a lawyer.

The mystery deepened when Ellie squeezed his hand, hard enough to hurt. He winced, looking down to see that the colour had drained from her face.

"What is it?" he asked.

She glanced up at him fearfully. "That's Josh," she said. "That's my ex."

There was no time to ask her what might be going on, as David and Michelle walked into earshot. Blake straightened his back, trying to make himself look as imposing as he could. Without thinking, he took a step forward so that he was standing defensively in front of Ellie. She gripped his hand even harder, giving him strength.

"Well, well, well." David's voice barely carried above the thrum of the rotors. "Blake Fielding, as I live and breathe."

215

"I told you we'd find him," said Michelle, her face creasing again as she looked him up and down. "We didn't need Josh after all. We could have just sniffed him out."

"Yeah, it's sad," said David. "How the mighty have fallen. One minute you're one of the richest men on the planet, the next you're rolling around with the pigs."

"Goats, actually," Blake spat out.

They both laughed, and Blake's blood boiled in his veins. He felt Ellie squeeze his hand again, not in panic, but to reassure him. Josh was cowering beneath the chopper blades as he made his way across the yard. He stopped behind the others, peeking past David's shoulder as if he was worried somebody might take a shot at him. Blake had no idea why Ellie had been dating him. She'd been batting *way* below her league.

"What are you doing here?" Ellie asked.

"Claiming what's mine," the man replied, giving her such a smug grin that Blake felt like he actually *was* about to take a shot at him.

He breathed slowly and deeply, keeping his cool. He was in enough trouble already. He didn't need an assault charge on top of everything else.

"Josh came to us with an offer," said David, raising his hand. He was holding a manila envelope and Blake knew what was inside it — the papers that would strip him of everything he had spent his life building. "I call that perfect timing. Shall we? A couple of signatures and it's done. You can't run anymore."

"Who said I was running?" Blake eyeballed David until he looked away. Coward.

"Where do you want to do this?" Michelle asked.

"Right here." Blake held out his free hand. He was furious, yes, but something had taken the edge off his rage. His head was full of dreams of him and Ellie waking up together in their farmhouse, of drinking coffee and eating freshly laid eggs together on the porch, of planting crops and raising livestock, and even wrangling goats in the mud. Nothing else seemed to matter anymore, and the thought of returning to

216

the boardroom and poring over thousands of lines of code seemed like the least appealing thing imaginable. He smiled at David, and it caught the other man by surprise.

"Not here," spat Michelle, swatting at a fat bug that had landed on her shoulder. "Inside."

"Where the papers won't fly away," added David, fighting to hold on to the envelope in the wind from the helicopter blades. "After you, Blake."

Blake paused for a moment, then turned and headed back to the house. Ellie walked by his side, not letting go of his hand until they reached the door. Isla had arrived before them and was looking at the trio of newcomers with murder in her eyes.

"I'm sorry," Blake said. "They won't be here long."

"I wouldn't stay in this pigsty if you paid me," Michelle muttered as she walked through the door.

Blake turned to her, positioning his body in a way that made her take a step back in frightened surprise. "Michelle," he said, his voice low and threatening, "the way I see it, you guys have spent the morning chasing your tails all over the English Riviera, looking for me. Why? Because you need me. If I don't sign these papers now, you're facing a legal battle that could sink this company for good. So listen to me, and listen well. You can say what you want about me, but I swear if you say one more thing about this gracious woman, or her house, or her beautiful, kind daughter, then I will take those papers and stuff them into the goat shed and I will see you all in court. How does that sound?"

Michelle's mouth fell open like a puppet with snapped strings and she looked away.

"That's an apology, right?" he said.

"Sure," she mumbled, turning to Isla. "I'm sorry."

"Enough of this," growled David. "I'm bored. Get me a table, and let's finish this thing."

He shoved past Blake and walked to the kitchen table, pushing Ellie's laptop and notepads out of the way. He opened

217

the envelope and pulled out a sheaf of papers, all covered in small legal type. Post-its pointed to at least seven places where Blake would have to sign.

Slapping it down on the table, he grinned at Blake.

"It's all yours," he said, pulling a pen from his breast pocket and holding it out. "Maurice left you a handsome severance package, enough to get by on for the rest of your life, really, if you behave. Any last words?"

"You're disgusting," said Ellie. "What you've done to Blake, you should be arrested for it."

"Oh, get over yourselves," said David. "Welcome to the world of business, sweetheart. I'd try to explain it to you, but it would go right over that pretty little head of yours. Blake was played, plain and simple. All these years people thought he was a genius and yet all it took to take him down were a handful of badly written fake posts."

"Hey," said Michelle, walking to his side. "They weren't badly written, they were carefully constructed. I knew people wouldn't believe it unless it really sounded like him, so I made it really sound like him."

She laughed, and David put a hand on the back of her head, pulling her close and kissing her. Michelle looked at Blake out of the corner of her eye and Blake recoiled. How had he ever found himself attracted to her? She was grotesque, and she was evil.

"But he's innocent," Ellie said. "You framed him."

"He was asking for it." Michelle broke free of David. "He's a loser. He was more interested in creating a wholesome, positive social network than he was in making money. And everybody knows money makes the world go round."

"I made you millions," said Blake, through gritted teeth.

"It's not enough," Michelle replied. "It's never enough."

"I can't believe I ever thought there was good in you," said Blake, and she laughed again.

"But that's you all over, isn't it? Blake the good man. Blake the kind man. That's why this is all so beautiful. You're the most decent person I know. You've never said anything offensive

218

about women in your whole life. You respect women, you respect everyone. And now everyone thinks you're a monster."

"And the beauty is, you admitted to it," said David, laughing. "Yesterday at the press conference. I mean, we were expecting some kind of fight and we were prepared for it, but in the end you just rolled over. You seriously couldn't have fallen into this trap harder."

"But why?" Blake said, his heart aching as he turned to his old friend. "I loved you, David. You were my best friend."

David's expression wobbled for a moment, then Michelle took his arm and clutched it tight. David seemed to steel himself. "No room in this world for nice guys," he said. "Just look at us, Blake. I've got it all, and you've got nothing."

At this, Blake smiled again. And to his surprise it was a genuine smile. He looked at Ellie and he felt nothing but happiness and relief. She was all he wanted. She was all he would ever want, even when they were old and grey.

"You know what? You two deserve each other." He turned to Ellie. "I have everything I will ever need right here. All these years I thought I was happy, but it was only when I met you that I understood what happiness even was. They've taken my company from me, they've taken my credibility from me, but they've left me with something money can't buy. You."

Michelle pretended to throw up. "Well, don't think your little flower here is going to save you. Because we're taking everything of hers as well."

"What?" said Ellie.

"LifeWrite," said Michelle. "It's a great idea, and it's ours."

"*What?*" Ellie said again, louder this time. She looked at Josh, who was skulking in the corner of the room. He walked to David and Michelle, dwarfed by both of them.

"That's right," Josh said. "Did you think I wouldn't strike back after what you said the other day? Do you really think I'd let you treat me that way? You wrote LifeWrite when you were with me, and I kept copies of all the code. I even helped you create it."

219

"That's a lie," Ellie said. "All you did was criticise and complain."

"It's your word against mine," he said. "You never copyrighted it, you never patented it. You left all your ideas and code lying around in those stupid little notebooks of yours for anyone to read. Which means it's as much mine as yours."

"No," said Ellie. She looked at Blake, tears in her eyes. "They can't do that."

"They wouldn't dare," Blake said.

"Oh, it's already done," David said. "We signed a deal with Josh this morning. Say hello to your soon-to-be-millionaire ex-boyfriend."

CHAPTER 35

ELLIE

Ellie's head spun, her heart pounding so hard she could feel it in her throat. She stared at David, his smug smile spreading across his face like oil over water, staining everything it touched. Beside him, Michelle crossed her arms, her icy smile cutting through Ellie like a blade.

She turned to Josh, hoping against hope that he would laugh, say this was all some sort of joke. But his wet grin was all the confirmation she needed.

"You're disgusting." Ellie's voice trembled with rage. "You're all disgusting. How could you do this?"

"I'll happily take you back, Ellie, if you beg me."

Blake was on the move before she even knew it. He towered over Josh, his arm raised, his fist clenched, ready to pound him into the dirt.

Ellie grabbed Blake by the shoulder and pulled him away.

Josh squeaked, scampering back. "I'll sue you," he whined. "I will, just you try it!"

"Sue me for what?" Blake said.

Josh looked for a moment like he might be about to hurl another insult at Ellie, but suddenly she was standing

221

right in front of him. Then she slapped him across the cheek, hard enough for the sound of it to echo around the room. He dropped on to his knees, howling.

"You are the very worst person I know," she said. "The weakest, most despicable excuse for a human being. You deserve everything that is coming to you."

"Oh, save the outrage," Michelle sneered. "You were careless. You didn't protect your precious idea. That's on you, sweetheart."

Ellie clenched her fists, her nails biting into her palms. "You can't just steal my work."

"Actually, we can," David said with infuriating calm. "And we have. Josh here was kind enough to supply us with everything we needed. The code, the concept, the pitch — it's all ours now."

Ellie turned to Blake, whose face was a storm of fury and pain. His jaw was set so tightly it looked like it might snap. She saw his hands tremble for a moment before he balled them into fists at his sides.

"This is illegal," Ellie snapped. "You can't just take someone's intellectual property. It's theft!"

"Prove it." David spread his hands wide as if daring her to argue. "You didn't copyright it. You didn't trademark it. You have no leg to stand on. And before you think about a legal battle, remember we have the resources to bury you."

Blake took a step forward, his broad frame towering over David. "You really think this is going to work?" he growled. "You think people won't see through you?"

"They won't," Michelle said, her confidence unshaken. "And even if they do, it won't matter. Perception is reality, Blake. You of all people should know that by now."

Blake's shoulders heaved as he took a deep breath, and Ellie could see the war raging inside him. She placed a hand on his arm. "We'll fight them," she said, her voice steady. "We'll take them to court."

"Sure," David said with a chuckle. "Fight us. Drag this through the courts for years. By the time you even make a dent,

222

we'll have rolled out LifeWrite as part of Heartbook, and you'll both be bankrupt."

Ellie's gaze darted back to Josh, who was hanging at the edge of the room, looking less sure of himself now. His smirk had faltered, replaced by a furrowed brow.

"Wait a minute." He stepped forward. "You never said LifeWrite would be a part of Heartbook. You promised me CEO, a board seat. You said I'd have a say in—"

"Oh, Josh," Michelle interrupted with a laugh. "Sweet, stupid Josh. Did you really think we were going to let you anywhere near the decision-making table? You were a means to an end. Nothing more."

Josh's face flushed and he clung to the back of a chair to keep him upright.

"Enough," said David, losing his patience. "Sign it now, Blake, or face the consequences."

"I won't," he said. "Not unless LifeWrite is off the table."

Michelle let out a sharp laugh. "You're not in a position to negotiate, Blake."

"I'm not signing," Blake said, his voice a growl. "Not now, not ever."

David's smile turned wolfish. "If you don't, we'll move forward with LifeWrite anyway. We'll copyright it under Heartbook. Once that's done, Ellie won't just lose her company — she'll lose her reputation. We'll make sure the world knows she tried to steal from us."

Josh let out a noise like a dying mouse.

David pressed the papers closer. "You have a choice, Blake. Sign and walk away with your dignity — or let us destroy her."

Ellie's heart shattered at the look in Blake's eyes. She stepped closer to him, placing both hands on his arm. "Don't do it," she said. "Don't let them win. I'll figure something out."

"You won't have time." Michelle's tone was gleeful. "We've already started the process. If he doesn't sign, Ellie, your name will be dirt."

Blake looked down at Ellie, his expression softening. He reached up, brushing a strand of hair from her face. "This isn't just about me anymore," he said softly. "This is about us."

"Blake, please—"

He held up a hand, silencing her. Then he turned to David, his jaw tightening. "Fine," he said. "I'll sign."

"Blake, no!" Ellie grabbed his arm. "You don't have to do this. We can fight them together."

"I can't let them ruin your reputation," he said. "I won't."

David held out the pen and Blake took it. He moved the papers to the table and Ellie glanced at the mess of her ideas strewn next to them, the code she'd been showing Blake only moments earlier now sitting redundant on her laptop. Blake's hand hovered over the pages and for a moment Ellie thought he might change his mind. But then he picked up the pen and, with deliberate strokes, signed his name. Each movement felt like a dagger to her heart.

When it was done, Blake dropped the pen and turned to David.

"That was almost too easy," his old friend said. "You're even more pathetic than I thought."

"Come on." Michelle walked out of the room, her heels clacking on the wooden floor. "I'm sick of the stink of this place."

Josh followed, still rubbing his cheek and throwing Ellie a venomous glare, but she refused to flinch. *Let him scowl*, she thought. He deserved worse.

David lingered, his smugness faltering slightly as Blake spoke.

"You've taken everything from me," he said, quietly. "But don't think for a second that this is over."

David hesitated, the smallest flicker of something — guilt, perhaps — crossing his face. For a moment, Ellie thought he might say something human, but then Michelle's impatient throat clearing echoed from outside.

224

"I hope you find your freedom. You were a good friend, David. I'll miss you." Blake's words carried a weight that pierced Ellie's chest.

David's jaw tightened, his hand flexing at his side. Then, as if something inside him snapped, he turned and strode out without a word, slamming the door behind him.

Ellie let out a shaky breath, her pulse thrumming in her ears. She turned to Blake, who stood staring at the closed door, his shoulders tense.

For a long moment, the only sound in the room was the faint hum of the helicopter outside, its rotors beating the air in a cruel, constant reminder of everything that had just happened. Ellie crossed the room and slid her arms around Blake's waist, pressing her forehead against his back. His body was rigid, coiled with tension.

"Are you okay?" she asked, listening to his heartbeat.

Blake didn't answer right away. His hands came to rest over hers and he sighed, a deep, shuddering breath that seemed to release some of the weight he was carrying.

"Yeah," he said finally. "I think I am. But I'm sorry for what they did to you."

He turned around and pulled her close. "He had no right to do that to you." He kissed the top of her head. "We can fight it in court. We can get LifeWrite back."

"We don't need to," she said, breathing her words into him.

"Why? Of course we fight. It's your idea, they're not going to just steal it out from under you."

She opened her mouth to explain, but faltered as her gaze dropped to his lips. Before she could think better of it, she stretched up on her toes and kissed him.

Blake responded instantly, his arms tightening around her as he deepened the kiss. Everything else faded away — the betrayal, the anger, the lingering humiliation of Josh's smug grin. All that remained was Blake, his warmth, his strength,

225

and the way he kissed her like she was the only thing keeping him anchored to the earth.

When they finally broke apart, both of them breathless, Blake's hands framed her face.

"We fight," he said again, his voice softer this time, but no less insistent.

Ellie's lips curved into a grin as she shook her head and pushed her glasses back up her nose. Her gaze flicked to the table, and she nodded towards her laptop and the little red light still blinking away.

Blake followed her line of sight, his brows drawing together in confusion.

"It's still recording," Ellie said, her grin widening.

Blake blinked, then barked out a laugh — a real, deep laugh that made Ellie's chest swell.

"You're serious?" he asked, a slow smile spreading across his face.

Ellie nodded, unable to suppress her own laughter. "Everything they said. All their lies. It's all on the laptop."

Blake looked at her like she'd just handed him the world.

"You're brilliant!" He brushed his thumb across her cheek. "Absolutely brilliant."

Ellie shrugged, a playful glint in her eyes. "I mean, I didn't do it deliberately, but I'll take it."

"Let's make sure we've got everything." Blake stepped over to the laptop.

Ellie watched as he bent to check the file, his movements careful but quick. Her heart swelled with a mixture of relief and something else — something deeper. Whatever happened next, they weren't going to give up. They were going to fight back.

And this time, they were going to win.

226

CHAPTER 36

ELLIE

It had captured everything so perfectly that it was as if the camera had been set up to do exactly that. The beautiful irony of it all, Ellie thought, was that when David had pushed the laptop across the table, he'd positioned it in a way that framed the place where they had all been standing. David and Michelle were in the middle of the movie, their smug expressions captured as if by a master director of photography. Josh was there, too, just sneaking into the frame. Blake and Ellie were on the edge of the shot, and Ellie blushed when she saw herself march forward and slap Josh around the face.

"That was so cool." Blake put his arm around her and held her tight, and she leaned against him, resting her head on his shoulder.

"You should have hit him with a closed fist, though," said her mum, leaning over with a grin on her face. "Or a hammer. We need to celebrate, but first I need to go feed the zoo."

She walked away, and they watched the rest of the video alone, Ellie barely able to keep the smile from her face. The old laptop had performed admirably, every piece of dialogue was audible — right up until the last few seconds when Blake and Ellie appeared on the screen.

"*You're brilliant!*" Blake's words filtered through the speakers. "*Absolutely brilliant.*"

It went black. Ellie located the file on her laptop and duplicated it, then duplicated it again. Then she dropped it into an email and sent it to herself just in case the computer decided to explode. Only when she heard the *bing* of it landing in her inbox did she sit back. Her head was spinning, the adrenaline in her veins making her feel tired and heavy. The encounter with Josh had left her exhausted.

She looked over at Blake, with his elbows on the table, his head in his hands. His hair was mussed, his shirt still streaked with dirt from the yard. He looked every bit as drained as she felt, and something about that tugged at her chest.

Blake sighed and Ellie glanced at him again. He lifted his head, meeting her eyes with a faint, tired smile. "You okay?" he asked, his voice rough.

She didn't answer right away. Instead, she studied him, noting the faint shadow of stubble on his jaw, the way his blue eyes still carried a flicker of determination despite the exhaustion in them. This man, she thought, had given up everything for her. He'd lost his company, his reputation, and now he was here, in her mum's kitchen, fighting for a life he hadn't even known he wanted until a few days ago.

"I don't know," she admitted finally. "Are you?"

He chuckled softly, shaking his head. "Not even close."

That made her smile. She leaned forward, resting her elbows on the table and propping her chin on her hands. "What happens now? What does having this evidence mean in actual terms?"

"It means exactly what you think it means," he said. "It means everything."

"It means you're in the clear. Everyone will know that you didn't write those things."

228

"It means any court in the world will deny Josh if he claims he wrote LifeWrite," Blake said. "It would deny Michelle and David the copyright. It's yours."

Ellie nodded, relieved, but her mind was racing. "What happens to them? David and Michelle?"

"They'll lose everything," Blake replied. "The board will kick them out, no question. Jail isn't off the table either, not with the evidence we have."

"Would you want that?" she asked, testing the waters.

Blake met her gaze, his jaw tightening. "They deserve it," he said bluntly. "For what they've done, they deserve every consequence coming their way. They didn't just try to destroy me — they tried to destroy you, Ellie. They went after something you built with your heart and soul. People like that don't get my sympathy."

She studied his face, the sharp set of his jaw, the flicker of anger still simmering in his eyes. This wasn't the Blake she had met days ago. This was someone hardened by betrayal, someone who had fought to keep his composure while everything he'd built was ripped apart.

But when he looked back at her, the tension in his face dissipated. "Maybe I don't want them to go to jail," he said, the corner of his mouth twitching into a smile. "But when this all comes out, can we just let them stew about it for a little while?"

"Deal."

Blake grinned, the spark in his eyes returning.

"And you'll get it all back?" she asked. "You'll get your company back."

He nodded, but the expression on his face was almost one of disappointment.

"*Do* you want that?"

"I honestly don't know anymore," he said. "I thought I did, but so much has changed since yesterday. Right now, the only thing I want is this." He looked around him, then he

229

looked back at her. "The only thing I want is you. I love you, Ellie Mae Woodward."

Her lips parted, but nothing came out. Her hands moved on instinct, reaching up to cup his face, her fingers trembling slightly against the rough stubble of his jaw.

"Blake . . ." she whispered, her voice breaking. She stared into his eyes, searching for any flicker of doubt but finding none. "You mean that?"

"I've never meant anything more," he said, his hand coming up to cover hers. "It's not just that I want you, Ellie. It's that I need you. You've changed everything. You've made me see who I could be, what life could be."

Her heart was pounding so hard she thought it might leap out of her chest. She closed her eyes for a moment, leaning her forehead against his as tears slipped free and traced warm paths down her cheeks.

"You're not the only one who's changed," she murmured.

She felt his fingers under her chin, gently tilting her face up. When her eyes fluttered open, his gaze was so full of love it made her breath hitch. Before she could say anything else, his lips were on hers.

The kiss wasn't urgent or hurried. It wasn't about passion or desperation. It was deeper than that. It was the kind of kiss that spoke of trust, of commitment, of for ever. She melted into it, her hands sliding down to rest on his chest, feeling the steady beat of his heart beneath her fingertips. He held her like she was the most precious thing in the world, and for the first time in a long time, she felt utterly safe.

When they finally pulled apart, her forehead rested against his, both of them breathing heavily. Blake reached up and tucked a strand of her hair behind her ear, his fingers lingering against her cheek.

"You have no idea how much I love you," he said, his voice barely above a whisper.

Ellie laughed softly, her thumb brushing against his chest. "I might have an idea," she replied, grinning through her tears. "And for the record, I love you too."

They sat back, listening to the farmyard sounds through the open window. The goats bleated and the cows lowed, and the world seemed alive with birdsong. It was as if it was Ellie's first time in the countryside and she wondered why she had never appreciated the full extent of its beauty before. Why had she given this up for the smoke and bustle of the city? Why hadn't she moved back out here a long time ago?

Because she hadn't met the right person to be here with.

Her laptop fan kicked into gear, reminding Ellie that she had an important job to do before she got too carried away with the good life.

"So we send it," Ellie said, the excitement fizzing up inside her.

Blake nodded. "We send it. I'll email it to the board, and then my APEX group chat. One of those guys will know how to make it blow up."

"And I'll email it to all the news outlets," Ellie said.

"And I'll make brownies," added her mum as she kicked off her wellies and filled the kettle.

"Sounds like a plan, Mum," said Ellie. She pulled the laptop to her and opened up a new email. "Strap in, Blake," she said. "It's going to be a bumpy ride."

She fired off the file, passing the laptop to Blake. He typed a message, then emailed the video to the board. When it had sent, he closed the laptop lid.

"There's no one I'd rather be on the journey with."

EPILOGUE

One year later

"Careful, Blake!" laughed Ellie, as he carried her through the door of their farmhouse, almost banging her head on the lintel.

"Sorry," he said, not looking sorry at all. His grin was wolfish, his sapphire-blue eyes burning with something that had nothing to do with the champagne they'd been drinking all afternoon.

He looked devastatingly good. His hair was longer now, sun-streaked and perpetually tousled. His shirt was undone just enough to show off his taut muscles and tan, and his jeans hugged his body in all the right places.

The last year had changed them both. They spent most days outdoors, working the land, riding horses, and having ridiculous amounts of sex under the stars that made their past city lives seem unthinkable.

"You're impossible," Ellie murmured, her arms wrapping around his neck as he dipped his head and kissed her, deep and slow. His breath was full of strawberries and mint from the cocktails they'd made that morning, and for a moment, the world outside the cool, stone farmhouse ceased to exist.

He pulled away just enough to let their foreheads touch. "You are everything, Ellie Mae," he murmured, voice rough with emotion. "And I'm going to spend the rest of my life proving that to you."

Ellie's heart swelled, but she smirked mischievously. "Then I forgive you for nearly concussing me on our wedding day."

Blake laughed, carrying her deeper into their home before finally setting her down in their kitchen — though he didn't let go of her completely. His hands lingered on her waist, his thumbs brushing over the soft fabric of her wedding dress.

"You do realise you just got married in a sunflower dress, right?" he teased, trailing a finger along the thin strap over her shoulder.

Ellie grinned. "And you just got married in jeans."

He shrugged. "I mean, we do look pretty damn good."

She rolled her eyes and turned towards the window of the large country kitchen, looking out to where their closest friends were gathered outside, clinking glasses and laughing in the golden evening light.

The wedding had been chaotic, hilarious, and perfect. Nobody had worn suits. Nobody had worn designer gowns. Even the vicar had rolled up his sleeves and drunk whisky after the ceremony.

They had written their own vows and promised them to each other, barefoot in the farmhouse yard, with only the people who truly mattered watching.

Blake wrapped his arms around her from behind, pulling her against his chest.

"You make me so damn happy," she whispered.

His voice was a warm growl against her ear. "That's my job now. My sole purpose in life — especially since you're the breadwinner."

Ellie laughed, leaning back into him. He wasn't wrong. LifeWrite had exploded. Within weeks of launch, it had ten million users. Now? That number was staggering. The last time she'd checked her bank balance, she'd nearly fainted.

233

Her success was hers alone. And that meant everything to both of them.

After the infamous takedown of David, Michelle and Josh, everything had changed overnight. Fired without golden parachutes, forced into 300 hours of community service, and slapped with seven-figure fines. And, in a way, that had been a better punishment than jail as Michelle had to get her hands dirty. Social media, the means of their scheme to destroy Blake, had become their ultimate downfall as the ceaseless posts ensured their crimes could not be forgotten. Heartbook had recovered, but Blake had refused to return. He remained the founder and major shareholder but was no longer the CEO, letting the new board deal with the day-to-day stress.

A loud crash echoed from outside, followed by yelling.

"Oh, crap," Ellie muttered, looking out the window.

Devlin Storm stood laughing while Lissa and Blake's parents sprinted across the yard, trying to wrangle a goat that was currently devouring a wedding bouquet.

"Is it Bob?" Blake laughed. "It's always Bob."

The back door slammed open and Christian strolled in. His black Henley was unbuttoned, showing off abs that had half their wedding guests swooning.

Behind him, Darcy appeared, barefoot and grinning, her dark hair a mess from unscheduled goat herding.

Christian leaned against the doorframe, effortlessly cool as always, arms folded across his chest. "You two done sneaking off?"

"Hardly," Blake said, voice low.

Christian raised a brow. "Not my business, Blake, but your honeymoon is going to be short-lived if your parents get eaten by your goats."

"Oi, newlyweds!" Devlin grinned, appearing behind Christian and Darcy, throwing an arm around Christian's shoulder. "We have a situation."

Ellie sighed. "Definitely Bob."

234

"I swear to God, Ellie," Blake groaned, pressing a kiss to her shoulder. "You promised me no more goats and we adopted your mum's whole herd. How did that happen?"

She smiled up at him. "Because you love me. And Mum values her veggies enough to get sheep instead. She saw us coming."

Devlin burst out laughing. "See, this is why I love you guys. Your naivety is so cute."

Blake shot him a glare. "You know, Storm, there's a spare stall in the barn. I can absolutely put you in it."

Devlin clapped a hand over his heart. "Kinky, Fielding. But I'm taken." He winked at Darcy.

Darcy rolled her eyes, but her cheeks pinked.

"All right, farmhands," Christian said, pushing off the doorframe. "Let's go wrangle this menace before Bob eats the cake."

Blake groaned. "If that goat gets the cake, I swear—"

Ellie laughed. "Come on, Mr Fielding."

"Mr Fielding-Woodward," Blake corrected, grinning like a man who had everything he ever wanted.

Ellie's heart expanded to bursting.

This was it. Their life. Messy. Perfect. Full of chaos and love and goats.

And she wouldn't trade it for anything.

She glanced towards the kitchen table, where her trusty old laptop sat, still open.

"You coming?" Blake called.

"Yeah," she said, grinning. "Just a second."

She tapped open her profile page on LifeWrite.

A single line stared back at her:

Ellie Mae is now married!

She clicked 'update' and snapped the laptop shut, turning to run after the man who had changed her life for ever. For the first time in her life, Ellie knew without a doubt that she was exactly where she was meant to be. She'd spent years

235

believing she was cursed, that happiness would always be just out of reach. But she'd been wrong.

She hadn't been cursed. She'd just been waiting for the right person to share it all with.

And now she had him.

THE END

THE CHOC LIT STORY

Established in 2009, Choc Lit is an independent, award-winning publisher dedicated to creating a delicious selection of quality women's fiction.

We have won 18 awards, including Publisher of the Year and the Romantic Novel of the Year, and have been shortlisted for countless others. In 2023, we were shortlisted for Publisher of the Year by the Romantic Novelists' Association.

All our novels are selected by genuine readers. We are proud to publish talented first-time authors, as well as established writers whose books we love introducing to a new generation of readers.

In 2023, we became a Joffe Books company. Best known for publishing a wide range of commercial fiction, Joffe Books has its roots in women's fiction. Today it is one of the largest independent publishers in the UK.

We love to hear from you, so please email us about absolutely anything bookish at choc-lit@joffebooks.com.

If you want to receive free books every Friday and hear about all our new releases, join our mailing list here: www.joffebooks.com/freebooks.